FAKE CROWNE

THE CROWNE BROTHERS

CD REISS

I ALSO WROTE THESE

Iron Crowne ~ Enemies to Lovers

Crowne of Lies ~ Marriage of Convenience

Crowne Rules ~ Forced Close Proximity

Fake Crowne ~ Fake Relationship

Crowne Jewel ~ Enemies to Lovers

You might also like:

The *New York Times* bestselling Games Duet

Adam Steinbeck will give his wife a divorce on one condition. She join him in a remote cabin for 30 days, submitting to his sexual dominance.

Marriage Games | Separation Games

Monica insists she's not submissive. Jonathan Drazen is going to prove otherwise, but he might fall in love doing it.

COMPLETE SUBMISSION

CONTEMPORARY ROMANCES

Hollywood and sports romances for the sweet and sexy romantic.

Star-Crossed | Hardball | Bombshell | Bodyguard | Only Ever You

1

COLTON

My head weighs four tons. My front is cold, and my back is hot.

Something wet slaps against the side of my face.

"Colton."

My name is a string leading me out of sleep. Guy's voice. Impatient. Smell of chlorine and stale beer. Sound of birds. High-pitched *whee* followed by a *whrr* that's a good three octaves lower. The orange clouds inside my eyelids are too bright.

"Colton. Colton. Colton."

Shit. It's Logan, and I already have a splitting headache.

Blink, blink. The sun's low on the other side of the garage. Still too bright. My cheek is at the edge of the pool. Jan, the pool lady, in wraparound Oaklies and a trucker cap, pushes the vacuum under the water with a long aluminum pole. Forward, then back. *Whee-whrr.*

"Colton." Logan's voice is above me.

There's no rule against sleeping in the backyard and I

1

don't need his permission to be hungover. All I need is ten minutes to get to the bathroom to piss, then the kitchen for water and a few Advil. Then I need the rest of the day to sleep this shit off.

"Colton."

"Fuck off."

He and Ella are supposed to be away until next week, but here he is, live and in the flesh.

"It's my house, Colton. I don't fuck off in my own house."

I feel a steady pressure at my shoulder. His foot, pushing me harder and harder. Before I can get up, he rolls me into the pool. I catch my breath and hold it before going under.

It's fucking cold and loud down here.

I come up facing Jan from Luminous Pool Services. She's laughing and giving me a thumbs-up for not drowning.

Now I'm awake. I shake my hair away from my eyes and turn to Logan standing above me. He's in a fucking suit, of course, arms crossed, sun behind him so I can't really see his expression.

"What did you do that for?"

"So you can experience the toxic dump in my backyard."

"What toxic—?"

Just then, a jellyfish bobs onto the tile by his feet, which is impossible. It's a condom. Judging from the pearly spew of syrup leaking into the water, it's been used.

Last night, when I told Carmy to be careful, I meant don't fuck in the pool. I lost track of him and everyone else who showed up at my brother's guest house. Logan's put me up for the past year and change, and sometimes I forget the house isn't mine.

"I'll clean it up."

I get out of the pool. My hoodie's taken on a few gallons,

so when I stand, I'm a waterfall. That's when I realize my legs are bare. I'm in my briefs. Fuck.

"When?" It's a challenge to say anything later than now.

"You didn't call first. If you called, and said, 'Hey, we're coming home from wherever,' it would have been cleaned up already."

"You would have picked the rubber out of the water and left the rest for my wife to swim in."

He acts as if it's not too gross for anyone to swim in, which it is, but as if Ella's gonna get knocked up that way. I could tell him he shouldn't worry, at least it's not my rubber, and add a backhand about his own virility. That's what I'd normally do, but I don't. One, because I need to live here, and two, because my brain is too fucked for backhands.

"You want me to take care of it or not?"

He looks me up and down, making sure to judge me from head to toe, then says, "We talked about the parties."

Fuck him. We didn't talk. He said things and I nodded.

"It wasn't a party. It was a dinner."

My head hurts and I need pants. I go toward the guest house before I say another incriminating word. The patio table's a disaster. Amidst a garden of red Solo cups, a bong leaks brown water. One of the cups is half full of cigarette butts. It only takes one New Yorker with a pack of Marlboros to stink up the upholstery.

A toxic dump. He's right about that.

Past the sliding doors, my jeans are draped over the back of the living room couch. The coffee table is growing another red Solo cup garden, without the butts or bong. Thank God I won't have to deal with cigarette stink in the house. Logan comes in and scans the mess.

"Look." I put the jeans on my wet legs, which—as anyone

3

who's ever tried to teach me to cook can tell you—is like trying to stuff a raw chicken into a Ziplock. "This is just..." I kick hard to untwist the pants, then force my leg through. "It's a couple of garbage bags and a chlorine shock to the pool."

"Of course you know because you've done it half a dozen times."

He's right again. I struggle with the second leg.

It's his house. He used to ask me not to have parties. Now he tells me flat out, lays down the law, draws a line in the sand, whatever. I just had a few friends over to watch a ball game, then things got out of control.

I'm really tired of making that excuse.

"Go to the office or something," I say instead. "By the time you get home, you'll be able to do surgery in here."

He should just take my word for it and go, because I really have done it before. Instead, he leans on the couch, crosses his arms again, and watches me try to push a wet leg into dry jeans. Asshole.

"Where's Ella?" I ask because sometimes—not every time, but sometimes—she defends me.

"Florence, at some textile thing."

"*Pitti Filati*." Finally, I pull the waist up over my soaked briefs.

"That one."

"You're married to a *garmento*. Catch up, man." I leave my pants unbuttoned and head for the bathroom. I need to piss and brush my teeth. My mouth tastes as if I set a polyester shirt on fire then gnawed on whatever melty stuff was left.

Logan stands in the doorway while I take a leak that echoes off his tiles. No respect for a guy's privacy.

"You need to start working again."

4

I left the job in the Crowne mail room a month ago. It's the family company. I could go back. But yeah. I need a job. Just not that one.

I flush, button up, and wash my hands.

"I can't find someone worth producing." I put toothpaste on my brush and tap the wall that separates the guest house bathroom from the garage it's connected to. I built a studio in there and he's right, I need to use it.

"You're in Los Angeles," Logan keeps going as if he knows everything. If I ever act like this, I'll punch myself in the face. "People flock here to be musicians or... whatever. You're not looking, you're partying."

"Do I tell you your job? Because the parties are business." I brush my teeth. I feel as if I'm jabbing an enflamed brain with a hot poker, but at least it's getting the toxic taste off my tongue.

Logan's just not leaving.

"We need to talk," he says.

Of course he says it after I've started foaming at the mouth.

"Ee-ah-auking." I talk around the brush.

"You need to get your shit together."

"Eh-ah," I agree. Can't argue the sky's bright pink at high noon. Blue is blue.

"When you first came here, you were more or less all right. It was like you were trying. But when you quit Crowne, you lost all sense of responsibility. We all support you, Colton, but Ella and I... we can't have this going on anymore. It's not going to work."

"I 'oh-ee." My apology is frothy and a little defensive. I look at him in the mirror.

He looks away. "I don't want you to think I'm trying to

bust your ass or be your warden. But you're not doing anything. You've reverted to form. It's hard to watch."

I shrug. Coming from a workaholic, that doesn't mean much. Kicking my feet up without a computer open on my lap would be hard for him to watch. But the fact is, I've been in some kind of holding pattern for too long. I don't know what I've been waiting for, but that's what I've been doing. Waiting. Of course it's painful to watch.

"This isn't easy for me." He pushes back his hair. "You're my brother. I love you. But there has to be a limit."

My brush stops. I knew this was coming. Like anything you expect but can't predict, I didn't think it'd happen today. Trying not to act bothered, I look down and brush harder.

"I'm going to give you time," he says. "A few months. If you can't get it together, Mom and Dad have space at the house."

"Uh-uh." No way. I'm not living with my parents, even if they can comfortably host the entire Wu Tang Clan without crossing them in the halls. "I'll 'igure i' ou'."

"There's a reason."

"Ih 'ine."

"I don't want you to think—"

"Eye-eht-iss-fine!" Forcing the f sprays toothpaste on the mirror.

"Ella's pregnant."

"Ah." I spit and rinse, then wipe my mouth with the back of my hand. "Congratulations."

"I'm sorry to do this but..." He waves, indicating everything in his purview that I fucked up.

"I get it. You don't want the kid pulling latex jellyfish out of the pool or being around Uncle Fuckup."

"You're not—"

6

"Whatever, dude. Use different words if it makes you feel better." I snap a towel off the floor. There are three under it. I pick up those too. "Give me a few days. I'll be out of your hair."

I have no idea where I'm going. I can couch surf. Get a sound engineer job.

"Look, you don't need to go so fast. I don't want you crashing at some loser's place. I'll never hear the end of it."

Ella may not always take my side when I fuck up, but overall, she's got my back. That's one thing. Using her ain't gonna cut it though.

"Okay, look." I jam all the towels into the hamper. "I'm not trying to get between you and your wife and I'm not trying to stay where I'm not wanted. I hear what you're saying, and you're right. If I was you, I'd be kicked out already, or you'd be, if you were still you. Whatever. I'm not even mad. I'll tell Ella it was my idea." I punch him in the arm. "I got you."

I brush past him to leave the bathroom.

"Liam said he made you an offer," he calls.

My brothers talk about me more than I talk about myself. It's been a fact for so long, I'm not even annoyed.

Our brother Liam's a talent manager. I've barely heard from him since I came back to Los Angeles. Then I got a call last week about a client who needs development. Singer. Somehow—in a town full of music producers—I'm the only one who can make her EP. I have a gift for developing talent, he says.

So does he, for blowing smoke up assholes.

"I told him no. Now I'm telling you... no."

Logan follows me through the house like a honey badger on a bee.

"You should do it." He's over my shoulder down the hall.

"I said I'd figure it out."

The headache's roaring, but when I hit the living room, the sight of it pisses me off, and I know I'm not going to sleep until it's clean.

"And I said there was time." He's scanning the war zone while I pour two Advil into my palm, add a third like a woman having a bad period, and drop them down my throat as if they're coated in applesauce.

I'll take responsibility for the mess, but I'm not owning up to the guilt on Logan's face.

"How many times do I have to say it's fine?" I ask. Rhetorical, of course. There's no number on it.

"Do you ever shut up?"

I make the zipped-lip sign and stack used cups. Logan sighs, hands in his pockets, looking at the mess.

"So, until you can get stable and go, here's what I want."

Oh, Logan wants something. Fan-fucking-tastic. If I could only put money on any of my brothers setting the terms and making the rules, I'd be richer than Dad. All of them have ended up being dictators in their own way. Some days, I wonder if our sister, Lyric, and I are even related to them.

I hold the stack above the overflowing trashcan, trying to figure out if there's space for it. I get it into an empty space on the side, and half the tower goes in, but the other half...

I was going to mop anyway.

"What do you want, Logan?" I make another stack. "Or did you just want to watch me clean up?"

"I want you to use the studio you built in my garage."

"What do you think that's going to change?" I ask.

"Once you start working again, you'll stop this nonsense."

"I have no choice. I can't move. I don't have the bones."

"The what?"

"The bones. The bread. The money. For fuck's sake, don't you even watch television?"

"I'll loan you—"

"No." I drop the stack of cups in the bag and cut the air with my hands, because one hundred percent, absolutely not. "I appreciate everything you've done for me. Gratitude, man." I tap my chest with my fist. "No hard feelings." I crouch for the spilled cups.

"Of all of us, you're the smartest."

I dump the pile in the sink and lean on it, head bowed. "Jesus, Logan. I'm fucking trying to be good here."

"You don't have to try to be good, dumbass. You are good. You're just not doing it right."

He thinks he's saying something nice, but he's not. He's dressing up my life in his rules and showing me how much better it looks. Of course it looks better in a fucking suit. The problem isn't wearing it for an hour. The impossible part is walking around in clothes that don't fit day after day.

"Can you just let me clean up?" I ask.

"Say you'll think about it."

"You'll think about it."

"Funny." He claps me on the back and walks back to his house.

By the time the sky is sunset pink, my headache is more of a stiff neck.

I've flipped the patio cushions to hide a cigarette burn and brought the garbage out back. The house is clean, the pool is sterile, and you can't smell cannabis or tobacco unless the air is still and you breathe real hard.

The guest house is nice, but the studio is my space. I set up one side of the control room with some mid-century stuff Jab's grandfather was getting rid of—a lime green chair, an orange couch, a cabinet set. One of them has a turntable inside it. Logan had left a box of old Pez dispensers in a corner of the garage, and I built narrow shelves over the couch to display them. Then I built shelves for all my records, so I can listen to old shit that doesn't remind me of all the ways I fucked up. Of Tamika. The lawyers. Of the disappearing money I'd demanded—so sure I could use it to prove something.

I proved something all right.

The orange couch is a few feet from the sound board, which is under a window looking through to a soundproof-ish studio I can't get myself to use. Not since Tamika. That board. That mic. The cables and monitors. She's inside them, a reminder of losing it all.

Hydrated, with a nasty headache raging from behind a locked door marked ADVIL, I stretch out on the orange couch. I'm exhausted. Fully awake. Heavy as a feather. Light as a rock. Fine, really. I can sell my shit and go anywhere. Or I can live with my parents. They live in fucking Bel-Air for Chrissakes. Who's luckier than me?

This shit with Logan is getting old anyway. Having coffee with him and Ella in the morning. Chilling with her stepmom, who's a cool lady, and her buddy Amilcar.

The thought comes... and it's like getting T-boned by a car running a red light. I sit up as if someone just put a trombone to my ear and blew hard.

I like it here.

Shit.

I don't *want* to leave.

Cursing facts that can't be unknown, I get up and change the record to Max Richter. No words. No one telling me anything. Just *da-da-DA da-da-DA* over and over.

When I took my inheritance and split, I was hopeful I could make something of myself without my family connections. I went to Memphis, Detroit, Austin. As soon as I settled in, or even when there was a threat of feeling at home, I'd get a call from a friend in another city, or I took off to hear a new act and never came back. I left behind half-done deals and artists who trusted me when I didn't trust myself.

Then I landed in Nashville, where I met Tamika, and settled in one place, built her the studio, and produced her music. Her leaving was bitter medicine. It tasted like my own.

I should leave again. Take to the road. See what I find.

But the pull to do that is gone.

I'm not attached to Los Angeles, but I like having my family close by. I like this back house. I like this corner of the garage and my old album collection. I like my fucking Pez-collecting brother and his knocked-up wife. Ella being pregnant reminds me that I also like babies.

I wrangle my phone out of my pocket and call Liam.

Here goes nothing.

2

SKYE

I sing like no one's watching.

Up ahead, the light goes red at the song's chorus. I'm lit by the purple flashing neon of a smoke shop to my left with fill from the streetlights through the windshield. Perfect. I stop at the crosswalk and turn down the song so I can hear myself, instead of Tamika's gut-punch voice.

I got this. All major scales. Auto-tuned to death. Slow tempo. Repeat, repeat, big uplift, and repeat louder.

The windows are rolled up, but it's not as if I'm behind soundproof walls or anything. My old Toyota leaks sound like a colander leaks water, and as I hit the bridge with everything I've got, I worry that someone will hear me.

No. The city's loud and I'm just a voice. I'm as good as alone. The guy in the crosswalk with the backward baseball cap and his hands in his jean pockets can't hear me. I sing to him. To the wave of hair trapped behind the cap buckle, swaying with his stride.

"Don't be scared," I belt from the bottom of my lungs. *"You*

know you're safe with me. Don't be sorry..." I close my eyes and put my hands over my heart for the big notes. *Don't be my friend, don't be my... Don't be don't be don't be...*" The last *e* morphs into an *oo* sound so Tamika can stretch it into seventeen syllables, and every one of them is for the guy crossing the street with his hands in his pockets. I take my hands off my heart and stretch them forward, opening my eyes toward the end of the chorus.

He should be on the sidewalk by now, but no. He's still standing there. In the whitewashed glare of my headlights, his eyes are a sharp, clear blue.

"Shit." I gulp a bunch of air.

He's my age or a tad older—mid-slash-late twenties—with a face that's approachably handsome in the whitewash of my headlights. He puts up his hand to cut the glare and turns all the way around to face me. I don't know whether to apologize, or shrug, or panic that a stranger heard me grabbing for the outer reaches of my range. Usually, the third option would choose itself by making me incapable of breathing.

Even though I wait a split second for the anxiety take over, it doesn't. I count down. I'm fine. No panic at a stranger hearing my voice. No shit-sure belief that a rando can see through all my pretentions to the lack of talent beneath, thinking things about me that I won't ever know, tying himself to me by his opinions. None of that.

Great. Fine. I'm not having an anxiety attack. But Crosswalk Guy isn't moving. We're looking at each other through the windshield, me in wide-eyed "what the fuck do you want?" and him with some kind of curiosity.

If he thinks he knows me, he doesn't. I'm not interested in meeting a random guy in the street and I don't want to play a game of chicken with him. Why doesn't he finish crossing?

From behind, a loud blare jolts my attention.

The light is green. Crosswalk Guy takes a step in my direction.

Jesus Christ. The SUV behind me swings hard to get into the left lane, which is already moving, to the tune of screeching and honking.

I roll down my window and lean out. "Can you move?"

He just stares at me. It occurs to me that he could be having some kind of mental break.

"Please?" I add.

"Can I talk to you for a minute?"

What the... is this guy hitting on me in the middle of Wilshire and Western? What kind of psychopath behavior is this? It's terrifying, but I'm not scared. I'm just angry. I don't even tell him to fuck off. My actions will speak for themselves.

Once my head's back in, I close the window. The light's gone yellow, and I have a split-second opportunity to go, so I take it, swerving around him and through the empty intersection at the last second.

In my rearview, I watch him avoid getting hit by a car and run the rest of the way across. When his foot hits the sidewalk, I breathe a sigh of relief.

My mother acts as if Los Angeles is some kind of lawless dystopia.

Maybe she's right.

Turning off Wilshire, I pull into the underground lot on Serrano Ave. I'd park on the street, but the lot is free if you bring a receipt from the karaoke place on the third floor, which is where I'm going. I park in the back so I don't have to pay for the valet, which isn't free no matter where you get a receipt from.

I reach for the phone in the passenger seat. As I disconnect it from the charging cable, my mother's ringtone comes from it. I've owed her a call for days, and the call can't go on too long if I'm driving, so I answer.

"Hi, Mom."

"Oh, Skye!" My mother sounds pleasantly surprised I picked up. "How are you doing?"

"Fine." Still a lie, but close enough.

"Did you get the package I sent?"

The box had all the forms, brochures, booklets, and directories I'd need to enroll in med school in the fall, when my one-year deferment ends. I checked for the earliest deadline for all of it, closed up the box, and shoved it under my bed before the anxiety exploded in my chest.

I'm not finished with Los Angeles. I haven't done anything but make friends and keep a job making coffee. I'm not ready to go yet. And I like it here. I like it a lot.

"I got it. Thank you."

"Do you need help filling any of it out?"

"Most of it is online. I can do it."

"Your father's excited for you. He says he'll introduce you to the dean if you like. Make a smooth transition in."

"Okay. That sounds good."

There's a pause. I should say something. Offer a bite of my day-to-day here or tell her I'm making headway with music, but I've been saying that for two years and every half step forward has seemed more meaningless as the clock ticks.

What made me think I could become a singer in twenty-four measly months? People with twice my talent take ten times as long.

"So," she says. "Have you met anyone special?"

My entire brain snaps to attention. She hasn't asked that in a long time. She used to bring it up when she wanted to know if that special someone was a man or a woman so she could either worry I wasn't in a phase or hope it was permanent, depending on the special person's gender. When her friends found out I was bisexual, she dared them to have a problem with it. If the ladies of the Grosse Pointe Women's League wanted to judge, she could judge them harder.

She's a complicated person.

"Define special," I ask.

"You know what I mean. I was just wondering."

She's right. I know exactly what she means. Her worries about my sexuality have switched over to discomfort with the geography and precarity of my career choices. They've morphed into a need to make sure I had a solid career to salve the loneliness every "confused bisexual" must suffer from.

She wouldn't accept anyone judging me, but that didn't mean she understood me.

Like I said, she's complicated.

"Wondering if I'm going to stay here for them?" I ask.

"Skye. Why do you always think I have some ulterior motive for asking about your life?"

Maybe she's right. Maybe I'm the problem. As mothers go, I could have done a lot worse.

"I'm not focused on that right now, Ma."

"I know, I know. And yes. I'm sorry. I admit it. I worry you're going to get attached and stay there."

It's hard to be mad at someone who cops to their shortcomings.

"It's all right. I get it."

"So, how is the singing going?"

"Honestly?" I sigh. If she can be honest, I can too. "It's hard. Really hard."

"What about that agent who signed you?" Despite her wanting me to come home and have the life she's dreamed of, she's annoyed on my behalf. She wants me to succeed as much as she needs me to fail my way into med school.

"Still hard."

"Isn't it his job to make it less hard?" I half expect her to offer to call Liam Crowne herself and give him a piece of her mind. How dare he not hand her beautiful, perfect, talented daughter the entire world on a silver platter?

She isn't just complicated. She is—without a doubt—the most complicated person I've ever known.

"He's trying, Ma. We're all trying."

Jeannie is already singing "Brokeback Blues" and Becca is otherwise taking charge of the entire operation, assigning songs so that we build slowly to a crescendo fifteen minutes before we have to vacate, and wind down by the time they kick us out.

Starsong Karaoke's private rooms hold twelve people max. We have ten people so far. A bottle of vodka. A tray of wings. They set up three mic stands in front of the huge screen, give us access to thousands of songs in four languages, serve food and drinks, and let us sing our hearts out behind a closed door where no one can see or hear.

When I got to Los Angeles, I assumed this cost a fortune. It doesn't.

"You saved two spaces, right?" I ask Fátima, my roommate and manager at the Starbucks on LaCienega. She has long straight hair parted in the middle and a pretty little mole over her lip that I used to kiss when we were sex buddies.

"Yeah, who's coming?" She squeezes a lime into her vodka and soda.

"Liam Crowne."

When Liam signed me, it was such a boost to my confidence that I worked in the studio for three whole days. Then, knowing there were people who would eventually hear me... People I didn't know... Strangers who would judge me based on their own feelings and thoughts and the kind of day they'd had instead of judging me based on my voice and what I was trying to do... It made me crazy. All I could see was their big eyes, their big ears, their invisible scowls. I'd never know what they said.

Tripping over that fear has been the story of my time in Los Angeles. Then Liam found me at a karaoke bar like this one, drunk enough to sing without the private room.

Liam has zero-anxiety status, which took his time and patience. He had enough of the second thing to make the first seem irrelevant. He believes in me, and after all the work he's put in, I believe in him.

I'm fine with the guest list until Fátima reminds me of the math.

"And?" She wants to hear who number twelve is, and I'd made such an effort to forget.

"He's bringing his brother."

Fátima's eyebrows go up a little. "He's got four brothers. The builder, the CEO, the mysterious one, and—"

"Colton," I say. "Which one is he?"

Jeannie finishes and it's Evan's turn to sing her jazz-style version of "I Will Survive."

"Why do you look like that?" she asks instead of telling me which one is showing up.

"Like what?"

"Like all your blood stopped at your neck and made a U-turn back to your heart?"

"I forgot to be nervous until now. I don't know him and he's some kind of producer."

I've crashed and burned with every producer Liam's put me with. It's not that I'm hard to work with or that my songs are bad. It's the anxiety that attacks as soon as they bring in the musicians because I'm sure they can hear the flat notes, the utter lack of dynamics. They compliment me because they want to get paid. Or they want to get in my pants. Or they just want to get it over with.

Thinking about it makes me miss a word. Or a note. Or I cough. And sure, they say it's normal, but all I can think about while I'm in the middle of the song is every place I could fuck it up.

Something in my brain decides the only way to avoid these horror scenarios is to stand there and do nothing.

"Okay, *mija*." Fátima sits on the low table in the U of couches so she can face me. "Let me remind you of something about LA that I've told you a million times. There are all these rich fuckers living on the top of that hill, and I know as much about them as our neighbors. So yes, that family is rolling in it, and yes, they had, like, six babies in a tub of money, but Colton... he's the worthless one. That boy's a Bible story."

"I'm sorry, Fátima, but that can mean a lot of things."

She rolls her eyes. "He took his inheritance early and ran off looking for the 'next big thing.' Blew half of it throwing open-bar raves and most of the other half on lawyers."

"Nothing criminal, right?"

"Stupid baby shit. Anyway. He spent another chunk building a studio because he did, eventually, find the next big thing." She smirks at me. "Tamika."

"God, I love her."

"Well, so yeah. She came to Gavin McCormick with a demo, and he listened because a Crowne boy produced it, and—supposedly—it was all wrong. Like, everything wrong. But he heard something special and 'bought out' her contract. Or ripped it up. Or started fucking that Crowne boy's girl, stole the song, all his ideas, made the exact same composition with exactly twenty-two percent changes, and anyway... that's where the rest of the lawyer money went to."

"Did he get anything?"

"*Nada*. Not a dime. Sad face." She traces a frown. "I guess if you have that many kids, one of them's going to be a fuckup, no matter how rich you are. You feel better?"

"I see what Liam's doing, you know. He's trying to save his brother and serve his client at the same time. Clever."

"Stick with Liam." She winks at me. "He's got bad luck, but he's not a fuckup."

"Noted."

3

COLTON

Once I finished cleaning up, I took a nap, and now I'm really fucking late. Liam buzzed me seventeen times, and I slept through until the eighteenth. I brushed my teeth and ran here without stopping for a second except in the middle of the street because someone was singing in her car, and she was really something.

But I was in the middle of the street, and late, and anyone that good already has producers lined up out the door.

Liam's waiting right outside the elevator. "You're fucking late."

"Yeah. Sorry."

We're in the hallway of an office building in Koreatown, and even my mumbled apology echoes. The lighting makes my brother look green.

I'd do anything for Liam. I owe him. When Malin died, I was thousands of miles away and checked out. Totally incommunicado. I avoided any news about the Crownes, which wasn't easy. When Tamika told me, months later, that

21

my sister in-law had died suddenly, I la-la-la'd her at first, then realized the funeral was long over. Too late to send a card. So I did nothing. The next time the family heard from me, I was going to be so different my apology would mean something.

Different never came home, but the apologies did.

"Come on." Liam starts down the hall. At the end of it is a whiteboard sandwich sign that with an arrow drawn onto it.

"How's Matt?" I ask.

"Better. Only sucks his thumb at bedtime. I can't get him to quit."

"He lost his mother." We turn at the sandwich sign.

"Thanks. I forgot."

"Sorry."

"Stop apologizing." He stops at a set of glass double doors and puts his hand on the bar but doesn't push it. The lobby beyond them is painted white but lit with colored lights. "Listen. This girl. She's a little…" He looks for the word. "High-strung. No. More like… under certain circumstances, she gets nervous."

"Okay." You can say that about anyone, pretty much, so I don't know what he's trying to say.

"So don't be a dick."

"Don't be a… when am I a dick?"

"Just… don't be…" He sweeps his hand up and down, from my head to my feet. "Come on, man. Stand up straight. Be a serious person."

I'm about to argue that I am a serious person, but I have no proof, so I reach past him and push the door open.

The lady behind the counter smiles as we approach. "Welcome to Starsong."

"Crowne," my brother says, taking out his wallet. "Liam

Crowne." He snaps his credit card on the counter. "This is the card I phoned in. My party's already in room six, yeah?"

Her face lights up like Dodger Stadium. This is why I hate telling anyone my last name, because I can't follow it up with "I walked here because I don't want to spend money putting gas in the car." But Liam doesn't seem to mind how his name changes everything, so here we are, walking down a hall with soundproof doors on either side, behind a woman with dollar signs in her eyes.

For a moment, I wish I was back in Austin, or Detroit, or Nashville. Even Memphis.

Maybe not Memphis.

Dollar Sign opens the door to the corner room. When the door opens half a crack, a song spills out like a wave, hitting that thin slice of note that can cause a physical reaction. The chills. The note you make them sing the song a thousand times to hit. The singer is exhausted but let's go one more time and it gets pulled out of a place that's left after they've given up. Thom Bastardo called it the Malice Note, because they hit it out of spite. Ricky Rubia said it came from the crack where the artist's broken. That's the note. That's the way it's done. That's what's flooding the hallway when the hostess opens the door.

As soon as I walk in, the singing stops as if someone's yanked the needle off the record. The cheesy music keeps going and Liam gets in my way before I can see who's at the mic.

A bunch of eyes are on Liam and me, but I'm looking for that voice. I can't tell which one she is.

Am I desperate to get to work like Logan wants me to? It's impossible that I'd hear a voice I want to work with twice in one night.

A tall woman with straight hair parted in the middle gets up to sing "Gloria," and her friends cheer her with, "Fátima! Fátima! Fátima!" Liam talks to some guy with a ring on every finger.

"Colton!" Liam calls me over to sit next to him. He's moved on to talking to a girl with a nose ring and soft pink bob and another girl with a ponytail tied at the back of her neck. Even without makeup, the second girl's olive skin is all satin glow. "This is Skye."

He introduces me to the ponytail girl, and after an awkward pause, she does the intro for Pink Hair. "This is Becca." We shake hands. "She's a DJ."

"So, Skye here," Liam interjects, "is the voice I was telling you about."

Up until he gives me that context, I thought anybody else in the room was the singer in question—except for the one hacking up "Gloria" and selling it for parts—but I lean back a little until one of the spotlights right behind Skye is right in my face, squint a little, then hold up my hand to block it out.

"This is going to sound weird but..." I drop my hand. "Did you drive here in a silver Corolla?"

"Did you walk along Wilshire and cross on St. Andrews?" She smiles and sips her vodka-and-something, and we both know her question is an answer. She's the girl in the car singing "Don't Be." Liam said she was nervous, but I've encountered her twice now and I think he's talking about the wrong girl.

"And just now, when we came in?" I ask. "That you?"

"Yeah."

"You stopped in the middle of the song."

She shrugs as if she doesn't have to answer to me. Good. She doesn't.

"So, you're Colton Crowne?" Becca asks. "The same one who—"

"Probably?" Whatever it is, I don't want to hear it, so I dip down for the last glass on the tray and scoop up some ice. "You guys need a refill or nah?"

They're both good.

"Gloria" ends to cheers and whoops. I'm thinking I got out of Dodge, but Becca has something on her mind.

"So, Colton," Becca says, "I heard Tamika's demo on Soundcloud before it got pulled. It was good."

"She is who she is." I try to shrug it off with a simple truth. I worked with the most talented woman in the business until I didn't.

"No, I mean the sound was super lush. How'd you do it?"

"Plug-in."

"The Neve?"

"Nah. I programmed it myself. Down at the code level."

She raises a pierced eyebrow and looks me up and down as if she has to reassess me. That's why I don't usually tell people shit like that. It changes the math. I don't know why I said anything at all.

"Really fucking good," she says.

"Not good enough."

"Skye!" someone calls. "You're next."

"Oh yeah," Becca says with a little clap. "I put you on 'Wings of Gold.'" She grabs the remote from the stand and makes a shoo signal with both hands. "Go, go."

"I... uh..." Skye glances at me, then at the stage.

Between the crosswalk and what I heard when the door opened, I've heard enough, but I wouldn't mind hearing a whole song. I'm not made of stone.

I shrug, and as if me not caring one way or the other is motivating, she goes up to the mic.

That's when the door pops open. A waitress comes in with carafes of soda on a tray. Becca holds the remote to start the song, then pulls it back. There's a man behind the waitress. Big blond in a leather blazer and tie-dyed T-shirt, wrap sunglasses pushed up his forehead so they look like big, black eyebrows.

Gene Testarossa. Formerly of WME Agency, now with Glendora Records.

Liam jumps up and greets him.

"That's thirteen," Fátima murmurs to Becca. "I can go." Her lashes drop as she looks at the piercing in the other chick's lip.

"I have to stay." Becca shrugs a little, a distinct flirt in her eyes.

"I'll go," Skye says. "I'm tired anyway."

"Don't worry about it," Liam says. "Everyone's been paid. Skye! I want you to meet someone. Gene, you know Colton."

Ten people are here for a good time and their buzz is being shot out of the sky by my brother's industry gladhanding—which I'm part of whether I like a good time or not.

"I'll go," I say, but no one hears me.

"Colton!" Gene shakes my hand. His iced-out Piaget clicks when he claps my bicep hard enough to force me to take a step to the side.

Fátima looks pretty aggravated and Skye's holding the mic, wide-eyed, as Gene holds out his hand for her.

"Heard a lot about you," he says when Skye takes it.

"Um... I..." She looks at her manager, but he's making room for Gene on the couch.

It's good to see Liam back on his feet after Malin. He's getting out. He's working. But Jesus Christ, bringing Gene Testarossa into any kind of room has big bull-in-china-shop vibes.

"'Wings of Gold!'" Becca cries, pointing the remote at the machine. "Skye. You ready?"

Skye doesn't nod or say she's ready to go. She just stands there with the microphone under her chin, other arm dropped straight along her side. Her eyes are directed at the tabletop with its little puddles and bunched-up wing-sauce-streaked napkins, but they're focused somewhere in the middle distance.

Then her brows knot in the center, creasing a line at the end of each eyebrow.

I'd bet the last $650 I have in the bank that she's not singing tonight.

Becca and Fátima look at each other. Becca nods, then Fátima approaches Skye, who looks up as if shocked to find herself on stage with a microphone.

"We're thirteen." Skye puts the mic back in the stand. She's going to leave to make it twelve, which Liam paid good money to keep from being an issue.

"I gotta split anyway." Waving to everyone, I turn to Skye, who's already removed herself from the front of the room. "You finish up."

Before anyone can tell me I should stay, I'm out of there, heading down the hall to the little counter where Dollar Sign is standing in front of an iPad, and down the stairs thinking this'll keep anyone from following me.

Wrong again.

COLTON

The night is pretty cool and Wilshire's pretty dead, even for a Wednesday. A bus rumbles by like an empty dragon. The Serrano light turns green for no one in particular. I start across the boulevard when I hear my name. It's Liam.

"Call me tomorrow," I say. "I'm going to bed. I still have this headache."

"Wait." He's out of breath from chasing me. "Listen. Please. She's good, I'm telling you."

"I know she is."

"They're good songs, and she doesn't micromanage the compositions. The instrumentals we have will still work. But we don't have all the voice. She gets nervous and clams up."

"No shit?" Sarcasm is humor for times shit isn't funny. "I know stage fright when I see it."

"If she doesn't know everyone in the room... she chokes. Locking down a public studio, it's just not enough. In Logan's garage, it's just you."

"She doesn't know me."

"Everybody likes you. You'll be friends. She'll sing. Done."

"Great. Thanks for the offer. I mean it. I appreciate it." I put my fist to my heart. "But it's a nah for me."

"She's really good, Colton. I'm never going to be able to look myself in the mirror if I don't do everything I can for this talent."

Who am I to call him a liar? He believes in this girl, and Liam hasn't been passionate about anything outside his son and his dead wife for a long time.

"If she can't get up on stage in front of people, she's a studio backup singer. Period. It's a good living. Let her make it." The light's changed back. I punch the button again.

"You owe this to yourself."

"I'll talk to my accountant." Beating up the button isn't working, and there's just enough traffic to make jaywalking dangerous. I go to the Serrano side, figuring I'll make my east-west crossing first, just to get out of this conversation about who owes shit to whom. But Liam's not deterred by a new crosswalk.

"What she needs is a voice whisperer," he pleads, really getting on my last nerve. "That's you."

"I never shoulda told you guys about that."

"*The Fader* told me and everyone else."

"Fuck *The Fader*, fuck that guy, and fuck his article. I had a legitimate claim and he made me out to be some butthurt boyfriend Tamika Clark stepped over, and it wasn't like that."

"I know." He holds out his hands to slow me down, but for real, fuck that too.

"He gave McCormick—the dude who built the biggest piracy site in the fucking world—a halo and wings. The last quote was McFucker taking credit for my work because a judge skipped lunch. And right before that? Paragraph right above? That fucking hack puts this quote that the lawsuit 'got emotional for everyone involved,' just to kick me in the nuts."

"That's not what it said, Colton, and you know it."

"Read between the fucking lines."

Serrano's empty. I step off the curb before I go off on my brother for another hour. I've managed to keep my shit together for months, especially in front of my family. I'm not going to lose it even further in the middle of the street.

But Liam won't accept a truce. He knows exactly what to say to get me to stop in the middle of the street with the light counting down.

"You put Tamika's shit all over the radio."

I turn around and pace back to the sidewalk.

"Did I? Who produced it?" I already know the answer. The talent I dropped a couple of years of my life on made it big once I was out of the picture. "Not me. So I don't know what you think I whispered."

Liam scoffs. He thinks he knows something about anything. "You just quit the mailroom at Crowne. Do you have any plans at all?"

"They don't even need a mailroom. They have email."

"You have more potential than any of us."

"Okay, I'm done. We're cool. I gotta go." I cross Serrano Ave.

"You're walking? This isn't New York, Colton. You don't just *walk home.*"

He's right. This isn't New York. You don't just cross when you feel like it either. But I'm looking forward to walking a few blocks to get my head together, then another few to forget whatever just happened. So fuck this light and fuck my brother, who's getting on my nerves right now.

"Colton!"

"Whoa!" I slap the hood of the silver Toyota Corolla that stops an inch from hitting me.

In the street's floodlights, Skye looks stricken, both hands gripping the wheel, mouth contorted into a grimace, and that little cute knot of concern between her eyebrows.

"I'm sorry!" I hear her through her open windows.

"It's okay." Holding up my palms, I show her there's no harm.

"I'm sorry!" she repeats, blinking hard. "I'm so sorry!"

"Seriously, it's cool."

The traffic light glints green, then yellow, then red, against the two lines of tears down her cheeks. Aw, man. I don't like that.

I'm one step from the sidewalk, where I should be, but Liam's there and part of my brain is still in the five-seconds-ago world where it was important to get away from him, so I go to the driver's side. She puts the car into park and wipes her cheeks with her fingers.

"See? I'm fine." I lean on the top of the door. "It's cool."

She sniffs, and I realize her eyes are pretty red. She didn't start crying when she almost hit me. Nah, that started before she even got in the car. In this kinda state, she has this delicacy about her, and she's fighting it. I like the delicateness —it's interesting. And I like the fight. That's even more interesting.

"What are you crying for?" I ask.

"Because I'm tired."

"You cry when you're tired?"

"Yes. Yes, I do." Skye sounds annoyed with herself. "It's late and I got up early for work."

My defenses break down without a sound. Her frustration when she sniffs back her sob isn't right. She doesn't have to get on herself like that, and if no one ever told her that, well, I'm not going to leave it unsaid.

"It's a pretty cool valve. We're all born with it." What am I saying? Do I sound stupid? I must, because she doesn't even smile.

"I'm a toddler, okay?"

A city bus belches along Wilshire. Liam leans into the open window on Skye's passenger side. I ignore him. I'm not talking to him right now.

"No, I didn't mean that," I say.

"Of course she's tired," Liam says across the car. "You were late."

My shortcomings are common knowledge. You could print them on the front page of the *LA Times* except they're not breaking news. But him coming at me like that in front of Skye, who shouldn't matter because I don't know her—but who weirdly does matter... that pisses me off. And pissing me off ain't easy.

"What did Gene say?" Skye asks.

"He's a little confused by the deer-in-headlights problem—"

"Hey." I say it softly because I've already yelled tonight. "Shut the fuck up."

"So, what's your plan?" Liam demands from me.

"Mine? I'm going home."

"Gonna jerk off? Spend what you have left on beer?"

"Mom ever tell you minding your business is free?"

"You already came crawling back broke like a guy in a Bible story."

"Where's my fatted fucking calf?"

"You guys!" Skye tries to interrupt whatever's happening

across her front seat, but she went from taking up my entire attention to barely even there.

"You owe me," Liam growls.

"I *owe* you?"

"Guys!" She throws up her arms, not crying anymore.

"For leaving. For hiding. Running away… whatever you did. You. Owe. Me."

"Get in fucking line." I point behind me at the endless, imaginary line of aggrieved people that follows me around.

"Okay, I'm out." Skye snaps her seatbelt and opens the door, slamming it into me.

Because my arms are off the door, embracing the crowd of people I owe things, I'm caught totally off balance and fall on my ass onto Serrano Ave, which hasn't had a car go down it since Skye almost hit me.

But in Los Angeles, an empty street doesn't stay empty for long. For the second time, I'm at the wrong end of screeching tires. From where I'm lying, the SUV seems like a hundred-ton tanker, and I'm sure I'm done. There's no way it's going to stop in time. Everyone in that line behind me is going to have to get their satisfaction elsewhere.

Skye moves for me, and I put my hands up to tell her not to, but she's so fast I don't realize she's grabbed my wrists until she pulls me up, falls back, and inertia launches me forward into her car, against her, pushing the air out of both our lungs.

I'd get off her, but she feels nice, and she's a good anchor while I catch my breath.

And also, she's gripping my jacket so hard that if I do pull away, she's going to rip it.

"You're okay." She's stating a fact she hasn't accepted yet.

"I think so."

"I am so sorry."

"Jesus Christ!" Liam cries from the sidewalk. "What the fuck?"

The SUV's door slams. Skye is still holding me close to her.

"It's fine," I say. "Are you okay?"

"I thought I killed you." She loosens her grip and smooths down my jacket.

"Dude, he literally jumped"—it's Eugene Testarossa, making excuses to Liam—"in front of my car, and you..." He points at me. "Are you doing it again?"

"Doing what?" Now that I've been freed, I get off Skye.

"You guys a thing?" He looks at Skye as if he hadn't seen her upstairs. She's new to him. Full of possibilities. "Because if you're a thing..."

"No!" Sky says. "We are—"

Liam cuts her off. "You caught them." He stands between us and Gene. "Definitely a thing, but they're not talking about it for obvious reasons."

"I can get with that. Yeah. Patterns. Tells a story. Nice." He's bobbing his head like a dashboard ornament, agreeing with some brilliant idea he just had though I can't say I have a single clue what he's talking about. He points at Liam with his finger-gun. "Let me know when you have something." He taps his ear.

"Will do," Liam agrees, but Gene's already in his SUV, which roars forward, slows at the corner, and runs the red light.

"I don't like guys like that," Skye says.

"Nobody does." I comb my fingers through my hair and realize I'm not wearing my cap.

Skye reads my mind and scoops it up from the place

where the street meets the sidewalk, swatting it against her thigh to sterilize it.

"Thanks." I pop it onto my head.

"Well." Liam straightens his jacket. "Tonight was a wild success. No need to do it ever again. You two, as far as Glendora Records is concerned, are now a Thing with a capital T."

"Hold on..." I say.

"What the..." Skye says at the same time.

"You heard me. We'll talk about it tomorrow. I'm going to go home and drink a bottle of vodka. Colton, do you need a lift?"

"Still gonna walk."

"Skye, you're okay to get home?" He's already backing up.

"Car's still running so..."

"I'll take that as a yes. Good night." He pivots on the ball of his foot and strides to the garage with the speed of a New Yorker in danger of being two minutes late.

"Will he really drink a bottle of vodka?" Skye asks.

"Just one. Small one."

She spins to me, the two lines between her eyebrows fully engaged in her concern. I want to touch that shape. Press it. See if it's as tight as it seems. I put my hands in my pockets.

"A whole bottle? Is that safe?"

"The flight attendant cuts you off at, like, three, so..."

She smiles and gives me a little shove. "I'm sorry I couldn't sing 'Wings of Gold' when he came in. New people make me nervous."

"Next time I won't be new." There won't be a next time, but I don't want to deal with that right now. We just went through something together.

"Especially since now we're in a Thing with a capital T."

"He's gonna wake up hungover and realize he hit optimal maximum weirdness."

She looks back at her car. "I guess I should get to bed."

"Drive safe." I back into the street, toward the crosswalk.

"You sure you don't need a lift?"

"Nah, it's close. But thanks."

"It was nice to meet you."

"Same."

She gets into the car. It takes me a second to get back onto the sidewalk. Skye pulls up to the red light and waves to me.

I wave back and decide that at this point, the walk home won't be any fun. I don't need to be with my thoughts as much as I'd like to explain to her, right now, why Liam's going to get someone else to produce her EP.

I knock on her window. She rolls it down.

"Yeah?"

"Changed my mind."

"Get in." She clacks the locks open and I get in.

5

SKYE

My dashboard ornament bounces side to side on a spring. On top of the spring sits a yellow smiley face with arms sticking out where its ears should be. Colton pokes it and it swings back and forth.

His right proximal phalanges are tattooed with LIVE, one letter for each finger.

"That's Lemony," I say. "Sometimes, I pop him when I'm in traffic. Makes me smile instead of get so mad I cry."

"I think I need one." He leans back, stretching into casual I-never-gave-a-fuck-and never-will posture, knees spread, one elbow on the door and one on the center console.

"You don't seem like the kind of guy who ever gets angry."

His left fingers are tattooed with the word FREE.

LIVE FREE

I wish.

"Anger eats the soul," he says.

"I think that was fear."

"Anger eats something then. Definitely fucks up a good

time. Traffic, though? I get a little mad. It's part of the LA experience." He taps his knee with two fingers, then three, then two twice—a beat string for the song in his head. His hand is huge.

"Is it hard work hard to be this laid-back?" I ask.

He scoffs. "Yeah." He looks away as if remembering something specific. "I got a PhD in shrugging."

He taps Lemony with a quick wrist. A leather strap is wrapped around it along with a string of wooden orbs and a thick-linked silver chain. The red highlights at the edge of his knuckles turn green.

"You want to tell me where you live?" I ask.

"Left." He barely straightens with renewed attention. "Right on Hudson. Take that past 4th. Can't miss it. Stupidest house on the block."

I snap the blinker and check behind me. "Can't wait to see what a stupid house looks like."

"Looks like a guy's ego."

"I'm familiar with that architectural style." I turn onto Wilshire.

"Where you from?"

"Grosse Pointe. It's a suburb."

"I know it. I was in Detroit for a while. I hear it's nice." He flicks Lemony then settles back against the corner between the seat and the door in that chronically-relaxed slouch.

"You keep saying 'nice' like that's a word you use when you mean something else."

He shrugs. "What do you think I mean?"

I match his shrug and raise him a questioning chirp from the back of my throat. "Anyone else, I'd think they meant rich, or clean, or safe. But you? I think you mean bland."

"To my Detroit people, it's got a big dystopian vibe."

"You know dystopian doesn't mean 'nice,' right?" I don't want to assume he's stupid, but that's the only explanation for what I'm hearing.

"Thanks, Merriam-Webster. I know what nice means."

I stop at the light and look at him. He knows what nice means, because of course he knows what dystopian means. It's not a hard word. But his smirk isn't covering over offense at the insult.

"Nice is a place so boring it makes you want to burn it down?" I ask.

"Yeah. So, 'nice,' you know?"

"I do know."

"Do you know we're on Hudson and your blinker's not on?"

I stick out my tongue at him. He's funny. I give him a pass and snap the blinker.

"What did Liam mean?" I ask, turning onto Hudson. "By... I don't know, all of it? Does he expect us to actually... you know?"

"No. Jesus. No. I don't know what he expects. Gene, I don't know what he expects either." He mindlessly drags his knuckle along the edge of the window. "Nah. That's not true. I know what he expects."

"Well, let me in on it."

"Guys like Gene Testarossa, they don't care about anything but how easily they can get ice in their watch. Liam calls? Maybe ice. So he comes. The girl he reps, she's cute. Definitely some ice. Can she sing? Well, he doesn't know that, and maybe he's willing to work around it and maybe he's not, but if Colton Crowne's with her before she's hot, same as he was with Tamika, well, it's easy fucking bling. And the easy part—" Colton turns to me. "Guys like that get their rocks off on it being easy. It's a status thing. If what's hard for everyone else is easy for him, then he's at the top of the pile. No money can buy him what *easy* can."

"Huh. I never heard it put like that. But yeah. Things being easy is its own status symbol."

"It's on the right. Middle of the block."

I find the stupidest house on the block, where stupid is defined by its size and nothing else. There are so many parking spots I have to check the sign twice because this can't be legal. Turns out it is.

"Stupid House Station." I put the car in park. "Connections for Silly Place, Dumb Mansion, and the Armpit of LA Shuttle. Watch your step, stand clear, get your keys out."

"Thank you, conductor." He opens the door. The light goes on and the dash beeps incessantly. "That was fun."

"What can I say. I'm a good time."

Without getting out, he shuts the door. Light off. Beeping stops.

"Look," he says. "About producing your EP…"

"Forget it. Liam tried. He's a good manager, and I know I'm kind of a tough case."

"You are, man. Tough fucking case."

"He's a trouper. You don't have to be. It's fine. We can still be friends."

"No. Let's do it."

"I'm sorry?"

"You have a lot of guts, and I feel like… I don't know. Someone like that might be cool to work with."

"I'm really cool to work with, except the…" I take a deep breath. I'm deeply ashamed of the performance anxiety, but I'd be more deeply ashamed to have an attack in front of him if he thinks I'm actually dying. "There's a reason I haven't been able to get anything down."

"Liam told me." He doesn't seem either concerned or dismissive. I'm not sure if I should be annoyed with him or grateful he took the revelation off my plate. I decide on the latter. "My studio's in the back. Right down that driveway."

"Great." I didn't expect this to be easy and I'm not sure how to feel. A minute ago I was enjoying myself, and now that's all turned into pressure to try again without freezing.

"The studio's not as stupid as the house," he adds.

"Yeah. Okay. Yeah. Thank you."

He gets out and waves, walking backward. He doesn't turn until I wave back.

I watch him move into the shadows. The lights that line the edge of the walk go on as he passes. My phone buzzes, so I check it before driving off. It's Liam.

—look what showed up on DMZ—

A photo slides in. It's screenshot from DMZ and a link. A picture of Colton pushing me against my car and me grabbing his jacket. Everything else is cut out. Liam. Gene. It's shot from a little above, through a windshield.

The headline under it reads: HAS COLTON CROWNED THE NEXT TAMIKA?

What? I tap the link. The article is short and breathless. Colton Crowne, who "discovered" Tamika in Memphis and who was "viciously" cut from credit or royalties by Gavin McCormick, may be nursing the next baby star into the sky.

They don't even know I'm a musician.

I could be a lawyer or an accountant.

But that wouldn't get clicks. No one cares about that story.

Liam follows with a text.

41

—**You guys**—

Colton is on the chat. I look at the driveway. The path lights have gone dark, but I can see him standing there, looking down with the screen glowing on his face.

"Fuck!" he barks, moving enough to turn on the lights.

That's when I know he's seen Liam's messages. He looks at me and, seeing I haven't moved, jogs over while his brother's texts ding.

— **This is gold-plated**—

—**A gift from the gods**—

—**We're on second base before we even get to the plate**—

Colton stops. Types into his phone.

—*What are you talking about?*—

—**You guys together in public coronates Skye**—

This feels more real than when Liam mentioned it before.

I don't have long to do something… anything… or I have to fulfill my promise to my mother and take up last year's deferment to University of Michigan Medical School. Being coronated, as Liam calls it, makes that possible. Without an electric shock to the process, I don't have a chance. I'm dead in the water. Pursuing a music career and med school at the same time isn't possible without a clone.

But I want clarity, so I text the chat.

—*You mean you really want us to pretend we're fucking?*—

I hit Send before I rethink the word fucking to describe

what I'm not doing with Colton, who answers from halfway back to the car.

—*That's what he means*—

He could have told me that himself. Instead, he stands there as Liam's message comes in.

—**That's what I mean**—

I'm about to text that I'm in. I'll do it. I'm thrilled actually. But it's not just about me, so I wait for Colton to come to me. I open the passenger window. He doesn't come. Instead, he sends a message.

—*You know Gene took this right? From the angle?*—

I look back at the photo. Yeah. It was taken from the SUV before Gene got out. Maybe he took it to get evidence in case he'd hit anyone or maybe he was thinking that fast. That's secondary to the fact that it found its way to a gossip website.

A notification drops over the picture. A text from Colton.

—*So, no. Fuck him. No*—

Once that comes in, I look at him as he puts the phone in his pocket and starts back my way.

I want to be coronated. I want it to be easy. I need the boost to start before the walls close in.

They've been closing in for months. Ever since last year when I applied. Before that, when I took the MCAT without studying. I thought I was so clever, setting myself up for failure. I wasn't clever enough to get the answers wrong though.

That's fine. It's fine. I'm okay with it. Screw the coronation. I can't make Colton do something he doesn't want to do. He has every right to refuse. But I'm still reeling from the transition between hope and regret. For a minute, I was in a world where I had a head start and I'm just as suddenly back in the status quo.

He's coming this way. I don't want to talk to him. I don't want to hear the reasons he thinks it's a bad idea. Not right now, because he's probably right and I just want to sit in my disappointment alone.

Before he reaches the car, I drive away.

COLTON

"Get the fuck out of here," I murmur in the dark as I answer the group chat, then silence it, because I'm not even going to be party to this trashfire plan.

Stupidest idea ever. Insulting to both of us, but especially Skye, who shouldn't need a PR stunt to be noticed. Then she drives away, and I figure she's pretty insulted by the suggestion. I don't blame her.

I told her I'd produce her EP, and I meant it. But now it's not just a favor for my brother or something I'll do because Skye seems like a cool person. Now I'm going to do it to prove I'm not an asshole like my brother.

She needs to know I'm not on board for gimmicks, so I grab her number from the group chat and shoot her a text.

—Call me tomorrow. We can start whenever—

Walking past the gate and along the side of the big house, I hear Ella laughing. She's home from Italy, pregnant, and the reason I have to move out. Cool, cool. Nice reminder of pressure I forgot to feel for a couple of hours. Great. Now I'm fully jacked up.

All energy, I get to the back house and pick a beer out of the fridge. It's a lot. Skye. Her voice. The anxiety problem I gotta work around. My brother's nutbag PR ideas and Gene Testarossa's duplicitous ass.

One song should be a cover. Totally fresh take on a love song.

I take a swallow of beer then put the bottle to my forehead.

She writes her own songs. Helpful if they're good. A pain in the ass if they suck.

The garage is attached to the kitchen, so I'm there in a few steps. I leave the bottle by the couch and hit the studio.

The piano keyboard is set up. My kid self did what he was told and took his piano lessons, practicing like a good little nerd, but once the kid was gone, the man knew how to do something he'd never forget. I hit the keys, but I have nothing.

This is not the keyboard I need to fuck with right now.

I wander back to my laptop and tinker around with the coding behind the lush plug-in, thinking about Skye, her voice, the anxiety between her eyebrows, and eventually lapse into the way she felt when my body pushed hers against the car. The way she gripped my jacket. Like a wild horse I'd only be able to tame for a few minutes. She was pure energy.

Without windows, I lose track of the hours. When there's a knock at the door, I look at my watch. It's eight in the morning already.

46

I hope it's not Skye. I stink. Another knock as I cross the kitchen. She's getting impatient. Good. Me too.

Figuring I'll let her in and jump in the shower before she can catch a whiff, I open the door.

It's Liam, launching into it without even a hello. "I need you guys to do the fake thing."

"Fuck." Half annoyance, half disappointment. A little resignation, because I should have counted on any one of my brothers not taking no for an answer.

"Hear me out." He's sharp as a knife, fresh and clear-eyed, smelling like aftershave and toothpaste.

"No." I walk away from the door but leave it open. I need food.

"Good!" Liam throws up his hands, but not in the I-give-up way. It's more I-dig-your-concept. "Say it again. Put it on a loop. When you're in front of me, deny it like you're on trial. I don't care. This is for the cameras."

"Liam." I stand straight. No slouch. No shrug. "No."

"It's not international diplomacy. We're not making an arms sale. It's entertainment, and your job."

"I never said—" I stop myself when I notice his mouth twitching on one side. He's trying not to smirk. He knows I agreed to work with Skye, and there's only one way he could know that. He spoke to her first. "Fuck off."

Food. I can't think without it. The fridge has four beers and cheese slices. Open jars of olives, but I'm not feeling the green ones right now.

"I agreed to cut an EP. That's the job." I stick my nose in the milk. Gone. I check the cabinets. Cans and boxes of soup. Spices. Where did I get a tetra pack of two percent?

"Your job is to support the talent. Look." He sits on a stool

47

on the other side of the island. "There are a thousand new songs uploaded every day. You're competing with YouTube, and TikTok, and Soundcloud's still a thing. We're up against every preadolescent with Pro Tools. We got twelve-year-old girls with voices like angels singing to their stuffed animals. Okay? And you can make magic—yes, music magic. But the real magic is Tamika's first producer—the guy whose heart she broke—"

"Jesus, Liam. Stop." I grab a can of black olives.

"—back home like a prodigal son, getting back up on his feet with a new voice. A girl from Detroit."

"Grosse Pointe actually."

"Arriving in Los Angeles with ten dollars in her pocket. Stop. Don't try to correct me on the details. The girl gets off the bus with a duffel bag and a dream, ready to bust her ass climbing the ladder, and she meets *him*." Both hands indicate me as if I'm some kind of prize. "A native of this all-or-nothing town, finally come home broken and humiliated. And their love lifts them both. She fulfills her dreams. He redeems himself." He claps once, keeping his palms together and shaking his head with his eyes closed, as if he's in some kind of reverie.

"Were you always like this?" I don't know this guy anymore. Malin wouldn't have tolerated this shit, but it's never a good time to bring up the potential disappointment of his dead wife.

"I'm better than ever."

"It's a gimmick." I rummage around for a can opener. "She doesn't need it."

"It's a story," he pleads.

"It's a setup. Gene set this up."

"He needs a story."

"You're not Hans Christian fucking Ander—"

"Gimmicks sell. And don't tell me lying to the celebrity-media-complex is some kind of ethical line in the sand."

"No, you dumb fuck! Because I did this already and it was a fucking disaster."

"But it was real that time."

I find the can opener and open the olives.

Yeah, it was real, and that's what made it so shitty. I'm over it now, but there's no way I'm walking that road again.

"I moved on, Liam." I toss the can top in the sink. "The relationship... that's done. I have nothing. No feelings for my ex. I want her to be happy. That's it. It's not like that anymore. But you're right that I'm not over it. I can't move on from all the shit that came with that relationship until fuckers like you stop describing me with words like 'humiliated.'"

Pinching out three olives, I flick the can to his side.

"You want your cache back? Go to dinner with a beautiful woman on your arm." He snaps his fingers and points at me to punctuate his point. "Kiss her cheek. Tell the press you think she's hot."

The olives pop between my teeth and wash salty brine over my tongue. "They're going to compare her to Tamika."

"You're finally getting it." He plucks out an olive and eats it.

"And they're going to dredge up everything... in public. You're trying to put me in the same situation I just woke up from."

"That's why the story works."

"You're a stubborn fuck."

"Because all of us have so much more to gain than lose. Especially her."

He's right. I take the can. If I don't do it and Skye's career flounders, it'll be on me, because I refused to do this fucked up thing.

Wait. This tango takes two.

"Hold on," I say, eating olives like popcorn. "You talked to Skye already. If she was going for this, you would have led with it. So you came to me, figuring if I agreed, she'd change her mind. Right?"

"She's in, Colton. If you're in, she's in."

The olives are soft and salty, and the can's almost empty.

"Great," I mumble. "Fucking fantastic."

He brightens as though someone hosed the dust off him. He can sense I'm bending his way.

"You know," he says. "If I had to pick any of the six of us to have to depend on, you'd be the last."

It'd be easy to get hurt over his lack of faith in me. But he has motives, so he'll say what he thinks will work—and he's also right. Dependability isn't exactly my middle name.

"Thanks and go fuck yourself."

He slides the can back to me then rubs his face. When he lowers his hand, his cheeks are red. He's my big brother again, not shaving yet, face bitten by the Cambria cold. "Look, I've been treading water ever since Malin died. Just getting Matt to preschool is overwhelming, and I have help. I can't believe everything my wife was doing while I was out there thinking I was busy."

"Imagine Mom."

"Six of us." He huffs then shakes his head.

We take a second of silence thinking about everything our mother—despite all dad's money—gave up for us. I take the last olive and throw the can into the recycling. The clatter wakes him from his thoughts.

"Yeah, what I'm trying to say is... every day I'm

confronted with Malin being gone. Matt needs me. I can't be a power player anymore. I got that. I accept it. But then I heard her… this talent…" He points out the window at the Skye who isn't here. "Finding her made me feel the way I was before, when I woke up in the morning pumped to move mountains one rock at a time. Now I'm down to ten clients. Half of them do commercials. She's all I have. If I let her slip through my fingers, I could live to be a hundred and I'll never find another one. I'll never get this chance back. She can't fail. I can't let her."

"Then don't, man. It's your deal." Even as I push it all back onto his plate, I'm cracking. I wasn't here when he needed me. I took my money and abandoned everyone because I thought I was too good, too smart, too cool for all of them.

"Yeah." With regret, he gets off the stool. "I thought it would be fun, but you probably don't need any more fun added to your schedule."

That's the most compelling argument he's made. Hanging out with Skye *would* be fun.

"Talk later." He goes to the front door.

Liam's acting as if this is it and… no. This is not it. We have to do the EP. Is he out? What I want with Skye, I don't even know. All I know is I'm not done. I also know I'm not going to walk away without finishing the job. That's what got me into trouble in the first place, but I'm a leopard and I got spots.

Liam's hand is on the knob.

"Couple of weeks," I blurt. "I have to protect myself. I'm not going through that again. I'm not going to mix all my hurt feelings and shit up with the work. Okay? That's not going to happen again."

His hand slips away. "Okay?"

"Public breakup. No hard feelings." The hard feelings with Tamika were the least of it once the lawyers were involved. "And I get sole production credit. Me. Forever. You're my brother, but I want a contract. It's lawyers now or lawyers later, and they're cheaper now. I'm not getting sucked dry again because she decides I don't have the right connections."

"Wait. What are we talking about?"

"She goes and fucks Gavin McCormick or whoever and comes back to bed thinking I'll just sign all my work over... I need to have a contract to hold up."

"Back to bed?"

"Whatever!"

Liam's in front of me, hands gripping my shoulders. "Hey, kid?"

"Forget it."

He squeezes the bottom half of my face. "Gonna happen different this time."

I push him off. I don't want to think too hard about getting cornered into this, because in the end, it's about the music. No more, no less.

Skye better agree to—no, swear to that, signed in blood, or this whole thing is off.

7

SKYE

Dr. Solomon had been recommended by Dr. Haversham, who'd been listening to my problems since I was eleven. Her office is in an old Hancock Park mansion that's been divided into therapeutic spaces. She's just the middle-aged side of elderly, seventy-percent gray, without a stitch of surgical maintenance. She has the energy of ten psychiatrists and the confidence of a woman who had to be twice as good to get half as much.

She leans on the left arm of her chair and crosses her legs in the other direction. The black leather cushions squeak. Both of our chairs are curved wood that cups the body with black leather cushions and a matching ottoman. Her office is furnished in mid-range mid-century furniture she got from her grandmother, who bought it new in the actual mid-century. Kids' board games are stacked on a teak table, and a matching bookshelf is stuffed with psychiatric literature.

"So," I finish telling her everything from karaoke to Liam's phone call at seven in the morning, "Liam's going to talk to Colton about it again, thinking maybe he can convince him, and if he wants to do it, we do it."

"That's a lot."

"Last night was the absolute definition of a lot."

"What story are you telling yourself about it?"

I sigh. Yeah. The problem with me isn't what my life *is*, it's what I tell myself it is, and I rarely have anything nice to say. "I haven't really processed it all yet, which is a good thing."

"You haven't had time to engage triggering thoughts."

"Yeah. Once I'm out the door, I'm sure I'll get around to calling myself a worthless, fake-talent—"

"Stop."

"Right." I'm not supposed to say the things I use to hurt myself, even if it's to illustrate a point because it'll start a loop I can't get out of. I should know that already. I've gone from joking around to panic attack too many times. "I'm fine." I close my eyes and inhale, paying attention to my breath. "I'm fine."

"Do you need to go to the next step?"

"I don't think so." The next step is humming—not singing —the "Star-Spangled Banner." "I have it."

"Good." She uncrosses and recrosses her legs in the other direction. "So, you want to do the thing your manager—"

"Agent."

"Thank you. Your *agent* suggested you pretend to be in a relationship. And you think this is a good idea?"

"It can't hurt, right?"

"Maybe not." She shrugs.

"I'm probably going back to Michigan in August, so it has a sell-by date."

"It could also create openings for negative triggers to get through."

"But that's the case with anything new I try."

"Touché."

"All I have to do is manage it. Keep control."

"Why not try the Lexapro again?" she asks. "I know you don't like some of the side effects."

"Mindfulness doesn't give me diarrhea."

"Can't argue with that. We could try something else. Effexor? Maybe Klonopin…"

"Klonopin made it worse, and Effexor backed me up so bad I wished for Lexapro. Tricyclics do nothing, and taking beta blockers off-label makes me nervous, which defeats the entire purpose."

"I hear you. You don't want medication."

"I'm not judging anyone who does."

"I know you're not."

"I just don't like the way I feel on them, and no, I don't like being anxious all the time either, but that's who I am. It's what I do to myself, not what some pill is doing to me."

"That makes sense. And you've been working very hard to manage it."

"I think it's working. Last night, I was in a situation that normally… I'd have an anxiety attack, and I didn't."

"No, you almost got hit by a car instead."

I laugh a little and shake my head. "He wouldn't have let that happen."

"Who?"

"Colton."

"Is he an Avenger?"

I laugh. "Is there one who's really easygoing? Whatever Man to the rescue? Chill Dude will save us?"

"Captain No Problem? You think that's a man who can make things happen?"

"No, but he's a guy who can make things *not* happen."

"Ah."

"He was very good-looking which... you know... makes me into a wreck." I laugh nervously. "But he didn't. I had nothing." I draw a circle around a heart that palpitates like mad around beautiful, confident people.

"Why do you think that is?"

"Maybe you cured me," I say brightly.

She smiles a little. That's what she does when she knows I'm avoiding the subject at hand. Forty years of treating anxiety means she doesn't miss a trick.

"I think... this sounds gross... before he showed up at karaoke, Fátima told me all about him and his problems. He's made some bad decisions. Lost all his money. Had his heart broken. I guess that made him as human as me. That really does sound gross."

"It doesn't."

"Uh... yeah, it does. I'm feeling better about myself by thinking about his problems, so it's very, very kind of gross."

"Is it possible everyone has problems? Everyone's having a hard time? Even the people you can't see? You're worried about strangers judging you and your work. Every one of them is suffering in some way. Have you considered some of them might feel a little better because of your humanity?"

"No. And I don't mean no, I've never thought of it, I mean no, I've considered it and I think it doesn't matter. When people like a song or whatever, it's just a song. There's no investment in it existing. If my voice or my song isn't there, they'll listen to something else. But when they hate you—like, if they're offended by the way you sound and it's not like you can do anything to convince them otherwise? Then it's personal." I sit straight, because I'm done, and I'm right, and I have spoken truth.

Dr. Solomon clears her throat, straightens her shirt, and leans in the opposite direction. "I want you to think very hard about doing this particular PR stunt with this particular man."

"Why him in particular?"

"You've expressed a connection with his humanity." She starts with her pinkie and counts off toward her thumb. "A sympathetic telling of his story. You trust him in a way he hasn't earned and you can't explain. And critically, you describe a strong physical attraction." She folds her hands in her lap. "If you spend time pretending you're in love with him, you might wake up to realize you're not pretending."

"I didn't come halfway across the country to get a boyfriend."

"Let's put a pin in that, okay?"

"I mean it. That's not what this is about."

"I believe you. I get it. You're in the driver's seat."

"Exactly. This is one hundred percent about my career. Falling in love with him—and by the way? Yes, he's good-looking... but not every handsome guy is my type, so whatever? But falling for him would make this whole thing complicated when actually? It only works if we keep it simple."

"Noted. Good. We have seven minutes. Would you like to do some visual mindfulness?"

"Sure."

For seven minutes, I focus on an egg-shaped sculpture, but all I can think about is whether or not Liam got Colton to agree.

"Fuck frappes," I say when Fátima tickets another three in from the drive-thru.

I'm a buzzsaw behind the bar. I move like a dance, pulling drink ingredients from my muscles, counting syrup pumps, calling out names, hot, iced, half-caf, no whip, please can you add more cream, thank you, thank you, I said oat milk, do you know how they treat the cows, thank you, this isn't how my name is spelled, I also have a cake pop, can I get a straw, what are you doing after your shift?

The sun's shadows are just starting to cross the parking lot by the time our shift is over. I'm drained in a way that's satisfying—almost peaceful.

"You were on the spot today," Fátima says.

"I figure I can be the attending at the ER in, like, northwest Detroit, no problem."

"Does that pay?"

"A little more than our current employer. Benefits aren't as good though."

We reach our cars on the far side of the lot. That's the first time I hear my phone buzz all day, but that has more to do with being busy than being unbuzzed.

I open my messages. Mom. Liam. Liam. No Colton. So no plans for a session. I don't know if that's a good sign or not. Feeling too good to deal with any of these messages, I put away the phone.

I told Fátima everything about last night except the possibility of the fake relationship. There's something too shameful about even trying something so risky for the sake of my career, and something even more risky about telling another person.

"I'm hitting tumbling class," Fátima says.

"Should I pick up dinner for you?"

"Nah." She licks her lips and rocks her shoulders as if she's working up to telling me something. "I have a little date."

"With?"

"I'll tell you, but you have to promise not to make it weird."

"Why would I make it weird?"

"Because she's in our crowd. Like a friend. You know."

"Is it...?"

"Stop. Please don't guess."

"It's Becca."

"You guessed. It's going to get weird." Her shoulders droop.

"It wasn't weird with us. We're fine."

"Okay. Stop right there. You're, like, some ice-cold bitch with no feelings. Please do not take it personally, it's just a fact." She opens her car door. "I love you. As a friend. Now. Thank you and goodbye. If I'm not home tonight, don't call the cops."

She gets in and drives away, leaving me to wonder if I'm really an ice-cold bitch with no feelings.

8

SKYE

When I get home, my body feels drained and empty from work. I'm looking forward to sleeping like a dead baby.

Fátima and I live in one of eight two-bedroom bungalows that surround a clean and well-maintained courtyard. The sun is still peeking through the trees as I cross it with a bag of Korean dumplings dangling from one hand. The jacaranda tree in front of our bungalow dapples the setting sun against my doorway, and the periwinkle chair where the mailman leaves packages is now occupied by a man in a hoodie and backward cap, slouching as if he belongs there.

I stop while he's still in the distance, because no woman wants to see a strange man waiting at her door. Ever. But he waves. It's a casual flick of the wrist, but with that gesture, I immediately recognize the man I've only known in the dark as he sits in the dimming light of the day.

Walking again, I watch him stand and walk toward me. The gossip sites I scanned on break say he's damaged goods,

0

but the way he moves has a relaxed confidence that doesn't seem damaged at all. I can't help but envy it.

"Hey." He looks as if he hasn't slept.

"Hey."

He looks as though he's trying so hard not to do a head-to-toe eyefuck. Maybe because that's what I'm trying not to do. I don't even know where my anxiety ends and my own brain begins, because I'm *fine*.

He reaches for me. "Let me help." He takes a bag like a gentleman dressed in a Brooklyn Projects hoodie and backward cap. Chivalry doesn't usually come with a gold chain around its neck.

"Uh... so what are you doing here?" I'm hungry enough to chew off his arm.

"I wanted to talk to you." He lifts the bag. "What do you have in here? Smells good."

"You have my number."

He shrugs. Starts to say something. Shrugs with the other shoulder. Then laughs to himself.

"Seemed too quick," he says finally. "Push some buttons. Say hi. Talk a minute. Hang up. I figured this has more... here, there, up down." He laughs to himself. "What do I even mean?" He looks up through the space between the leaves, where the sun pokes through. In that light, his eyes are the color of frost. He looks back at me. "It has more dimensions."

I smile. I can't help it. He's so fearlessly vulnerable.

"It has three dimensions, exactly."

"Time is the fourth. If you..." He shrugs again. "Whatever. If it's a bad time, I can go away and make a two-dimensional call. Or you can..."

"No," I say. "There's a picnic table under the fichus." I tip my chin at the big tree on the other side of the courtyard. He follows my gaze, finds the table, and we head for it. "I hope you like mandu dumplings."

"Love them, but I'm not here to mess with your dinner."

"I ordered extra for Fátima, but she said no, which she always does, then she eats whatever I get."

He puts the bag on the table. He brushes away the dried leaves. "Well then, I don't want to mess with her leftovers."

"She'll be fine." I reach into the bag. "Consequences of saying no."

"In that case... you said mandu? I'm in."

I turn my face down so he can't see my grin. "There's plenty so... *bon appetite*, but in Korean."

"Baller. That's not Korean. Maybe K-town."

We take out the containers and place them in the center of the table. I run inside for cups, a pitcher of water, and utensils. When I return, he's standing by the table, scraping wooden chopsticks together to get rid of the splinters.

On my side, a set of chopsticks are already laid out. He catches me looking at them, then notices the forks I brought.

"Sorry, I assumed you'd use chopsticks."

I put down the forks. "And I assumed you didn't know how to."

He screws his mouth into a little knot and shrugs at both of our assumptions.

We sit across from each other. Dinner is packaged in plastic steamers. Paper towels are stuffed in the lower layer and doused with boiling water so they steam the dumplings lying on a grate above. This way, they don't dry out.

The chopsticks look tiny in Colton's hands. I hadn't noticed how huge they are. Maybe that's why he seems in such control of them. As if he could pick up a T-bone steak or a grain of rice with the same facility. He grabs a slippery dumpling and lays it on my plate. Then another. After the third, his courtliness and his competence are equally unbearable.

"Are you always like this?" I ask at the fourth dumpling, pulling my Styrofoam plate toward myself.

"Like what?" He takes four for himself and doesn't drop any of those either. He takes off his hoodie and wraps it around his waist. His T-shirt is tight over his chest with high sleeve cuffs that stretch over his biceps.

I look away to pour water into both cups. "You don't need to be such a gentleman, getting my food on my plate and whatever. I can do it."

"I can get my own water too, but thanks." He pops an entire dumpling in his mouth and takes a cup. His hand says FREE.

LIVE FREE.

Easy for his fingers to say.

This doesn't need to be so serious. It's just dumplings in the courtyard. I nibble the edges of one before biting it.

"Do you like them?" I ask after he pops the second.

"Mm-hm."

"It's a table set up on Wilton off Olympic. They Tweet 'open' and the line starts forming. They close up when they run out. So anyway, what the hell are you doing here?"

He grins, and I wait for him to say something like, "I'm eating dumplings," but he doesn't. He folds his fingers together into LFIRVEEE.

Fuck it. I put a dumpling in my mouth and chew. It's delicious, and I'm not doing another thing to pry out whatever's stuck between his motivations and his reticence.

"I didn't sleep last night." He dips the second-to-last dumpling in sesame sauce. "I was like a kid who had sugar packets for lunch." After eating it in one bite, he puts down his chopsticks. "I was testing my setup. Making sure, you know, just in case we did this—then I spent, like, two hours on the piano learning your songs."

Hand over my mouth so the entire dumpling doesn't escape, I nod, unable to express that I can relate to hyperfocus.

Once I've swallowed, I can speak. "You're a musician?"

"Nah. I'm not a performer. I can't make it through a whole song. But I can write what I think. Play a bit here and there to see if it sounds okay."

"Okay, so you were up all night noodling around."

"That's the word. Noodling."

"And then you slept and came here?"

"No sleep."

"Uh-huh." I peer into the dumpling container.

"Take it. I'm done." He pushes it toward me. Fine. I won't argue about food, so I pinch it out. "I wanted to explain about saying no to Liam."

"You don't need to. No is no."

"You drove away like you were mad."

"I guess I was annoyed that I didn't even have a second to form an opinion. And I wanted that, but if you're a no, then what I think is whatever, right?" The last dumpling turns into the last half a dumpling, then it's gone. "And I didn't want to talk about it. Really. I just wanted to go home. I'm sorry. I didn't mean to be rude."

"It's fine." He shrugs and picks up his water. "Did you ever get around to forming an opinion?"

The correct answer is both simple and false. That is, no, I did not form an opinion.

It works. It's safe. He's rejected the idea already, so there's no reason to consider it. If I land there, he's on the spot to explain his own reasoning, giving me the option of going either way. But he's been part of a long day. I'm too tired to play games with him.

"I did."

"And?"

"I'm not too proud to manufacture some advantage for myself. I guess that makes me unethical and manipulative."

He hides his smile behind his cup. A little twinge of tightness starts in my chest. He knows what a faker I am. A fake, untalented, overambitious shell. I forget to tell myself I'm fine. My brain's too busy mentioning how obvious it is to him that I'm fake, and even if I make it, I'm still fake, and even if I spend my whole life living a dream, the day will come when everyone figures it out. And Colton Crowne will say, yeah, I kinda knew it the first twenty-four hours.

When he lowers the cup and I can see his face, I'm sure that's what he's thinking.

"This business isn't ethical," he says. "And any guy with the power to make decisions about your life will manipulate the shit out of you first so when he does fuck you over, you're nice and surprised." He shifts forward as if he wants to leap across the table at me. "Okay, look. I don't like being told what to do. That gives me a fucking rash. So Liam pushing me to cut the EP before I even heard you makes me itch. Then with the whole 'pretend you're dating' without asking you first? My answer's gonna be nah. Or fuck you."

"Why should he ask me first?"

He raises his eyebrows as if I've surprised him. "Just seems right."

"So, vibes?"

"Whatever. Vibes." He tents his right hand on the table.

He's wearing a thick silver ring on his right pointer. I don't like men who wear rings, generally. But specifically, I like this ring on him, because his hands are twenty percent too big and one hundred percent perfect. "But there's the third thing which I'm not looking to make a big deal out of, but it's kinda also the real reason I said no."

"Don't get me wrong." Mirroring him, I sit forward. "I'm curious. But pro tip? Quit while you're ahead. The first two reasons are enough."

"Third reason." He raps the table and sits back. "This scares the fuck out of me. For real. I already had a big public meltdown."

"I heard."

"I can't tell you what that was like. Knowing my entire family was reading about it, and maybe they were mad or disappointed or sad or who knows. Knowing they were out here watching that whole thing that was killing me? It killed me deader."

"But they love you."

"Yeah. That's the point."

His sleeves are so high I can see the tattoo on the tender skin inside his arm.

Everything. Now.

He's got his whole worldview inked into skin that fits him perfectly. He's more at home in his body than anyone I've ever met. Not just his body. The world. How can someone walk around not worrying about anything? Just being the way he is without apology or excuse. He's fascinating and terrifying.

Everything about him is attractive.

"Huh." He's a sign on a bus that's written in a language I don't speak but can kind of work out if I stare long enough.

"Huh, what?"

"I get it," I say. "Except for that last part, so skip that. Not wanting a repeat... I get it. Hundred percent."

"Good."

"Good."

I lean on the table to push myself up, but he stops me by putting his hand over mine. He's looking up at me in the deepening twilight and his palm is dry and warm and strong.

"So, we're on. Yeah?" he says.

"On?" I squeak.

He moves his hand away. "For something unethical and manipulative."

I have to sit down before I pass out. "Really?"

"Fucking with people." He shrugs. "Could be fun. Could fuck us both up. I can't go much lower. You might wanna sleep on it."

Do I? Will I wake up different? Will a rising sun illuminate a life full of things I'm unwilling to lose?

No. It won't. Every time he opens his mouth, I trust him in a way he hasn't earned and I can't explain.

"I'm in. Seriously. And thank you. Okay." I pick up the packaging, smash it small. "Wow. We're really doing this."

"Hold up." He moves the bag away after I stuff what I have into it. "Anyone in my family can tell you, I need rules."

"Okay. Whatever you want."

"If either one of us starts catching feelings, that part of it is done. I'm not going there again, and trust me, you don't wanna visit."

"Fine. I'm not worried about that on my side."

"Really?"

"Backward baseball caps... not my thing."

"Then don't wear them." He takes the bag.

I snap it away. "Can I make a rule?"

"This should be good."

"I need to know that when you're talking about me to people, you're only ever saying nice things."

"Don't piss me off and I won't."

"Even if I piss you off."

"Fine," he says.

"And..."

"You wanna make more?"

"It's obvious. It's practically attached to rule one." I crunch the bag down and realize I missed a container. "No sex. Not that sex always makes feelings, but it's complicated and we're going to be busy."

"Fuckin' right." He nods and knocks on the wood again. "Okay. Last one."

"Go."

"Liam sent me the music tracks and your best takes."

"That's not a rule."

"You're an alto."

"What?" I gasp.

"You're out of your range."

"I'm a soprano."

"You can *hit* soprano, but you're an alto."

Banging my palms on the table I stand over him. "No. I played Cosette, not Eponine. I was Glinda, not the green fucking witch."

With my shadow falling over his face, he looks up at me with those big blue eyes and that half grin that holds half a million contradictions, and I feel as if he's the one standing over me, lording his power or whatever I'm failing to do.

Of all the things that were said in the past half hour, this is the one that's blinding me with rage.

"You want to know where you're going to make your money?" He taps his thumbs together. "Here's a hint. It ain't with big notes."

I'm done. He's trying to take something away from me, and I won't let him. It's mine. "I was Maria, and I made big notes and danced at the same time."

"Singing with your heart." He puts his FREE hand to his chest.

"You don't know shit about my heart."

He looks away, taps the tabletop once, twice, then stands. "Let me help you clean up."

"I have it."

He ignores me and puts the top on a container.

"Colton, really." I take the container. The lid falls off.

He picks up the top and I hold still so he can put it back on. His hands engulf the plastic, holding it in place as he seals the lid with his thumbs. The container tilts, and he cups the downward side to keep it from tipping over. His pinkie brushes past the side of my hand, and it's like a million little sparks leave a trail behind them.

Maybe backward baseball caps are my thing?

That'll be my secret. He'll never know it. I pull away before I turn into pure electricity. I have the empty container. I don't even know why we were bothering with the top. I don't know why he's here, really, or what I want to do with a conflict that shouldn't be. Grabbing the empty bag, I stuff the container in it and—before he can help—walk to the courtyard trash can.

My thoughts are jumbled and my feelings are confused. I can't locate a center.

But I'm not anxious. The thoughts that start an attack haven't shown themselves. But... thinking about not thinking them is as good as thinking them.

Faker. He's heard your fuckups and he knows you're a faker.

Crap. It's starting.

He can tell you have no talent.

Dr. Solomon would call that illogical. He wouldn't offer to spend his time developing my talent if he didn't think it existed.

It's a favor to Liam.

He's bored.

He knows.

By the time I dump the trash, I've lost control of the entire narrative in my head. Panic is setting in. He can't be here. This cannot happen in front of Colton Crowne with the LIVE FREE tattoos on his big hands and the blue eyes and crooked smile. He needs to go and the only way to get rid of him is to tell him what I want one way or the other.

I'm going to say no thank you, but that would be obeying that punishing voice.

Fake faker.

"I don't know why you feel like you have to convince me." I try to sound casual. "You want to try something different, who am I to say you're wrong?"

He knows you have nothing.

"We'll make something cool either way."

"Sure." I start for my bungalow.

He walks astride. The sun is almost gone. It'll be night in a few minutes, but it isn't yet. He's going to walk me to my door and all I need to do right now is collapse.

I stop. "Nothing personal. I can get back myself, and it's a straighter line out if you head that way now."

"Good idea." He backs up and waves. "Can you come tomorrow? Like noonish?"

"Yeah, sure."

"You gotta park on the street. My brother likes the driveway clear."

"Okay."

A handful of teens walk around him, and behind, while on the sidewalk, a guy pushes a stroller while holding a toddler's hand.

"Colton?" I say before he turns his back to me.

"Yeah?"

"I'm not an actress. What if I'm not convincing?"

He looks left, then right, then puts two fingers in his mouth and whistles at the teens. The boys turn first.

"Rate this," he calls to them, then comes for me, hands gently taking the entirety of my jaw.

I hold onto his wrists as his face comes toward mine, blocking out the sun. When his lips touch mine, the hair at the back of my neck stands up and my arms breaks out into goose bumps, as if my skin is thickening itself against the vulnerability that comes with feeling this good.

It only lasts a couple of seconds, but it's enough to know if I'm going to fake it with anyone, it'll be Colton Crowne.

Still holding my face, he looks up at the kids. "Yeah, or nah?"

"Nah!" one calls. Guy. The rest are ignoring us. "Fuck her and I'll judge."

My middle finger communicates how much I give a shit what he thinks. The kid offers me his crotch. Colton drops his hands into a careless shrug. *What are ya gonna do?*

"I'm convinced," I say. "We're on."

"Cool." He steps back. "I'll see you tomorrow."

I nod and wait for him to turn around, but he doesn't.

"Go." He shoos me. "I'm just gonna make sure you get in.

From here." With the sun behind him, separating his feet and putting his hands in his pockets, he's the perfect silhouette of a guy who's not moving until he decides he's moving.

So I turn away and let myself in the house, waving once before I close the door. Through the window, I watch him walk to the street with legs that are too long and a gait that's unbearably loose and easy.

How does a person get like that?

He's real. You aren't.

"Seriously," I tell that stupid voice as I snap the curtain closed. "Shut the fuck up."

But my mother's voice—*It's too hard. Art is for your spare time. You'll starve*—braids with mine—*You're worthless, no talent. Only a fake would have to fake*—and another voice that's starting to sound like Dr. Solomon.

You don't have to hurt yourself.

Breathe. Say words that help.

I kick off my shoes, drop my bag on the floor, and put a pot of water on to boil. Teabags. Cup. The voices are so loud, I crouch on the kitchen floor with my forearms over my ears, my fingers laced together, and my forehead on the linoleum.

Meditation doesn't work against a bully. Mindfulness won't stop the taunts the mind creates.

My chest hurts. Blood pounds through my veins. My lungs are the size of pinto beans. The cause of the attack doesn't even matter. Colton's nowhere near the cause or the cure. It's me. All me. And I know my heart's not going to explode. I know I'm not going to die. This is just a record skipping in my brain. It's not going to play the rest of the song until the needle gets a nudge, and I don't have the power to move it.

"I'm fine," I tell the floor. I don't just say the words. I hear them. "I am fine." The word fine loses its meaning. "Satisfactory. Decent. Solid. Fine. Fucking *fine*."

The words are too automatic. My mind does its own thing while my ears hear them.

Fake-fake-fucking-fake.

I have to control both. Lock them down. Push the needle away from the scratch. I am fearsome. I am afraid of myself. This house is going to come down before I submit to this shit.

You're wasting your time.

"Fine!" I scream into the void between my mouth and the floor. "*Fine!*"

My breath bounces back against my lips. I feel it, and not the pain in my chest. The bully thoughts peek around the corner.

Fa-

"Fine," I say in a low voice, testing my alto.

The breaths come slow and even for another minute while I create a buffer between the two voices. I don't even entertain the bully as a joke or a perverse test of my nerve. You can only ignore it.

The teapot hisses to not-quite-boiling, and I concentrate on every move, every feeling, every sound of tea preparation. I am the picture of mindfulness.

Fine. Really. I'm fine. Just thirsty. If the pain in my chest has lessened, I try not to acknowledge it, because naming victory tempts defeat.

The teabag tab hangs off the side of my cup like a Christmas ornament. Fátima's out for the night with Becca. The house is mine. I'll go to bed early and sleep late. Get to Colton's stupid house at exactly noon. I hum the "Star-

Spangled Banner," waiting for the whistle, and realize I'm not nervous about failing in front of him. He'll know if I mess up, but he won't have secret thoughts, because we're both faking it.

At least we're being honest about our dishonesty. That's how you live free.

9

COLTON

If my math is right, Logan's wife isn't all that far along, but she's really showing.

Standing in the middle of the studio, she's looking over the cables and corners. The floor has carpet remnants in shades of puke yellow and diarrhea brown. The outside-facing walls are covered in acoustic foam. The rest are still raw sheetrock. I've set up a microphone and music stand, but it's otherwise bare.

Ella never complained about the noise from the build or Jab and Carmy coming in and out, but she never came in to check it out either.

"With the right motivation," Ella says from the other side of the glass, "a guy can do a lot of damage."

The first studio I built was in Tamika's basement in Memphis with this exact same equipment. This time, it was easier and faster because my head wasn't as far up my ass.

I press the intercom button. "Thanks, I think?"

"You're welcome, definitely." She comes into the control room.

"If you want to turn this into a playroom or something, it can come out easily. There's already foam on the walls for a little guy to bounce off."

"We have a playroom." She's looking at all the knobs and edges, following cable lines from end to end without responding to my offer. "I didn't know you had it in you."

"Because I didn't tell you."

"Why not?"

"If I told you, I'd have to explain why I came back, why I wasn't going to do this anymore, and you'd say, 'Oh, Colton, you should,' and then my brothers would have *ideas* and shit. Fuck that, man."

"I wouldn't have pushed you."

"Yeah, but I didn't want to even explain what had happened while they all looked at me like, 'How do you fail at such easy shit?' You know how they are."

"I do. And I'm glad you're back to doing what you love." She pats my arm and looks over my shoulder. "Hello, there."

Turning, I see Skye in the doorway, clutching the shoulder strap of her bag.

"Hey, come in." I hold my hand out to her. "Skye, this is Ella. My sister-in-law."

"You're the designer?" Skye holds the handshake long enough to make me wonder if she intends to take Ella home. "From Papillion?"

"Yes, it's nice to meet you."

"That red sparkly dress Gretchen Rojas wore to the Grammys? That was you?"

"All Gretchen," Ella says, releasing the hold. "A gown's only as beautiful as the woman inside it."

"Wow, yeah." She's starstruck over a designer. What's she going to do the day she meets a real celebrity? Faint?

"Okay, Ella." I clap my hands. "Get the fuck out."

With a wave, she's gone. I close the door after her.

"She's amazing." Skye faces me after turning a full three-sixty, checking out the place.

"When you're up for a Grammy, she can design your dress. But we gotta get you there first."

She drops her bag into one of the avocado chairs and looks over the knobs and sliders on the board. Her hair is piled on top of her head. The little hairs at the back of her neck curl loose and fine. I could brush them aside and kiss her skin. I could do a lot of things and every single one of them goes through my mind, asking for just a minute of my attention.

"There's a fridge in the cabinet. Under the lamp, if you want something."

I wish she'd want something, but no. She's leaning over the board.

"I always wondered what all these knobs do."

"Most of them don't move that much."

She reaches for a level slider, and before I can think too hard, I'm behind her, my hand keeping hers from moving. She smells like the ozone before a rain.

"You trying to fuck with a man's knobs?" I ask.

"Is that supposed to be some kind of double entendre?"

"That's against the spirit of the rules." I take my hand off her but I'm slower to back away before taking one last whiff of that pre-rainstorm-in-a-drought smell. "Come."

She turns her face toward mine. Her eyes are webbed amber green, and her lips are fuller up close. The worried creases between her brows are bird tracks in the sand. If I

77

can see all that, I'm still too close, and since she brought up double entendres, I don't know if "come" means I'm asking her to follow me to the orange couch or if I'm commanding something else.

I move away before past mistakes become a pattern.

"I want you to hear something." I go to the shelves with my albums.

"This is nice."

The studio has always been good enough, but suddenly, I see it through her eyes. The old furniture. The strangers' wear on the corners. The scratches from a cat I never saw. It's not nice. I want it to be better for my artists. More full. More real. The little living space is the only place in the house that's mine, not my brother's, and it's cobbled together from junk. The technical part of the studio has the equipment it needs to and no more, but it's not her opinion of the garage that's nagging at me. She does the same corner-to-corner scan as Ella, but this is different. I wanted Ella to know her garage wasn't ruined. With Skye, I care what she thinks about me as a person. What does this little room say to her about who I am? Why didn't I pay attention to that when I put it together?

What's wrong with me? I didn't feel like this over dumplings.

"It's dorm-core," I say.

Her laugh is more of a quick *huh*. I'm not sure if she didn't think it was funny, or turned a chuckle into a scoff because she isn't sure if I'm joking. If I could see her face, I'd know, but she's leaning over the couch to inspect the Pez dispenser collection while I finger through my albums. Or I pretend to, because I know where Yaz is, and it's not the middle. I'm really watching her check out the Warner Brothers shelf.

"I've been thinking about you taking it down a few octaves, and I gotta say…"

"You're wrong?"

"I'm right." The record I need tips from the anonymity of the stack. "I heard your vocal tracks, and I'm right."

"I was nervous."

"So?" The record player cabinet squeaks when I lift the lid. "That gonna change any time soon or nah?"

"I already have a therapist." Her arms are crossed and she's leaning on one hip. "And I'm a soprano at a club every week."

"Yeah?" I haven't heard about this.

"Well…" She sits on the couch, leaning all the way forward with her hands fidgeting between her knees, talking fast as if she's afraid she'll bore me. "I'm behind the DJ— Becca. You met her at karaoke. It's a live EDM accompaniment. Kind of improv? Syllables but not words. It's called glossolalia but without the religion. Hopelandic, also. This Icelandic band does it."

"Sigur Rós. I've heard of them." I jump in to relieve her of whatever's making her uncomfortable, but I sound like a pompous ass.

I close the lid over the turntable. Forget Yaz. Alison Moyet is too low.

I know what I'm doing, but I don't know how to do this anymore.

"If you want to add a layer," I say, "or change something, there's a guitar and keyboard in there. That's good, right?"

"It's perfect."

I shrug. It's not perfect. It's adequate. Whatever. "I'll get

Liam to hire a pro if the comp changes."

"Where did you learn about music?" she asks. "My parents made me take violin and piano."

"My high school had a setup." I open the transparent fridge door. "Coke? I got the Mexican bottles with the real sugar."

"I should probably stick to water." She takes a deep breath. "I'm sorry."

"For what?" I get water for her and a bottle of Coke for me.

"We should prep and talk about it, but I'm... I know I seem really nervous, but I'm not that nervous, which makes me nervous."

"I am." I unscrew her top and hand it over, then pop the soda and let the cap click into the hanging cup.

"Why would you be?"

"Uh, let's see." I knock back a gulp of Coke. "The last time I did this, it went really well, but I fucked it up so bad I went broke. If I fuck this up, I can't crawl back home because I'm here already. I leave my brother with a studio in his garage he never wanted, and I'm going to have a reputation as a guy who can't finish what he starts. So..." I shrug and take a swig of Coke. "Yeah. It's fine."

"Have a Pez." She reaches behind her, takes a random dispenser from the shelf, and tosses it to me. I catch it and hold it up.

"Garfield. Funny shit." I open the drawer with the candy so I can fill it. "You like Pez?"

"More of a Skittles girl."

"Okay, Skittles, I told you what I'm nervous about. What's your excuse?"

"I told you. I'm not nervous."

"You're fidgeting." I sit next to her and lean back to put my feet on the coffee table while I fill Garfield. "Your body's all curled in on itself like you want to be smaller. Look, now you're blushing."

"I'm far more nervous about this public dating thing."

"Don't stress that. It's literally a few seconds between the door and the car. Do some body language for Gene Testarossa, then back to normal like that." I snap my fingers to show her how easily I can shut shit off. "This in here." I spin Garfield to indicate the studio. "This is what I gotta get perfect." I toss her the full Pez dispenser.

"I have faith in you."

"What about you?"

She pauses to take a sip of water and winds up chugging half the bottle. I can't stop watching the way her throat moves when she swallows. It's not special at all, and it's not like anyone else either. She lowers the bottle and replaces the cap, staring at it pensively.

"It'll probably be the same with you as it was in every other studio, with every other producer Liam got. I'm going to try over and over and my throat will tighten up like a dishcloth someone's wringing out. But I'm used to it now. Doesn't even faze me."

"Tell you what." I take the Pez dispenser from her. "Every take you do, we both eat a Pez. When Garfield's got nothing left to give, we break, and if you want to go home, you go. You want to refill... let's say"—I lean back and take a random dispenser from the shelves—"Homer Simpson, we start over."

"I hope you like Pez, Colton."

"Less filling than Skittles." I put both dispensers on the table. "Let me tell you my take on your song."

10

SKYE

Garfield. Homer Simpson. Boba Fett. The Tasmanian Devil. Snoopy. A lineup of plastic collectibles stands at the top of the board. I pull back Santa's head. A pink candy juts from his neck. If I never eat another Pez in my life, I'll die having achieved something.

Between every motherload, there's a break, and at every break, we change something about the track. The tempo. The key. The phrasing. I froze for the entirety of Squidward's dispenser, even though he was sure the lyric change would work.

"Last one," he says over the intercom, from the other side of the glass.

This sucks. The only upside to this string of failures is the breaks between. He shows me the board and explains the plug-in he developed that... well, I don't know what it does, but when he plays me back, my voice sounds as if it's in the room, not recorded.

Maybe I'm enjoying the spaces between a little too much.

"No," I say. "No break."

"You're getting tired."

"I can't, Colton. We sit around yacking for half an hour after every little character and it's getting late."

Did I just insult him? Does he think I don't enjoy his company? Because I do. I clear my throat. We're not here for that.

"I tell you what," he says. "Less head, more chest."

This guy. I already took it down, and yeah, it's better, but I'm tempted to bring it down to a fry to prove a point.

"You've wanted to do this all day," I say.

"Do what?"

I put a fist on my hip, and with the other hand, I jab my finger in his direction. "Make me Eponine, not Cosette."

"Guilty as charged. You haven't committed to Eponine yet. You can't start breaking rules on day one."

I did promise. I agreed to the rules, and we kissed on it. "Fine."

"Atta girl."

"Fuck you."

"I know. I'm the worst. Give me some scales so I can level you."

I sing, dropping down with each word. "*Colton Crowne can go fuck himself please and thank you.*"

"Lower."

"*He wants me to sing like a man in a whiskey bar but it's going too far.*"

"Up where you were on *whiskey.*"

"*Fuck him fuck him fuck hiiiiiiimmmm.*"

I stretch the last word and the change is so blatantly effective we just stare at each other through the glass. That was it. The note that makes your spine rattle.

Damn him for being right.

"Told you." He's gloating.

"You got lucky."

"I got lucky the minute you walked in." His hands freeze on the knobs, as if he expressed more than he intended.

He needs an escape hatch, so I give him one. "Let's go, Colton."

"One sec, Skittles." He does things with his sliders I don't understand. "Okay. Three. Two. You're on."

I breathe and sing, and sing, and sing my entire song from beginning to end without freezing or cracking. I'm off in spots because I haven't practiced it at this part of my range, but I keep going because it feels the way it's supposed to.

It feels good, and right, and like something strangers will want to hear.

"Yes!" he shouts.

We both whip off our headphones. He slaps open the studio door and runs in.

"I did it?" I know damn well I did it, but does *he* know?

"You did it!"

He grabs me and lifts me off the floor. There's no choice there. It's gravity. He squeezes me against the hard reality of his body so hard I feel the fullness of his breath against my chest and the warmth of it on my neck. He smells like success, fulfillment, of broken things made whole.

He drags his mouth across my cheek. It's a beeline to my lips.

When I put my hand on Colton's chest to push him away, I feel his heart beating, and I get confused, because there's the reality of him thrumming against my palm. Had he not been real before? Or has some kind of wall dropped away?

Neither. Both. I don't even know my own mind, so how can I know him?

He responds by pulling back harder, and we bounce away from each other like mismatched magnets.

"Cool." His hands are up as if he's pretending he didn't just try to kiss me, which he obviously did, and I somewhat less obviously wanted him to do before I had a hot moment of sense.

"You kids."

The voice comes through the speakers. We turn. Liam stands behind the board with his finger on the intercom button.

The ground opens up under me. I've been caught, parked in the garage in January, making out with Karen O'Toole in the back seat of dad's Chevy Malibu. Busted twice over. First, for being bisexual, but second and more importantly, for being sexual at all.

My cheeks turn a hundred shades of pink.

"It's nothing." It's the perfectly normal—borderline necessary—thing to say. "Just some..." I wave my hand at the word but can't find it.

"Exuberance," Colton suggests.

Liam leans into the glass, still pressing the intercom. A hand reaches up to the window and taps a Lego guy against it.

"Matt!" Colton cries and turns to me for a second, already halfway out the door. "My nephew's here."

He bursts into the other room with a roar.

"Who taps my magic glass!" Colton scoops up a little boy, who squeals with the pure terrified joy only a four-year-old can muster. "Name yourself."

"It was Kay Jay!" He holds a little minifigure in Colton's face.

"Katherine Johnson. Cool. You know who else is cool?"

"Who?!"

Colton whispers in the boy's ear, and they both look at me.

"'Dis one?" Matt points in my direction.

"*Very* cool."

"Hi, Matt. I'm Skye." I hold out my palm for a high-five. If I remember my brother's kids correctly, that's the age-appropriate greeting.

"Say hi. Go ahead. She only bites after sunset."

Matt slaps my hand.

"Nice to meet you," I say.

Matt buries his head in Colton's neck as if he's too shy to meet someone so cool, then gets over it a split second later.

"Look!" The boy gives me the figure. It's a Black lady with glasses holding a chart with a moon, Earth, a rocket, and scientific formulas.

"Katherine Johnson." I have no idea who that is, but I act as if I do, then hand it back. "Totally cool."

"I told him you'd know what those numbers mean," Liam says to Colton before addressing me. "How is it going?"

Colton and Matt canoodle over the tiny chart the minifig is holding. I guess it's up to the most biased person in the room to do the reporting.

"Really good." I try to sound deeply honest, but Liam doesn't look as though he believes me. "For real. It took all day but definitely, we got something. Definitely."

The urge to backpedal is so strong I'm almost willing to lie and say it's terrible when I know it isn't. I want Liam to manage his expectations. I need to underpromise and overdeliver. That's what Dad always said. Set expectations you can easily exceed.

That works as a strategy if you're confident about what you can achieve and clear about your own limits. Without one, you're blind to the other.

"Colton can play it back for you." I point at my producer, who's crouched by Matt, inspecting the minifig's little chart.

Matt taps the piece and asks, "What it?"

Colton looks up at me with big blue eyes as if he's not a minute over thirteen, making out in the back seat of a parked car.

I don't know what his expression means, but I assume it's him telling me to believe in myself. Sell it. Stop underselling success.

He's right, and the voices are always wrong, except when they're not. I can't sell it.

COLTON

"This one." Matt points at the formula. "What it?"

"Um…" I glance at Skye, who's looking back at me, and in my heart, I'm begging her to just pay attention to Liam for five seconds so I can answer Matt without inspiring a fucking tidal wave of questions.

She turns away and smiles at Liam.

"We got my vocals on 'Like Love,'" she says. "I can't wait for you to hear it."

Matt taps the tiny chart impatiently.

"It's Newton's Law of Universal Gravitation." I speak low. "It describes how everything in the world is attracted to—"

"What's this big one?" He points at the longer series of letters and symbols at the bottom of the piece. Fucking Lego. Wouldn't occur to them to just make something up or put another rocket or something there?

"—all day…" Skye continues. "But it's right. I'd play it back for you but—"

"This is the calculation for the distance... right here, and rotation of the earth which is..."

"Colton!" Liam barks.

"What?"

"Pause the nerd shi—stuff a second and play the song."

I give Matt back his figure and get in my seat to play the take. The raw recording only gets a few seconds in before Liam reaches over me to click it off.

"Why does she sound like Kim Carnes?"

Skye's mouth tightens and she looks at me with lasers shooting out her eyes. Matt sits next to her and puts Katherine Johnson in her lap. The glare is diverted.

"It's the hook. Stop talking and listen." I put the song back on, and yes, Skye starts rough. That's the way we designed it and that's the contrast with the second chorus, then the bridge where she hits it, then hits it harder.

"Whoa," Liam mutters.

"Told you." The song finishes and I click off.

"I am so good at this." Liam turns to Matt, who's showing Skye how Kay Jay's arms and legs move. "Matt, you're talking to a star."

"She's cool," he says, stating the obvious with zero sarcasm.

"I'm not," she whispers as if sharing a secret. "I'm just Skye."

"That's where they put the stars though." Matt points directly at the ceiling.

"All right." Liam claps and stands. "I'm satisfied. Skye, good job. Colton, finish up three more."

"We got 'Don't Be,' 'Tunnel Vision,' and a cover." I wave my hand as if it's nothing. Easy peasy.

"What's the cover?"

"Give us a minute. We'll figure it out."

"I need 'Like Love' ASAP. I can try to get her into Shooting Star."

"What's that?" she asks with Matt on her lap, which is probably why he answers.

"It's a rock falling from the sky that gets burned up when the air goes *bang-bang-bang-pfft*."

"It's a showcase," I say. "Out in Mojave. They have it during a meteor shower. No lights allowed. You play in the dark while the stars come down. It's nice."

"Nice?" Liam scoffs. "It's a label executive nomination. Twelve labels get one slot each, and as far as I know, Glendora hasn't filled theirs yet."

"So you can ask Gene?" She has real hope in her voice. Hope is great, but you can't hang your hat on it.

"It's not that big a deal," I say.

Liam scoffs. "It's the prelude to a bidding war. It's a big fu —just a big deal."

"No pressure," Skye mumbles.

If I could kick Liam under the table I would, but he's not in range of my foot and there's no table.

"No pressure. Really. There's more than one way to skin this cat," Liam says. "Just... guys, you two can't let this get messy."

My hope that he'd forget what we were up to when he walked in was misplaced from the jump. Skye and I both know what he's talking about.

"It's not going to get messy, Liam." She seems serious—as if she thinks he has legitimate concerns that are any of his business.

"Here's the thing." Liam's about to explain what I don't

want explained right now. I feel like shit already. "Promoting new talent is ninety percent luck and I hate luck. Luck doesn't care how good you are. Luck's a fu—darn tease. You minimize her. You make it harder for her to operate. That's why we're doing this fake... stuff. We didn't invent it. It's done all the time, and when it's fake—really fake—they can tell. So don't get me wrong, I'm glad you guys have chemistry. That helps. But what's going to sell records is the breakup."

The breakup? I hadn't even thought about the relationship, much less the breakup.

Skye looks away from the figure that Matt's making "fly in the sky." She obviously hadn't thought it through either, but she seems more interested in the plan than gutted. She's got anxiety and nervous energy up the yin-yang, but she's wickedly ambitious.

"We'll break up," Skye says. "Not a problem."

I would have given him a "we'll see" or a "she doesn't need that to make it," but she's all the way in. Can't say I don't admire it, but it's also scary as shit.

"Good." Liam takes out his phone. "We don't need this turning into another disaster."

Another disaster? Skye's life hasn't been hit by a speeding train, so this is about me. My disasters. My messy shit. If I call him on it, we're going to fight, and I'm not into displaying how the Crowne brothers resolve conflicts right now.

He crosses his legs and taps his phone as if he's ready to take root right here. Matt's making the scientist walk across the floor on her little plastic legs. I love the shit out of the kid, but now Skye's on the floor with the chart, making Kay Jay chase it.

"Fine, Liam. Can you either help out or get out? You're messing with the vibe."

"Honestly?" Skye gets up. "I have an early shift tomorrow. So maybe we can pick it up next time?" She already has her bag over her shoulder.

"Cool," I say. "I'll walk you to the car."

"I'm right out front."

"It's dark." I grab my jacket.

"Really." She puts her hand on my chest and looks me in the eye. "I'm fine."

After a little push against me, she says goodbye to Liam and Matt, then walks out the door to the backyard. I won't escort her if she doesn't want me to, but I can watch from the doorway. The lights around the patio flick on when she approaches and dim when she passes.

"You want her." Liam's gotten up to stand next to me.

"Not my type. And I don't need a babysitter." I watch Skye go past the first gate. I hear the beep as she unlocks her car, and the door slap as she gets in.

"It would help me sleep at night if you had one."

"Take an Ambien."

The streets of Hancock Park are really quiet at night. When her car starts, I'll hear it, and I haven't yet.

"It's an idiomatic expression," he says. "Something people say—"

"A group of words established in cultural usage with a different meaning than the formal."

"There's Colton. Where you been, buddy?"

"I'm hungry," Matt says, rubbing his eye with his fist.

"We'll get you home." He picks up the boy.

The silence from the street is as unbearable as Liam. I leave, heading down the driveway, with the garden lights following me as I go through the gate to the street. Her car is right there with her in it, hands on the steering wheel as if she's blasting down the freeway at full speed.

Something isn't right. I pick up the pace, jogging across the lawn.

12

SKYE

As my voice came over the speakers, I tried to hear it the way a stranger would. If they didn't care about me, or believe in me, or had their career tied up in me, what would they hear?

It's almost like two planets
Colliding in space above
Throwing dust and granite
Spit of a kiss of
Something like love

Of course the audio was raw and it was the first good take. I have to do more and we'll choose the best. All that is obvious and true. But truth can only hold back the tide for so long.

And the truth? It has nothing to do with music.

I could feel a panic attack right under the surface of my skin, and if I didn't get out of there, I was going to collapse in front of two guys who were going to make it worse and a child who didn't need the sideshow. So I forced myself out to the car, where I could be alone.

My Corolla's right here. The car fob is at the bottom of my bag, and I dig around as if I'm being chased by a pack of wild wolves. Hitting the button, I get in and slap the door closed. My grip on the steering wheel is so tight I wouldn't be able to turn even if I was moving, which I'm not.

My heart beats so hard I shake, and the confusion has made new acquaintance with panic. My rib cage has shrunk to the size of a bran muffin, so my lungs can't really operate. I'm breathing as fast as a hummingbird, except I can't get any oxygen.

You don't have to do this I am terrible they'll judge me they'll say terrible things about my terrible voice they'll know the truth that I am nothing I am small I am not what I'm trying to become they see it they know.

Matt was a great distraction when Liam started making plans based on what he thought I sounded like, but with every word, I got closer and closer to being exposed in front of more and more people. Even then, I had it more or less under control.

Then Liam mentioned Colton and I ending a relationship that has never really happened, and the dam broke. There would be no Colton. No Pez at the break. No one to believe in me. Who could I trust if he was gone?

You don't even know him.

Got him fooled, don't you?

The yellow dude smiles at me, arms out for a plastic hug. I poke him. I try to think of nothing but the arc of his bounce.

"Breathe." The command is stupid. It's not like I have a choice. "Breathe, damn it. You're fine."

I'm fine. It's all fine.

You're going to fail at this.

Only because they won't see her gifts. They never do.

My mother's voice isn't coercive. There's no whining or whinging in the Phillips house. Even in my head, she sounds as though she's reading from a history textbook, and she's awfully sorry to deliver the facts as they stand, but she has to, because she loves me.

Med school will be here when you get back.

When...

Not if. When I've exhausted my options and come home. All my sad attempts at living a creative life will be a story I tell my kids to keep them from trying the same thing. I am my mother's daughter, after all.

Colton's arms around me, the soft touch of his lips on my cheek. The kiss I wanted so badly I had to scream at myself to stop it. If I'd kissed him, I would have fallen into a dark void of satisfied desire. And I wanted to, but I didn't. So it's fine, except all my mental discipline was used up and I had nothing left to stay cool while Liam dangled the prospect of failure...

... when you fail. Fail. Fail...

... by talking about success.

These are the thoughts I'm supposed to be watching out for. I heard them coming like footsteps down the hall, but I didn't stop them, and now they're a stampede.

The neighborhood is so quiet I can hear the traffic on Rimpau Blvd, a quarter mile away, but that's not as loud as my heartbeat and the terrible voices in my head stating facts, and my third voice, shouting that it's fine. I'm fine. I am not going to die. No one who doesn't already care about me heard a thing. It's all good. When I close my eyes, I keep my entire focus on my voice, saying out loud what I've only been able to think.

"I'm fine."

My throat vibrates the sounds. My fingertips press against the seam behind the steering wheel hard enough to keep me focused on the thread of pain.

"It's okay."

I'm not dying. It's just my brain skipping. Ignore it. Focus on breathing. On my voice. On the texture of the wheel. My mother stops speaking, but she's still tapping on the textbook.

I can shut her up, but future history is written.

"It's fine. I'm fine."

Facts now. There's no use trying to sound casual or flip. I don't even trust myself when I sound like that. Gotta be flat. Just the facts. One fact, two fact, red fact, blue fact. I laugh at myself, because my rib cage has grown enough to let me breathe, and the pounding in my chest has softened and slowed.

"I'm fine fine fine."

When I believe it, my eyes open.

Colton Crowne is in my face, and I gasp. How can he be so close? He's leaning over the hood of the car, into the windshield, staring at me, one lock of sun-streaked hair falling over his nose. Once my eyes are open, he jumps back, hands up to show me how harmless he is.

This guy isn't harmless. He might not mug me or kidnap me—he might not intend to do a thing—but harmless? No.

The windows won't open unless I turn on the car, so I just get out.

"I just wanted to make sure you were cool." His hands are still out, exposing his worldview inside his arm.

Everything. Now.

"I said I was fine."

He puts down his hands. "Okay, well, obviously you're fine."

"I am. Really."

"All right. You were baller today."

Believing him is easy, which anxiety hates. Anxiety knows that everything should be harder than it is. Easy things are lies. So I breathe deeply and exhale slowly before I have to shut myself in the car again.

"Thank you." Trying to stay calm makes me just calm enough to see how not-calm he is. "Are you all right?"

"Liam's just a dick. And..." He runs his fingers through his hair. "I guess I am too." He shakes the bees out of his head. "I'm sorry about what I almost did back there."

"What you...?" I realize he's talking about the kiss-that-almost-was. "Oh, that? Well, next time you can be the sensible one."

"No one who knows me would put money on that."

"I trust you."

He looks away as if I said something wildly inappropriate. We drift into a space where anxiety is the only sound.

"Okay, then," he says, breaking the tension over his knee. "Can we do Wednesday?"

"Come hear me," I blurt. "I told you about the vocals I do?"

"The glossolalia."

That word rolls off his tongue as if it's a normal part of his vocabulary, but I don't even ask myself why, much less him.

"Becca is spinning at Fountain on Tuesday night. If you're around, you should stop by."

"Might do that." He backs toward the sidewalk.

"You'll have to look hard," I add. "I'm not front and center."

"Solves a problem, doesn't it?"

"It does. Okay. I have to… um…"

"Go?"

"Yeah. I guess tell Liam he can come, but he already knows."

"See you Tuesday night, Skittles."

"You don't have to come."

"I won't see you anyway with your invisible vocals."

He's not going to turn around until I'm in the car. So I get in. He leans down to look in the window and mouths, "Lock it."

I push the lock button to seal the car. He comes back and knocks on the glass to wave goodbye before walking back to the house.

13

COLTON

I spend the night getting that first song into some kind of shape and send it to Liam with the invoice.

My sleep schedule is totally fucked up, or exactly how it should be. Depends. I like sleeping in the day and working at night, when no one's around to bother me or tell me to grow up or they're gonna kick me out. A guy can think between one and five in the morning, then pull the drapes and sleep for ten hours. A guy can noodle in the studio so hard he really convinces himself he's got everything under control, especially his dick and, more importantly, his heart.

Unless Jab comes around in the afternoon and you don't wake up, so he gets your brother to use his key just to make sure you didn't die on his property.

"He's breathing," Logan's voice slides through my blissful fucking slumber.

Someone taps my cheeks with cannabis-saturated hands. That's Jab.

"I think he's warm."

"Go away." I push Jab's meaty hand off my forehead.

"Man, how hard I gotta knock? You know what time it is? I ate lunch already."

"I'm going to work," Logan says.

I open my eyes. Can't see shit through the fog. But I'm one hundred percent sure it's Saturday. Guess that explains why he's going in after sunrise.

"Thanks, man," Jab says to my brother.

"No problem." An out-of-focus form leaves the room.

My mattress tilts when Jab sits on the side of the bed.

"What time is it?" I put my watch close to my face. It's the crack of dawn.

"Noon. Why are you sleeping? You sick?"

"I'm not sick."

"You got a Covid test you can take?"

"Fuck off, man." I sit up. He's already rummaging around my medicine cabinet. "I don't have Covid. I was in fucking deep wave. Give me a minute."

"You're usually up by now." Giving up on the test, he stands in the bathroom doorframe. He's not that tall—just under six feet, like me—but so wide, he barely fits through it without turning sideways.

"I was in the studio late." I push off the covers.

"Really?"

"Long story." I rub my eyes red, but at least the fog clears.

"Tell me on the court."

"Cool, cool."

I have no idea what I'm going to tell him.

Logan's not too rich not to have a basketball hoop in the driveway. He's even beat me at one-on-one a time or two. I'm not that lucky against Jab. He's a big guy, but he's agile as fuck, and when he covers me, I'm covered.

"Fucking around," I say, dribbling with my back to the net. It's the second time Jab's asked me exactly what I was doing in the studio, and it's been the same answer both times.

"So you're feeling it?" He moves with me whenever I try to turn.

"I'm feeling your dick in my ass, motherfucker."

"Don't expect a reach-around."

I fake and turn, duck under his outstretched arm and shoot the ball. It's in. I catch it on the way down and flip it to him.

"Come on." He smacks the ball on the concrete. I swear it goes flat. "What are you doing in there?"

"You calling me a liar?" I try for the ball. Fail. Guard.

"Yeah." He shoots. Rims it. I get the rebound. "Halley said she heard you're producing someone. People in accounting don't shut up, you know that."

Liam's agency's footing the bills, and of course it never occurred to me that Jab's girlfriend working in accounts payable for a completely different company would find out. Not that I'm trying to hide it, but news travels by jet around here.

"It's fucking Saturday." I dribble. The ball does not go flat.

"They all go out on Friday."

"It's a favor for Liam." I spin to shoot, but he's got me covered and palms the ball, backing up but not shooting.

This is going to be a thing. Jab's in finance because he loves it. Halley does accounting, because, like everyone else, she has to eat, but she's a musician and songwriter. She had some songs ready to go out with, and when I built the studio, she asked me to put them together for her. I begged off. I told her the room wasn't ready, which was a lie. The room was good to go. I was the one who wasn't ready. Now I'm going to have to answer for it.

"You only working with white girls now?" His throw arcs into the sky and through the hoop. Nothing but net, but I've lost track of the score. "That it?"

"Shut the fuck up." I have the ball, but I hold it without making moves.

"Gotta ask, man, because Halley asked you months ago and you were all nah, nah, nah, not yet. You got this whole thing"—he presents the garage like Vanna White—"and don't do anything with it until now?"

"I know what I did."

"But why?"

Putting the ball on my hip, I basically stop the game entirely. "I told you why. It got my brother off my back."

"Sure, man." He starts off the court.

"Dude." I hold out my arms, letting the ball rest on one palm. "Do I ask you why you take a deduction or whatever the fuck?"

"Not the same." He darts back onto the court, slaps the ball away from me, and dribbles. "Accounting has answers. It's math. This shit you do isn't like that. It's whatever you want it to be." He takes a shot. It bounces off the rim then goes in. "You do or you don't do. Halley's great, but you don't *do*." He passes the ball hard into my chest. "Why?"

"You know you're stepping over a line, right, Jabari?" I use his given name because I'm done fucking around.

"Yeah, I do. I love her, and if you think I won't cross a few lines to make her happy, you don't know me."

I've known Jabari Davis since ninth grade, and I'm dead aware of how many lines he'll cross for people he cares about. Tossing the ball to the side, I go to the U of couches around the glass table and throw myself into a corner that overlooks the pool. Jab follows, taking a flat plastic case from his pocket.

"I just need to know, honestly." He tips a joint out of the case and snaps it shut. "Is it because Halley looks like Tamika?"

"They don't look anything alike."

"You know what I mean." He lights up.

"I know what you mean, and I'm not gonna get insulted about it. You're welcome."

"You can fuck yourself." He hands me the joint. I haven't smoked in awhile, but I take it.

"Would that I could." I cough and hand it back.

"I know, you'd never leave the house. So, you gonna make me whole or what?"

"I have to finish this EP with Skye."

"Skye's the white girl?"

"Yes. She came through Liam and if I produce her and don't wreck the place like the last time you came over—"

"Me? There were, like, a hundred people back here."

"Yeah. That time. Then I don't get kicked out."

"Okay, not to tell a man how to live but... what? Are you a grown man? Get your own fucking place."

I shake my head, staring at the sparkling pool. Once I get paid for producing Skye, I can get an apartment with a pool and couches. I can rent studios with better equipment. I know how to run that kind of business. It's not that big a deal on the surface, but my resistance isn't on the surface.

"It feels like leaving again," I say.

"Getting an apartment?"

"Yeah. Logan's not half the dick. Ella's having a baby. My parents are half an hour on the 10."

"And the 405, for real."

"It's not so bad. Liam needs me. Liam—who doesn't need anyone. And I'm here. I have roots. My life's trash, but at least I'm *here*."

Jab flicks the hot tip off the joint. "You're fucked up, you know that?"

"Yup."

"And you're not really here."

That's the kindest accusation anyone's ever laid on me, and it's the most correct. Obviously I'm not running away, but the fact is, if I was fully committed to staying, I'd put together some kind of income and a place of my own, instead of giving myself an excuse to feel shitty because I'm living in my brother's guest house.

"Tell you what." I get my feet off the table and lean forward. "Halley's fucking good, and I have nothing planned. So tell her I'll get her an EP together."

"You tell her." He puts the leftover half-joint in the case. "And while you're at it, you can tell her it's because you believe in her, not because I came here and beat you on the court."

"I won't be lying."

"When?"

"The guy who tells me the party starts at six when he means ten is trying to nail down day and hour?"

"Yeah. I want it in white boy time."

"Arright. Tuesday night, Skye sings at Fountain. Come with."

"Hold up." He goes fully upright. "Is she the one who sings nonsense with that DJ?"

Jab may be in finance, but nothing marginally cool in Los Angeles gets by him.

"Yeah," I say.

"Fuck. She *is* good."

"Yeah. She is."

I must sound wistful or dreamy or something, because his head's tilted and his eyes are a little wider.

"You aren't... no. No way. Not again."

He doesn't have to spell out what he means. I know exactly what's surprising him, because it's not surprising. Falling for women I produce is a pattern, just as planned.

"I'm not. But..." Am I supposed to keep the fake part of the fake relationship a secret from him? I don't want to lie to my friend, on the one hand. On the other, Halley isn't my friend, and he's going to tell her. That's how shit gets messy. "It's complicated."

"Dude, you think about doing that shit with Halley and I'll... I don't know." Jab shakes his head, but he's got nothing to worry about. There's nothing real or lasting between Skye and me. Nothing at all.

"It's not serious. It's actually just..." I hate lying. Fucking hate it. "Don't worry, all right?"

"Tell you what. I'll get reservations at Bungalow for after. You bring Skye and tell Halley you can't wait to get her in the studio. All right?"

"Deal."

We shake on it.

It's kinda nice to have a plan.

14

SKYE

"I'm on my way out. I have a gig tonight."

I shouldn't have picked up the phone. I'm eating the last of the last tamale with my bag slung over my back because I didn't realize I was starving until I was one foot out the door.

"I was wondering if you needed any help filling out those forms." My mother sounds like a lion imitating a bird. She wants to sound harmless and chirpy, but she could roar at any minute.

"Not yet." I chew and swallow while tossing the corn husks.

"There's a deadline, dear."

"I know." Plate in dishwasher.

"You have to be there for registration in late August."

"Okay. Yes."

"Skye? Are you taking this seriously?"

"I am, Mom. I'm just one foot out the door. I'm singing tonight. I told you? The Tuesday night thing?"

"Behind the DJ in the dark?"

"Yeah, and also? I'm making an EP. That means extended play and—"

"You told me, sweetheart. Months ago."

Her voice asks what it's going to be this time, and all I have is that this time it's going to work. The other tries were with the wrong people. I'm going to finish it with Colton and it's going to be a hit.

I can't say that again.

"I'm up for a spot in a showcase. It's called Shooting Star. If I make it, well, it's in late August so..."

"You can't miss registration after you deferred for a year already."

"I know. But this would be a case where—"

"Where you have a chance. Yes. I've heard this song. How does it go, again?"

"I mean it, Mom. I'll know whether or not I made it in time to go home, and I may defer my promises, but I always keep them."

"Okay, darling. I know you do. I trust you."

"Thanks, Mom."

"I love you, sweetheart."

"Love you too."

I cut the call and put my hand on the doorknob and freeze, stopping my brain before it says horrible, cruel things.

"I'm fine." I take three breaths, keeping still as I pay attention to the position of my body, the sounds outside, the beating of my heart, the warming doorknob under my fingers—until there's not a single punitive, ugly word in my head.

Done.

The voice is beaten before it even arrives, and I leave the house victorious.

The Fountain is on Fountain Ave, which runs from Silver Lake to West Hollywood. When asked how to get anywhere in this town, either Lauren Bacall or Bette Davis—referring to the traffic on Sunset—said "take Fountain," which might have been funny if you lived here and knew what she was talking about, and also may have been true back then. These days, you're better off taking Sunset at rush hour.

Becca has single-handedly turned Fountain's Tuesday nights from dead zone into city-wide reduced productivity on Wednesdays.

The club building used to be a car repair. It has a Scientology school on one side and a gas station on the other. As clubs go, it's tiny. By midnight, the crowd is packed in, and the energy is barely containable.

Becca is spinning with her big blue headphones. I stand behind her, scanning the crowd for Colton, who said he was coming, but who knows? Even he said he's not reliable.

Becca moves an ear cup away and leans back toward me. "Has it ever been this packed?"

I shake my head. It hasn't. "You'll be doing Ibiza by next summer."

She flicks her hand, dismissing my optimism, and goes back to her laptop.

My phone vibrates in my pocket. Liam calling. I dismiss it. I'm busy, and even if I picked up, I wouldn't be able to hear him.

I know where my part begins, but Becca will give me a hand signal anyway.

I love doing Tuesdays with her. She wants my voice to add a bespoke element to her set. I can sing words, create sounds that could be words but aren't. I can break into long vowel sounds that add depth. She trusts me to improvise.

Nobody pays attention to me—they're too busy dancing and drinking, whooping and shouting. I've met a few of these people. They like how I add something different to the music that they don't hear anywhere else, but I'm sure they don't come here for me. Becca is the draw.

A text comes in. Thinking it's Colton, I peek at it.

It's Liam.

—We're here—

He must mean Colton.

—If u come to the booth by the laser orb I'll see u—

But among all the bouncing heads in the dark room, I already see Liam, and he's not with Colton. He's with Gene Testarossa.

Shit. Fuck. Shit.

He needs to ask before he does this.

Someone in this room is looking at me, and it's not just Liam, who I trust. A man is here to make a decision about my future. He's not my friend. He doesn't support me or believe in me. His literal job is to separate wheat from chaff. Wheat is a commitment for the label. Wheat makes you money. Chaff is free until he commits, then it gets expensive. If there's any doubt, I'm chaff.

I scan the room for Colton, but I don't see his backward

cap or wavy hair in the dancing crowd or the more likely spot at the static edges.

Becca holds out her hand, keeping time while the song changes.

Forget about Testarossa. Pretend he doesn't exist and never existed. He's a fiction, a name with no body, or maybe just an unreliable record executive who found something else he had to do on a Tuesday night.

He could be anywhere or nowhere, but no... he's right in front of me, talking to a young girl sweating through a dance floor break. Will he swing his attention when I start? Does it matter? Because the room is full of people, and I don't know any of them.

Fail fail fail fail

It matters. The fear of him hearing me has spread to every set of ears in here.

Becca makes the motion that means start, but I cannot make a sound.

She looks at me, hand moving to the next beat where I can come in. Makes the go sign.

Nothing.

I have nothing.

If I make a sound into this microphone, I'm going to have a panic attack in front of everyone. This has never happened at the Fountain—the one place where I'm fearless.

I'm pissed now. Partly at Liam. Mostly at myself.

Becca is laying out the beat for the next opening, looking at me with concern. I turn away and spot Colton approaching Liam and Gene. He faces me. Gives me a thumbs-up.

He's here.

Suddenly, I can breathe. It's not his presence that soothes

me. His faith isn't permission not to worry about the tightness in my chest or the judgments of strangers. He's a reminder that someone who matters has enough faith in me to design Pez handoffs as a routine. I have strategies. I know how to let this anxiety run through me. I am neither alone nor powerless. With careful concentration, I listen to the music in all its depth, feel the vibrations against my feet and the weight of the microphone.

It takes a few seconds of pure concentration. I'm still anxious, but I'm not frozen.

I don't need Becca to time me in. I know exactly what to do, and I break into a lament that's a joyful celebration of life, letting the music take me in harmony with what's already there. My sounds that don't make words, because words can lie. The phrasing and dynamics are truth. The mood and tone are under my control, molded and flowing with Becca's mix.

At the climax of my friend's penultimate set, I don't sing like no one's watching. I sing like everyone in the world is watching, and they can approve of me or hate me, but in the end, it doesn't matter when I'm singing.

Right now, tonight, I'm singing for Colton.

I don't think about what that means until—in a whirl and a bang—the set ends and Becca whips off her headphones.

"Damn, girl!"

"Damn yourself!" I jump off the dais in pure exuberance and find Colton waiting for me.

"That was—"

He never finishes. I throw my arms around him and kiss him. I don't stop. I kiss him right through his first moment of surprise. Through the following seconds of acceptance. Well after he puts his arms around my waist, I stay connected to him at the mouth, shutting out the hum of house music so I can focus on the way he rocks me back and forth.

He pops away, but not too far. A flashing light glints in the corner of his eye. It's the only thing in the room. The only light in the world is where the world reflects against him.

He'll think I was faking for Gene's benefit, but was I?

15

COLTON

I have friends everywhere, even at a Tuesday night gig.

Jellybean's here with Ned, standing in a dark corner. Carmy—who always told me to do a Tuesday at Fountain, even though EDM's not my thing—is right there. Rog is with his sometimes-girl, Ayla, and his brother Den. We're catching up for so long I almost miss her start, but the crowd gets tense, as if they know something is coming and it's not.

"If Idda known you liked this so much, I woulda gotten you in free," Rog shouts in my ear.

I tear my eyes off Skye to look at him as he gives me a "woulda done it too" shrug. I'd be totally in my rights to tell him to fuck off with his free shit when he makes bank in finance, but rich kids love perks and swag more than money.

"Next time," I say.

He claps me on the back.

Becca's looking to the side and behind. I follow her gaze to Skye, who's as still as a statue.

"Shit." I pop out of the dark corner to where I can see Skye better.

After our eyes connect, she explodes into song, dipping from alto to mezzo-soprano. Her voice—separated from the constraint of words—lands the emotions. She puts it all out there for the entire set, and in what feels like no time at all, she's done.

At first, I don't know why Skye's kissing me. Exuberance is one thing, because—no question—she deserves to be pretty fucking exuberant. Then I hear Gene's voice behind me. I don't know what he's saying, but it's him, and he's the one who wants me to repeat my pattern. So it makes sense, and I gotta admit, in seizing this moment to do this, she's really smart.

I kissed her that one time in her courtyard to prove we could, but this is different. I can't tell if she means it or not, but it sure fucking feels like she does.

Could be that I'm putting my own shit on her, because the kiss happens too fast for me to figure out what's going on with me, and my dick definitely has something to say about it, which keeps me from deciding anything one way or the other. I just kiss the mouth that elevated EDM from the mechanical to the human as if I want to bring that voice closer, explore it, and return it to its owner on the tip of my tongue.

When I need to breathe, I pull away but keep holding her because once this is over, I have to figure out the yes or no of what just happened.

"Well, hello there!" Jellybean says.

"Oh, hey, Jellybean, this is Skye."

"Who's this?" Rog asks, and I spend the next five minutes introducing her around.

"I sense a party coming." Carmy punches me in the arm.

"Sure, sure. I'll let you know." I pull Skye away from my friends. "Sorry."

"They seem nice."

"I hope you're hungry," I say. "We're going to a late-night place in Santa Monica."

"We? Those guys I just met?"

"Other friends. They're around somewhere."

"Do they know?" She takes my hand, and I can't believe how easily her fingers slide into mine.

"I'm not telling them until after the breakup."

"The super smooth, no-hard-feelings breakup."

"That one."

"Cool." She looks around and catches sight of Liam scrolling on his phone. "Where's Gene?"

Liam tips his phone toward the record exec leaning into a girl's ear. She's nodding and sipping her drink through a stir-straw.

"What did he think?" I ask because it has to be positive. Just has to be.

But Liam shakes his head. "Just finish the EP."

"That's what he thinks?" She squeezes my hand hard enough to cut off the circulation.

Liam puts away his phone. "You do your part and I'll do mine. Okay?"

His confidence seems to relax her enough to loosen her grip. Blood flows back to my fingers.

"Okay."

"We should go," I say.

"Let me say goodbye to Becca." She releases my hand completely and disappears into the crowd.

"What did he say for real?" I ask Liam. He shakes his head again.

"He saw her freeze. If he doesn't think she'll be able to perform, she's useless."

My skin tingles and the hairs on my arm go straight up. "Don't fucking call her that."

"To him. Useless *to him*. This is a business, Colton. It's not a personal insult, okay? What's with you?"

"She'll perform. Tell him I said so."

"Just finish the EP."

"I'll do my job."

"Good." He looks at his watch. "I gotta go. Make sure he sees you walking out together."

With a slap on my arm, Liam leaves. Gene's right there. I should tell him she'll be fine. She'll perform when she has to. I swear it.

Skye lays her hand on my back, and I jolt a little.

"You okay?" she asks. Her eyes are huge and dark, and her lip gloss flashes pink and purple in the dance floor lights.

"Yeah." I put my arm around her shoulder and pull her close so I can talk in her ear. "Let's give Gene something to think about."

"Such as?"

I pull her closer and kiss that glossy mouth, letting my lips slide over hers. I kiss her as if I'm trying to hold her breath hostage. I kiss her as if she's perfect, incapable of failure, a winner.

16

There's one restaurant open this late. It's close, but too far to walk. Since Becca and I rode with her equipment in her pickup, I don't have my car.

Colton's car is a Mercedes Benz 300 from the 1990s that doesn't suit him at all. It has leather seats and all the trimmings of the era. He spends the ride telling me about his friend Jab—who he met in ninth grade and whose real name is Jabari—his girlfriend Halley, what they want from him, and why they've earned it.

"Jab heard I was in Austin for the SXSW and he took a week off work to fly there, hunt my ass down, and pretty much kidnap me."

"Why?"

"I didn't call. Didn't write. He wanted to make sure I wasn't in trouble."

"Were you?"

"Yeah. I was in trouble. But it wasn't drugs or the mob or... I don't know what he thought I was doing. I started

118

with a bunch of money from my parents. The last dime I was getting from them. That was the deal. We each get one shot to ask for one big thing. The OBT. Right? Could be a favor or pulling strings or whatever. I wanted my trust released early. All of it. And they pay the taxes. Oh yeah, I thought I was so smart to remember the taxes." He scoffs at his younger self. "He shows up and I'm going through that money like water. I couldn't shut the tap. To him, that was trouble."

"How much was it?"

"A lot."

"So, more than a thousand dollars?"

We're at a red light, so he looks at me, wrist draped over the top of the wheel, far hand rubbing his lower lip. I'm not a mind reader, but I know what that look is about. He's trying to see if I'm serious about that number. He doesn't want to insult me.

I keep my eyes wide and blink, trying to hide my sarcasm. I don't want to be so easy to read.

"What kind of doctor is your father?" he asks.

"Literal brain surgeon."

"He good?"

"The best. Everyone says so."

He nods and moves forward when the light turns green.

"Whatever he makes in a year," Colton says, "my OBT was more."

"Why did you ask for it all at once?"

He starts to answer at least three times. Once with a shrug, once with hands up, once with a vowel sound he clamps down on.

"Because." He waits so long to continue I start to think that's the sum of it. "I have four older brothers and a younger sister. All of them... every fucking one... even my little

119

sister... had a career. They were doing shit. They were successful as fuck."

"You all basically had a head start." I rub my fingers together to make the money sign.

"I had more."

"How?" I wait to hear about how he was given more opportunities than his siblings, but he shakes his head.

"The point is, even with everything, I had to catch up, and I wasn't going to do it here with all of them watching me. Waiting for me to be as good as the rest of them. I told myself I wasn't coming back until I could hold my head up around that table full of suits. Except Lyric. She doesn't wear suits. And she's kinda cool, but in that entrefluencer kind of way."

"What kind of way?"

He smiles, laughs, turns down a side street. "Influpreneur. Influpreneur?"

Now I'm laughing. "Entrepreneur and influencer?"

"There's not one word for that?" He stops the car and puts it in reverse.

"There are, like, five as of this car ride."

Still grinning, he puts his arm behind my seat and turns to look out the back window. There's a muscle that goes from the space between your collarbones to behind your ears, and when Colton turns, his seems like the most gracefully designed thing in the human body.

"I think I smell," I say, suddenly self-conscious. "It can get really hot up in that booth."

"You don't smell bad," Colden says as he faces forward, his arm still over my seat. "You smell pretty much"—he removes his arm to put the car into park—"good."

He opens his door. The light goes on. We get out and walk down the dark street.

"Colton." I put my hand on his arm to stop him. That's a mistake. My skin is more sensitive to him than I expect. I feel the softness of every hair, the hardness of muscle and tendon, and the warmth of the blood going through his veins. I take my hand away as if I've been burned. "I need clarity. Are we pretending to be in a thing? When we go down the block, are we acting like there's... you know." I gesture back and forth between us. "Because it's not a Liam-approved event, and it could be for nothing. On the other hand, it's LA and there's always someone somewhere."

He looks away, then rubs his chin. "Probably. Yeah. Unless you don't want to."

"There might not be anyone to see us."

"True. So, no. Just business."

"But what about Jab and Halley?"

"I told him it's complicated."

This is stressing me out. I hate not knowing what to do next.

"So we don't have to pretend, but what if—"

"Okay." He puts his fingertips on my lips. I like his touch. I like that he feels intimate enough with me that he can do that. But I push them away because I don't like being told to be quiet. "You're going back and forth. We'll only be here an hour. So let's pretend. Just in case. Okay? I'll hold your hand. Put my arm around you. Spank your ass when no one's looking."

"What?"

"Joking."

"Don't give up your day job... oh wait, you don't have one."

He spanks my ass and I laugh.

Bungalow. The cozy name must be some kind of ironic joke to someone cooler than I am, because the restaurant is made of glass and steel, with cones of cold light coming from the concrete floor. A light mist hangs in the air between the street and the glass. It has the powdery smell of the dry ice machines my school used in *Wicked* whenever a witch needed to disappear.

I have never felt so underdressed in my life.

Colton and I are led to a table where I meet Jabari and Halley. They seem really nice, and they're wearing the exact right clothes for the room. Unlike Colton and me, who look like a couple of assholes giving the finger to everyone who bothered paying attention.

At least—according to the guy sitting closest to me—I don't smell bad.

Colton doesn't know how to sit up straight. His feet are tilted, bent, leaning on the edges of his sneakers... but always far apart. Same for his arms. They're stretched, bowed, draped over the nearest piece of furniture. At any given moment, he's a photo of a cat captured mid-leap.

"Did you major in music at Michigan?" Halley asks.

She's so stunning I can barely think. It's not that I want to have sex with her—though if push came to shove, I wouldn't say no—it's that she's so polished I can't believe she's really present.

"Biochemistry." I answer the question about my studies into my wine glass, which is already down to the last tablespoon.

"That sounds hard."

"I had a knack for it." I hide behind my glass again.

Halley was just talking about how nervous she was for her GMAT, and here I am, telling her my education was easy. But she doesn't seem put off. She did well enough to get her MBA from Howard University and wound up heading the accounting department at Warner's, three floors above "that big, handsome guy from Finance and Procurement."

"I was supposed to apply to med school right out of undergrad." I put down my glass and Jab fills it. "But I wanted to try this first. So my parents agreed to help me. They cosigned my lease and paid the car insurance for a year."

Jab holds up his glass. "To your parents."

We click and get back to eating. I narrate my life between chews.

"After the first year, I said I'd apply to med school, and the deal was I'd promise, cross my heart, that if I got in, I'd go. And I got into Michigan. Again. But it was right about when I got this fabulous agent."

"Liam," Colton murmurs.

"He is pretty fab," Halley says.

"So I had to stay." Everyone at the table seems to agree. "I had a job at Starbees, so I didn't need the money anymore, but I did promise, so I said, just let me defer another year and see what happens with that."

"When was this?" Halley asks, looking a little concerned.

"About a year ago."

"So what's happening with that?"

"I figure, I get into this Shooting Star showcase or I go home and become a doctor."

Colton stops chewing. "What?"

"I need something to tell them. This is it."

"That's not how this works," he says. "It's a process. It takes time."

I shrug and raise my glass. I don't know where all my wine went, but I drain the last drops.

"Past performance is no guarantee of future results," Jab says, filling up my glass when I put it down.

"He says that all the time." Halley jabs him.

"Well, it's true." He tries to refill Colton, who puts his hand over the glass.

"Driving."

"Cool, cool." He puts down the bottle and turns to me. "Have you ever heard this guy bludgeon a piano?"

"Uh... like the rock guys with the guitars? In, like, the seventies?" I make a smashing motion.

Jab chuckles. "No, like a guy with lead fingers. This dude. Fuck. We were all studying and he was like nah. I'm going to make Fats Waller spin in his grave instead."

"Those who can, do." Colton puts his arm on the back of my chair as if the person in it belongs to him. I don't belong to anyone but myself, but I like feeling as if it could be true. "Those who can't, produce."

He gets a laugh out of us.

"Was it worth it?" I ask Colton. When he seems to not understand me, I add, "Failing..." I address Jab. "What class was it?"

"Differential calculus. And this little leprechaun didn't fail anything but the jazz pantheon."

"Jab!" Halley scolds.

"It's true. Honey, when you meet Fats up in heaven, you ask him."

"I mean calling the man names. And he's normal size."

"Thank you, Halley." Colton leans forward. "And maybe, for me, practicing piano *was* studying. You thought about that?"

"No. Because that's stupid."

Our food comes. I didn't know Colton had it in him to pass diff calc. You never can tell about a person, I guess, and sometimes the things you can't tell are nice surprises.

"So, Halley." Colton jabs his fork at his food. "When I finish Skye's EP, if you're still game, we can do something..."

He talks business with Halley. He's going to work with her too, and that's great. I'm glad he has a plan after me, in case I suck.

Colton's phone is next to mine. They both buzz. He's still talking when he flips his over to read it, then puts it back face down, barely pausing. I check mine. Liam's texted the group chat.

—Hello? Earth to the hottest couple in LA. You've been spotted—

Colton puts his arm over the back of my chair. I feel his thumb run along the back of my neck with a touch so light and casual it sends a shudder down my spine. I hide behind my wine again. Pretending this is totally normal, and at the same time, I'm looking all over the room for someone who looks like they even care. There's no one. Am I blind or is Liam fucking with us? Does Colton just believe it? He must, because he's doing the pretending thing with his thumb and telling him to stop to text Liam is out of the question. I don't want him to stop touching me like this. Ever.

They've moved on from business, but I'm barely listening, because Colton's hand has moved down, teasing the skin under the edge of my shirt. My glass is filled again, and I realize how tipsy I am.

"You admitted you were trying to get thrown out." Jab responds to a story about Colton vaping behind the middle school building with a girl named Nina. "Bar none, you were Mirman's worst influence."

"Who's Mirman?" I ask.

They look at me.

"She's not from here." Colton lays his hand still on my back, looking at me with a half grin. "You all right?"

"It was just a question."

"It's a school," Halley says. "West side."

"East of Encino," Jab adds. "Or my dad would have put me at Harvard-Westlake. But you were coming from where? North of Sunset and west of Rexford?"

"You can just say Beverly Hills." Colton leans into me and drops his voice too low for anyone but me to hear, and considering he's moved so close I can feel the warmth of his face... that's pretty low. "You sure you wanna keep playing the pretending game?"

"I feel like we're winning." I just want to kiss him, and I've drunk away a bunch of my inhibitions. Someone's watching us. A stranger with an opinion I'll never know, and I don't care. All I care about right now is what Colton Crowne thinks. "Do you want to keep going?"

"No."

No is definitely a rejection, but he's not moving away.

"But you will?" I move a little closer. Our noses touch, shift, slide to the right until the sides fall into place like books on a shelf.

"Yes." He whispers against my lips a moment before they touch.

He may not want to play this game, but his kiss wants to exist. It gently asks for recognition, then demands to be known. It goes on longer than it needs to for anyone to take a picture and send it wherever. It goes on until I get dizzy and have to push him away.

Colton grabs his soda. Halley's eyebrows are raised. Jab's rolling his eyes and tapping his fingers on the table.

"Sorry," I say, picking up my wine glass, which is unexpectedly full again.

"I mean for *real.*" Jab pushes away his half-empty plate. "Get a damn room."

Halley laughs while, under the table, Colton squeezes my hand.

Right outside the restaurant, the fog machines sound like lawn mowers and the smoke smells like baby powder. I realize how absolutely wrecked I am.

Jab hands the valet his ticket, then looks at Colton. "Ticket, bro."

"We parked around the corner."

Jab scoffs.

Halley speaks quietly to me. "It was really nice to meet you."

"Same." God, I hate feeling this unbalanced. "You seem really cool and even when you talk, I can tell you can sing."

She tucks a strand behind her ear. "Thank you."

"And your makeup is, like, on the spot. Whenever I do mine, I look like... blerg."

"Your man doesn't seem to mind."

My man? Oh, right. That guy with the jacket hiding those arms, and the hair that's just a little curly and always the most perfect kind of a mess. The one who doesn't say bad things about anyone and who never blamed anyone else for his shortcomings.

The valet brings Jab's blue Tesla around. We say goodbye, and they zoom off. It's just Colton and me.

"I like them."

"Where's your car?" he asks.

"I can't drive while the world is so swim-swimmy."

"Yeah, I mean you can barely walk." He puts his arm around my shoulders, holding me up while we walk down the street. "Is it going to get towed, is my question."

"It's at Becca's." I lean into him. He feels so good, but also, I feel like I'm going to puke. "Downtown by the zippy overpass."

"Are you going to be able to get to the studio in the morning?"

"Yup. Fresh as Febreeze. I don't get hungover. Not my thing. I just sleep through it. But!" I hold up a finger as if I'm having a eureka moment. "If we go to your place, we can start earlier."

"You're a really cute drunk. Turn here." He guides me down the dark residential street. "When you said if you don't get into Shooting Star, you're quitting, did you mean it?"

"Yop."

"You're just... what? Leaving LA and going to med school? Based on one thing?"

"Based on everything. I have designated that meteor shower thing in the desert the straw that breaks the poor camel's back. And I told my mother, so now I can't walk it back."

"That's a tough show to make, Skittles."

"Whatever. Did you want to do that kiss or not?"

He loosens his arm, as if I'm telling him to stop holding me up, which I am not, so I pull him closer at the waist.

"What do you think?" he asks.

"I think it doesn't matter what I think. You asked if I wanted to keep playing and I said yes then you said no."

"You don't know whether I wanted to kiss you or not?" He stops, looks down at me. "You can't tell?"

"Am I psychic?"

He looks down the block one way, then the next. "Is anyone watching us? Do you see a single camera? 'Cos I don't."

"All I see is you."

With the hand that's not around my shoulders, he takes my entire jaw and holds it still. "No cameras."

"None."

"Good."

He kisses me again, and this one doesn't ask permission to exist. It's decisive, and it's made of yes. I get the message. I like the message. I enjoy the message, but I push him away when the combination of closed eyes and open mouth becomes unsustainable.

"Sorry," I say.

"If you don't want—"

"I do. You do that any time you want. Unless you want me to make sentences and not little squeaky sounds, then... hold up." I stop and put my hands on my knees. It took two minutes and a kiss to go from feeling happy to feeling the weight of my impending mortality. "Some guy didn't punch me in the stomach and run away, right?"

"I think that was Jab pouring."

"He kept filling it." The crack in the sidewalk keeps moving around.

"He forgets we're not all six-three and two-eighty-five. Here."

At first, when the earth goes out from under me, I assume I've fallen down drunk, but I never hit the ground. I'm in Colton's arms, carried down the street. I put my arm around his neck to stabilize myself, but it doesn't work. My stomach thinks it's on a stormy sea.

"Colton."

"You're not gonna make it home, are you?"

"Nope." My mouth fills with saliva.

"A few steps to my car."

"That's a nice jacket. I don't want to throw up on it."

"You won't."

My stomach is now completely over this nonsense. It twists and lurches. My throat signals a cough, but I tell it to wait. I'm pretty sure I can do that one time before my willpower's overridden by physical need.

"Here." He puts me down on the edge of the curb, at the back of his old Mercedes.

I lay my hand on the bumper as the next cough forces itself through and the rest of dinner is history.

17

COLTON

"We're here," I state the obvious, turning on the kitchen light. The fluorescents make her look even more tired and sick.

"This isn't my apartment." Her voice is raw but manages to stay melodic.

"You said—"

"I know what I said." She takes half steps in.

I try not to smile. Telling her that her snappiness is charming would be rude when she's suffering like this, so I fill her a glass of water and take down a bottle of Advil.

"I can take you home, but then you have to get up yourself in the morning. And I mean morning."

"It's fine. I'll stay here. We can keep the rules. We didn't break them, right? By kissing when no one was watching. The rule was sex. Kissing isn't sex."

"Last time I checked." When I turn around, she's bent over with her arms at her sides and her cheek on the counter.

"You have a lot of red cups. Solo cups. One, two, four, six bags. And three boxes of garbage bags right on the counter."

"Hey." I push her hair off her cheek. "Take these."

"This is a real glass." She gets up, steadies herself, and takes the pills.

"I usually hide them when people come over. Safer that way."

"Solo cups everywhere and not a drop to drink from one. Shit, that makes no sense."

She hands me the glass half-full. I won't take it. "Finish."

"Yes, Mom." She finishes the water, and I watch her throat move, resisting the urge to touch it.

She hands me the empty glass. "I'm sorry."

"For what?"

"Embarrassing you."

"Nah."

She bends her fingers back, counting the second infraction. "Splashing puke on your car."

"It's my dad's old car and it's been through a lot. I'll wash it off."

"Making you host me. Taking your Advil. Forcing an unforced kiss out of you."

"It's nothing. For real. And no one forced anyone. Come on. I have an extra toothbrush."

She counts off her fifth infraction. "Using your extra toothbrush that you bought for I-don't-know-who but I hope she's nice."

I lead her to the bathroom and flip on the light. She leans over the counter to look at her face closely.

"I'll bring you something to wear."

"Oh, blah." She sticks out her tongue in the mirror.

"Are you gonna puke again or you're okay without me?"

"Get out." She unbuttons her pants and I catch a flash of tender skin. That's my cue to split if we're gonna stick to the rules.

Get out. Her voice is husky and overused, but still has a smoothness. Maybe her octave wasn't what was bothering me. It was the slick, buttery pitch that made melodies out of regular sentences when she wasn't trying for lift.

There's a thing I need to hear, if I could just place it.

Everything I have is too big for her, so I pick out whatever, drop it in front of the bathroom door, and knock. "Shit to wear, right here."

"Thank you!"

I head for the garage, trying to pluck the sound she needs from the tip of my pointy little brain. Hearing the voices as I flip through my albums, I search for the sound of her. The place in her range that's commercial but not generic.

I want to sell it, angel food.

That's what Tamika said when I tried to find that sweet spot with her.

I am not here to make art no one hears.

In the end, she did it my way, and it sounded fantastic before her big-ass motherfucking new producer McCormick changed it just enough to wipe me of credit and cash, but not enough to make it suck as much as he does.

"Come on, where are you?" I say in frustration just before I find exactly what I'm looking for. "Ah!"

She comes to the garage wearing the Troubadour T-shirt and gym shorts I left for her. She looks tired but she's standing straight, so that's good news.

"I'll get the bed set up in a minute." I tilt the artist out from the E section. We're on a first-name basis.

"I don't want to displace you?" She leans against the doorway.

"It's a one-bedroom." I tip the black disc from the sleeve without showing her the picture on the front.

"I'm aware."

"You and me? In the bed then? Sure."

"I mean, I'll sleep on the couch."

"I thought you were trying to test my willpower." I open the turntable cabinet.

"It's mine I'm worried about."

Record in my hand like a shield, I freeze. Only my eyes are moving. They go from her bare feet, locked together around me, her legs, bent over my shoulders, her arms, over her head, the shape of her breasts—

I shake it off before I get to her face and what it's gonna look like when she comes.

"You're whiskey-voiced right now," I say, putting the record on the turntable.

"From vomiting in the street?"

"You always have it. The vomiting just brought it out."

She stands next to me, watching as I drop the needle. "You don't want me to sing right now, do you?"

"I want you to listen." I touch my ear.

She throws herself on the orange couch, lying with her arms over her head and one knee bent.

I sit on the edge of the cushions with my arm on the back. Her eyes are closed, so I can look at her face without it being weird.

"This couch isn't for sleeping overnight," I say. "Couple of hours is okay, but more than that and it's a stealth torture device."

"I know this song. 'Someone to Watch Over Me,'" she says

when the first notes rise. How am I supposed to not touch her?

"Ella Fitzgerald was a mezzo-soprano who dipped into alto."

"My dad plays this stuff when he's looking in people's brains."

"Listen." I put my finger on her lips, trying to be playful, but I rest them there, then pull back her lower lip. I bend down at tell her, "Just listen," with my lips almost against hers.

Her breath is toothpaste when her throat makes a little cracking sound. She opens her eyes. I sit up, exposed doing something I promised I wouldn't.

Her hand comes from over her head and touches the arm I'm leaning on against the back of the couch, running the length of it.

"Skye. The rules."

"When did you stop 'studying' at the piano?" Her air quotes sway like the ocean. She's not slurring her words and she puked a lot of excess, but she's still got booze in her blood.

"End of ninth grade, I guess?"

She drops her hand, twists her lips, tilts her head as if my answer would fail a lie-detector test.

"What?" I ask.

"Who takes diff calc in ninth grade?"

"It's a long story." I'm about to get up to change the record, turn it up, turn it down, stare at the way it goes round and round, but she stops me by grabbing my wrist.

"Is it?"

She puts my hand on her breast, and it's clumsy as shit

which is enough to bury me even deeper. That's it. I kiss her with my whole fucking face.

What am I supposed to do when I have more blood flowing to my dick than through my brain right now?

This, man. Just this. The doubts creep in between kisses.

"We can't catch feelings," I say.

"I can't catch. That's why you'll never see me playing frisbee or softball or whatever sport involves catching." She clutches my shirt, trying to get her hands under it.

"I mean it."

"So do I. Even if you throw feelings, I can't catch them. They'll whizz right by me or I'll drop them."

I get on the couch on top of her, which causes a blinding pressure in my balls. I want to get inside her so bad. She's not blind drunk, but she's not sober either.

She grabs me behind the neck and tugs me down to her, and fuck, making out, I can do. I kiss her like no one's watching. I kiss her sloppy, tasting her face and teeth, pushing my erection between her legs.

"Yes." She groans and slides herself along the shape of my cock. "Please, Colton. Let's do it. Just once."

The whites of her eyes are webbed with red veins. She may be more clear than before she emptied her stomach, but the only thing she ever consented to when sober was a kiss. Not this. As bad as I want it, the morning regret is going to be unbearable.

I could just touch her. Taste her. Everything but...

Fuck.

I can't.

There's not ever going to be enough blood in my dick to take what she's not clear enough to consent to.

She pulls me into another kiss, and I start telling myself

it's fine. We're both adults and it's not as if she's giving mixed signals.

But I'm a liar and those are excuses. I take my face off hers. She pushes her hips into me and my God, I'd better get into heaven without a single question from St. Peter, because arching myself away from those beautiful, grinding hips is the hardest thing I've ever done.

"I'm sorry," I say, head bowed. "You are really fucking sexy."

"I have a condom in my bag."

"It's not that." I sit straight and take her hand, kissing the tops of her fingers. "If I ever fuck you, Skittles, you're going to be fully awake." I'm totally focused on kissing the inside of her wrist, her palm, savoring every crease as I tell her what I want. "When I tease your body, you'll feel every touch. When I lick you and suck you, you'll beg to come, and you'll be one hundred percent in control when I tell you to wait. I want you to feel everything. My hands and mouth on you. My cock deep inside you. If you still want it when you're awake, I'm going to fuck you unconscious."

I've kissed every knuckle and curve of her hand, told her not only that I want to break our rules, but how, and she hasn't said a word.

Taking my face away from her limp fingers, I look at her.

She's sleeping. Her mouth hangs open and her head's tilted exactly the wrong way. Her neck's gonna hurt in the morning.

"Chalk one up for impulse control."

Wedging my arms under her shoulders and knees, I pick her up and carry her to the bedroom. I'm fit enough to get her there, but I need both arms to do it. I can't turn the sheets, so I lay her over the comforter.

"Mmhmmn," she groans as I pull off her shoes.

"Do you want a blanket?"

"Hmn."

"Okay. Give me a sec."

I get the plaid blanket from the top of the closet and put it over her.

"Mmnn."

"Okay." I tuck it under her until she looks like a burrito with a head. She doesn't make another sound.

I get ready for a night on the living room couch, checking the medicine cabinet to make sure I have enough Advil for her headache. I should probably jerk off just to release the buildup, but nah. If she still wants it when she's clear-eyed, this one's hers.

18

SKYE

On the stove in my parents' kitchen, feet between the burners, steam from vegetable and bean soup rising up my skirt, I grip a carrot, touching the pointy end to my chin. My head rests against a sharp corner of the stainless-steel hood. People come in, but not Dad. Mom flips the bacon. The kitchen gets more and more crowded. He's coming. I realize I'm scared.

Of course, that was a dream. Every bit of it. Except the headache, which does feel as though someone's pressing a steel corner into my head. And the bacon, which has a smell in the real world, where I am, but which is also not home. Big glass doors lead out to a patio on a side of the house I've never seen before. The ceiling fan churns. A poster for the Dead Kennedys hangs between two windows. It's not quite straight. My God, I hope this is Colton's bed.

I fell asleep on the orange couch and somehow wound up here. I wasn't that drunk once I puked, which was gross and warrants another apology, but also helped me sleep well and shave the edges off the headache.

I get up on my elbows and look around. There's a tower of baseball caps on the dresser. Yup. Colton's bed. That's where I am. The space next to me is flat, the pillow undented. I slept alone. We kissed. My pants are on, and my honor is... well, it's irrelevant, because what did I do?

Not drunk enough to black out. I think? You don't know what you don't know.

Last night I did the glossolalia. But first, I froze because one guy was there.

In the bathroom, I replay it all. The crowd of strangers didn't know me from Adam. I was no one to them, no name, no reputation, no connection. I couldn't suck in front of them because I made no claims. I was invisible. I could have been a few lines of code in Becca's laptop.

But Gene knew where the voice came from. He expected me to have talent, and even the expectations of that one set of ears was too much for me.

I can't do this. There's no cure for social anxiety, but I at least should be able to get it under control for a single record executive.

Colton reminded me that I have ways of calming myself down, and I did it, but then?

Did I say anything stupid with his friends? There was a kiss, and vomit, then a kiss again. It's all a blur, but I know one thing. I asked him to fuck me. I practically begged. Fuck. A few drinks and I get so hungry for affection.

He rejected me, which wouldn't be the first time I got a no, but we had rules and I broke them. He won't trust me anymore. He can't. Who would?

I ruined everything.

A glass of water and two terra-cotta Advil sit on the night table with a note.

Morning S
Take these if you want, but def drink the water.
C

The *def* is what confuses me. At first, I smile because it's so *him*, but in the context of his controlled sobriety and my fuck-me-please-even-though-I-puked... well... it's a slap in the face.

Sitting on the toilet, I bury my face in my hands. I screwed this up. I was the one who wanted the fake relationship when he didn't, and so I was the one who drew up the rules so I could throw them in his face the minute I had wine with dinner.

I wash my hands, and that's when I remember something that seemed said from the other side of consciousness.

If I ever fuck you, Skittles, you're going to be fully awake.

Oh God. Wait.

When I tease your body, you'll feel every touch. When I lick you and suck you, you'll beg to come, and you'll be one hundred percent in control when I tell you to wait.

He said that. I did the thing I do when I drink and he put me to sleep with everything he wanted to do to my body.

Maybe not even everything.

My hands and mouth on you. My cock deep inside you. If you still want it when you're awake, I'm going to fuck you unconscious.

I want that. I wanted it before last night, but in a casual, sort of "sure, you're cute and we're both grown-ups," kind of way. Now, I'm pretty sure I'd pick up a Volkswagen if his dick was under it. And his hands. And his mouth with that licking and sucking he promised.

"Damn." I shake my head slowly, replaying his words in my mind while tingling warmth gathers between my legs.

He had to be drunk too. He couldn't have meant all that. And even if he did, I'm now somebody to do things to and not a professional anymore. This is done. Shot. We're over.

I don't know what to think. I'm going to walk right up to him and ask what the deal is.

Colton's leaning over the kitchen counter, eating bacon from a paper-towel-lined tray with one hand and scrolling on his phone with the other.

"Hey," he says. "How are you feeling?"

"Good. Can I have some?"

He pushes the tray toward me and goes back to scrolling.

I take a piece. I'll ask him in a minute. "Whatcha lookin' at?"

He doesn't stop me when I peek over him. It's a bunch of numbers on a chart, then a picture of a microphone, then more numbers and technical shit.

"Upgrade." He flicks away the page.

"Looked fascinating."

"Really?"

"No. I was just being nice." I take another piece of bacon before I even realize I finished the first. It's super crispy the way I like it, with a hint of burned carbon. "Where'd you learn all this stuff? Were you the dorky audio guy in college?"

"Nah. I skipped that part. Not the dork part. That, I perfected."

"Didn't your parents want you to go to college?"

"Fuck yeah they did, but nah. I worked in this studio in

Van Nuys. Ten rooms. Bands in and out twenty hours a day. Learned everything. Better than college."

Is he brave or dismissive? Did he do the smart thing? Or is this one decision why he's living in his brother's guest house?

"It hadn't occurred to me I could opt out of my parents' plans until I was almost out of Michigan State." I shrug and break my bacon piece in half. "I almost set the house on fire."

"Why almost? Couldn't finish the job?"

"I was applying to med school, like they wanted, and everything's online, but the schools sent all these catalogs anyway. We had a pile, like, this high on the dining room table. My mother was nagging me to, like, get to it. Deadlines approaching blah blah. Anyway, I set the entire pile on fire and the curtains caught so... that was fun. Got a new therapist out of it."

He laughs a little, nodding in agreement as he breaks the last slice of bacon and gives me half.

"Colton. I don't think I've ever said these three words in this order." He looks at me suspiciously, because I can't be about to say what he thinks I'm going to say... and I'm not. "About. Last. Night."

I'm made of cringe, waiting for him to tell me that whatever professional relationship we had is now over, but he's good for a spin around the bedposts if I'm good too.

"Yeah," he laughs. "I'm sorry. I shouldn't have taken advantage."

"Uhh, yeah, no. You didn't. I did. Alcohol makes me amorous. I should have told you. Little heads-up, you know, so you could be prepared to say 'get off me' the next time I have a drink. But it doesn't mean anything. You don't have to worry."

"I wasn't worried." Is he as defensive as he sounds?

"You don't have to be so nice about it."

"Am I being nice?"

"Yes. No. Whatever. You looked worried. But you shouldn't be. I don't get attached that way."

"Good. Cool. So, new rule." He pauses as if considering whether or not to say what he wants. "No more wine for you."

"Okay. Let's consider that bill signed into law."

We shake hands, which isn't how legislation is signed at all, and touching him seems like a bad idea all around, because when we let go, our palms slide against each other.

I shower at his place. I've used partners' showers before. They've used mine. It's not a big deal, but with him, using his soap and washcloth seems incredibly intimate. Wearing his sweatshirt and a pair of his sweatpants is too much like wearing him. It's clean, of course, but still has his scent.

Bunching up the shirt, I put my face in it, trying to sense the detergent over the him-ness that seems overwhelming. I can't. I put it on anyway. The bacon probably messed up my nose.

We unloaded one of his drawers to find stuff for me, laughing as I pretended to wear his ripped-up jeans, and the pile is still on the bed. It's a little chilly, and my nipples are showing through the plain tee, so I grab a dark blue hooded sweatshirt and pull it on. The front says MIRMAN SCHOOL. I have no idea if that's a real school or some in-joke, but it's got good coverage and it's warm.

The woman in the mirror is dressed for a day in front of the television. Whatever. I'm ready to get to work.

Colton's not in the living room or kitchen, but I hear voices from the other side of the glass door. I see him on this side of the pool, talking to Liam, who has Matt stepping on his feet, and a taller guy in black. Another group are gathered by the big house. Ella. A man with his hand on the back of her neck. A woman in her late fifties. Woman my age leaning against the pillar that holds up the balcony above.

Do I stay quiet and wait for Colton to come back or go out and say hello? I can't decide which is more polite, then Liam sees me and waves me out. That's my answer.

"Skye!" he says when I'm outside. "Come meet the family."

Colton intercepts me when I'm halfway there, eyeing the sweatshirt, or my breasts under them. "Where'd you get that?"

So the look was at least partly the sweatshirt.

"It was on the bed, and I was cold. Is it okay?"

"Yeah." He waves it away. "Listen, if meeting a bunch of people isn't your thing right now, it's cool. I can beg off."

"It's fine."

"My family can be a lot."

"You don't come from nowhere, Colton."

"Am I a lot?"

"You're a whole lot."

"All right, but if you get, like, anxious or whatever…"

"I'll let you know. Thank you."

The group by the big house has migrated over and I recognize Ella. It's been less than a week since I met her, but she looks bigger already.

"Skye," she says, "get ready for a lot of information."

"I'm ready."

"My husband, Logan." I shake hands with a tall guy in a Henley who seems as if business casual is as casual as he ever gets. "Dante. Colton's older brother." Very tall, wearing head-to-toe black. They're both incredibly handsome in the way Colton is, but as different from him as imaginable. "You know Liam, right?"

"Yep, And Matt," I say, looking at the boy. "Did you bring any Legos today?"

"I go get!" He runs to the other side of the yard.

"I'm Lyric." Colton's sister waves to me then scrolls her phone. "He sometimes invites me to his parties but mostly nah."

"I'm Doreen." The older woman takes my hand in hers. She doesn't seem old enough to shake this much or young enough to clasp me so tightly... or for so long. "I made them."

"I'm Skye. It's nice to meet you."

She's still holding my hand and looking deeply at my face, squinting a little as if I'm not in focus.

"Ma!" Lyric barks. "You're making it weird."

"Oh." Doreen lets me go. "Sorry about that. Just had this feeling."

"A tingle?" Logan asks, one eyebrow raised.

"Not sure. Anyway! Here we are. We'll set a place for you."

"Thank you."

I try to make eye contact with all of them but catch Colton standing there with his hands in his pockets, and I realize it's early in the morning, I'm wearing his clothes, and my hair is wet. This looks like something it's not... even to Liam, who's supposed to be in on everything it isn't. I clear my throat. "Um, I'm sorry to interrupt breakfast. I had a little extra wine last night and Colton was too much of a gentleman to let me drive."

"A gentleman?" Dante says, arms crossed, eyebrows raised in sky-high disbelief. "Truly, through and through, right, Mom?"

"Of course he is." She pats Colton's arm with the shaky hand.

He pats it back then looks up suddenly, facing her.

"We're doing a Logan and Ella, and I'm not gonna lie about it." He directs the last bit at Logan.

"Wait, what?" Dante exclaims.

"Oh, my God." Lyric laughs.

"Hold on," Liam says.

"We're not getting actually married," Colton says defensively. "But it's a fake thing, so don't get ahead of yourselves."

I'm frozen still, and it doesn't feel like the usual anxiety. Anyone in this situation would be a little stunned.

"It's business," Liam says. "Skye here is one of the most talented singers I've ever repped and he's producing her EP. Letting them get seen together, as a couple, it's just good PR."

"Well, you're being seen here in my backyard," Logan says, slapping Liam on the back. "So good work."

"We're working on getting her into the Shooting Star showcase."

"Is that the one we sponsor?" Doreen asks. "With the Music For All Foundation?"

"Yes," Liam says. "We should hear the good news soon."

"Should we have your father pull a few strings?"

"No!" I bark and immediately regret my tone. "Sorry. I didn't know that was possible, but please. No. This is... it's kind of a test for whether or not I should continue this career at all, and that would kind of defeat the purpose."

Dante chuckles—probably at my naivete. Logan shoots him a withering glance that does nothing to stop the laugh.

"Don't mind Dante," Lyric says. "He has no talents to test."

"Breakfast is on the table," Logan interrupts. "Come on, Skye, you can tell us all about working with this idiot." He takes Colton by the back of the neck as if he's used to manhandling his little brother.

"We ate," I say to a handful of disappointed faces. They must want to hang out with Colton and, by extension, me. "But coffee sounds good."

Doreen shudders a little and rubs her hands together.

"You all right, Ma?" Ella says as we cross to the big house.

"Just a little tingly."

"Ah." That seems to answer some bigger question for Ella, and she smiles.

I hang back to walk astride Colton. "I hope this—"

"It's fine."

"You sure?"

"Yeah, why?" he asks.

"You seem nervous."

"Nah."

"I promise I won't embarrass you."

"I'm not worried about you."

Breakfast has been laid out on the back patio, which is much bigger than the U of couches at the guest house. A woman and man bring covered trays to a side table. Another woman—who must be a mind reader—brings another chair. This is what money does when people come over, I guess. My mother has Jovie and Liza over to clean, but she always does the cooking and prepping.

"Lyric," Dante barks when we're all sitting, "put that thing away."

148

"Fuck right off."

"You could stand to be fully present for five minutes."

"This isn't one of your clubs," she sneers back without even looking up. "You don't get to make the rules."

"I do," Logan says.

Dante reaches over Liam with a surprisingly long arm and snaps her phone away.

"Hey!"

"All right," Doreen says in a quiet voice that gets everyone's attention. "Shall we eat?"

Doreen doesn't tell Dante to return the phone. He puts it face down by his plate. It buzzes with a notification. He puts a cloth napkin over it.

Colton is next to me, slouched in his seat. I'd have to turn a hundred-twenty degrees to see his reaction, so I don't—but I wonder if he's keeping out of my sight for a reason.

Food gets passed around. Sausages and fruit. Yogurt. Granola. One of the staff brings me a cup of coffee, my own little pitcher of cream, and a plate of sweeteners. I thank him with delight at being handed the exact gift I wanted. I put fat blackberries and thinly-sliced cantaloupe on my plate, consider rejecting the sausage since I just had bacon, and decide I need to fortify myself for the day and take one. I pass Colton the tray and he puts it back in the center of the table. He's only got a spoonful of eggs.

"So," Doreen says when everyone has their food, "Skye, I hope we're not all overwhelming."

"Because this is about half of us." Lyric doesn't roll her eyes, but her voice expresses the same thing.

"Yeah, Ma," Logan says. "Should've stopped with Colton."

Matt crawls onto Liam's lap. I finish the little cup of coffee in three gulps.

"I would have had six more if I could."

"*That* would be overwhelming." I manage to get a word in. "This is a manageable number of Crownes."

Matt pushes a little Lego vehicle across the table to me. I take it and mouth the excitement of *ooh* and *wow*.

"Are you from a big family, Skye?" Doreen asks.

"Just Mom and Dad and an older brother. He's a veterinary oncologist. Big house. Big, big house." They all look at each other, smirking as if I don't know what I'm talking about, and maybe I don't, so of course I keep talking. "He's got this orange sports car. It's so loud. Talk about overwhelming."

Lyric singsongs, "So sorry to hear about your dick."

"Lyric Crowne!" Doreen scolds.

"She's with me!" We high-five across the table.

"Tell me more about the sports car." Dante leans forward.

"The doors open." Matt shows me how his Lego car functions.

"Koenig... something?" Somehow, more coffee has appeared in my cup. "It's Swedish."

"And there's a guy inside." Matt points him out to prove it.

"There is!" I peek inside. It's not Kay Jay this time, but a little man in a spacesuit.

"A Koenigsegg CCR?" Dante asks.

"I'm dying of boredom." Lyric tries to snatch back the phone, but Dante's too quick.

"Sounds right." I hand the vehicle back to Matt and dress my coffee. "Anyway. Overwhelming."

"No need to be." Dante handles his coffee cup with casual domination, ignoring the handle in favor of the entire rim.

"Under the hood, it's just a Ford. It'll only go as fast as the tow truck pulling it."

I finish the second cup of coffee in a split second. I guess that's what makes me bold.

Leaning on my elbows, I look Dante right in the face. He smirks, and that's the only thing that keeps me from withering under his intensity. Fuck it. I was taught that one should never take a social gamble at the dinner table, but it's breakfast and I really think the Crownes are different.

"You aren't insulting the Ford Motor Company in my presence, are you?" I ask.

Silence. No one knows what to do with this, least of all Dante, who seems curious enough to shut up so he can hear what I'm about to say next.

"I'm from right outside Detroit," I say, making fists then spreading my fingers to loosen the joints. "So I hope you're ready to fight."

Logan laughs. He gets it.

"I take it back." Dante holds up his hands. "I'd never fight a Michigan girl over the merits of good old American engineering."

"Good," Logan says. "I'm not up to scrubbing your blood out of the Italian stone tiles."

"Like you ever scrubbed a thing in your life." Lyric's fingers itch to grab her phone, but Dante puts his hand over the napkin.

"Apology accepted." I grab a piece of bacon as if I already haven't risked heart failure this morning.

"Skye," Colton says, "you drive a Toyota."

I put my finger over my lips. "We don't talk about that."

Colton smiles, someone chuckles, Lyric finally gets the phone away from Dante. The family moves on to subjects I know nothing about, but their relaxed tone of gentle and sometimes not-so-gentle ribbing continues. Logan implies Lyric is going to age out of her "job," making a point of the air quotes. Dante jabs back at Logan for working in the family business. Doreen remains kind and equitable—the queen of a kingdom that will never be at war with itself.

My family is nothing like this. We prefer silence over conflict. Safe subjects over risky humor. We'll let the pot boil itself dry before turning off the heat, because we can't tolerate that the flame gets hotter and brighter before it clicks off.

There's a wiggle and pressure on my calves. It's Matt under the table.

"Hey. Coming up?" I pat my knees and he crawls into my lap.

"Don't do it," Logan advises me. "You'll be babysitting before you know it."

"She's busy," Colton adds. "We have a lot to do."

"Please just assure me and the entirety of humanity that you're not singing on this EP of hers," Dante says.

"Shut up." Colton's back to his deep slouch.

"Has he ever sung in front of you?" Dante asks me.

"No." I glance at the smiles around the table. This seems to be a running gag.

"Of course. You're alive to deny it."

Logan adds, "The Defense Department wanted to use his voice as a weapon of mass destruction."

"It was too dangerous." Dante shakes his head. "And if he accompanied himself on piano..."

"Jesus." Logan puts down his fork as punctuation. "The pain of that first Mirman talent show."

"This?" I indicate the name on my sweatshirt. "It's a music school? East of Encino?"

"It's a very good school." Doreen sips her coffee. "Colton was the only one who got to go."

"We should get to work," Colton says, starting to get up.

The rest of the conversation happens fast, with overlapping sentences, interruptions.

"Dante's just bitter his IQ didn't make the cut," Liam says.

"Three points!" Dante defends his IQ, which I didn't think needed defending. "And this little dweeb..." He flings his hand in Colton's direction.

"All of my children are smart enough for any school."

"He blew the roof off the thing," Logan says to Dante. "Your three points were irrelevant."

"Wait," Ella says. "There's a minimum IQ? Like 135 or something?"

"That was poor baby Dante's score," Lyric says in the direction of her phone.

"You didn't even take the test," he tells her.

"Not enough is not enough." She flips Dante the bird. "And 143 is 143. Right, Colton?"

"We really need to get to the studio." Colton's standing now.

But Matt's on my lap, making *brrt* sounds as he races his little car while Dante defends the soft spot where three IQ points should be.

"If I'd been a completely anti-social nerd—"

"He was not a 'nerd,'" Doreen says firmly while I'm busy putting two and two together.

"—I would have scored better."

"Mom's right," Liam adds. "He was just awkward and a little weird."

"Hold on," I say, twisting to see Colton, who's backed away a few steps. "Is that how you were taking differential calculus in ninth grade?"

"It was the easy version."

"Differential calculus for dummies? I don't think that's a thing."

"You'd be surprised. Let's just go."

"Matt," Liam says, "Skye has to go with Uncle Colton. Come on back, kiddo."

"Say goodbye now." Doreen stands and puts out her arms. "I'll be gone before you finish."

Colton hugs his mother. She pats his back and hangs on long enough for me to wish everyone else a good day.

On the way back to the guest house, I whisper, stopping outside the studio door, "Why are you acting weird?"

"This... what we're doing here? This is not a real relationship where we sit by the fire and tell each other secrets, okay?" He shoulders the door open. "We are a PR stunt. It's not that deep."

Did he think this the whole time?

Of course he did, because he's normal. He respects boundaries. He gets it. I don't. I'm too much. I went where he said, explicitly, he didn't want me to go.

When I close the garage door behind me, he's already at the panel, switching everything on.

"I'm not about to get a test score tattooed on my face."

"Should I not wear this shirt? Is this like wearing a test score?"

He looks over his shoulder at me, then down at the school logo. "You look good in it." He turns back to the instruments but doesn't touch them. "It's—" He stops as if the next word lodges in the narrow of his throat. "All the money stacked on top of all the test scores and having this brain? I was born two steps from home plate, and now I'm back at second. Who gets all that for nothing... for *free*... and still ends up living in his brother's backyard? I bust my ass every day on being the biggest fuckup in the family. So now you know."

He flips a switch and the board lights up.

"I think they're just joking," I say.

"They are. It's my problem. That talent show they were talking about? Fifth grade. I did 'When the Saints Come Marching In' on piano. Mom and Dad told me I was fantastic, but my brothers were assholes about it. They were honest, but you see how they are. And you haven't even met Byron."

"They were just messing with you."

"Fuck them. I won't even sing Christmas carols in front of them."

"Well now that I know you're the sensitive type—"

"I can take a note. Just not from my family. Go ahead. Give me a note."

"Wait a minute," I say.

"Any criticism. Go."

"You got this big act you do like you don't care about anything and nothing matters. But stuff does matter to you and that's why you're in your brother's guest house."

"Not hurt." He holds out his arms and literally punches his chest to prove he's rock solid. "Not even bothered. Try again."

"You know you're weird, right?"

"That's all you got?"

I've never seen him so serious. I find myself thinking of something hurtful to say, just so I won't let him down. I shouldn't say it, but then he waves me off and turns his back on me as if I've come up short.

Last night, my sad, horny little ass really did ruin everything.

"Fine." I cross my arms, and he turns back around. "About last night? I have a note."

19

COLTON

I want to finish last night's unfinished business. I want to kiss her so badly I tell myself I'm in a straitjacket. If I unwrap my arms to touch her, I'm only going to look like a guy who belongs in a straitjacket.

"About last night," I repeat.

"The kissing."

"Go ahead."

"Your enthusiasm was hot, but sloppy."

"Oh, you like a guy without, like, spit?"

"Or girl. Woman. I like both." She lifts her chin, daring me to have an opinion about that, which I don't really. "And I like spit. Spit's fun, especially at the right time."

"Then I want a couple more adjectives on sloppy."

"You were loose. Into it."

"If I wasn't into it, I wouldn't have done it."

"Would you have done more?"

"I think I made that clear."

"Imagine what it would have been if it was like the kiss." She blinks and leans back at a barely perceptible angle. "It was like a driving arcade game; the kind where you sit in a black pleather seat facing a screen and turn this kinda loosey-goosey, barely-screwed-on steering wheel. There are two ways to play those. You can stay on the road and finish, or you can drive to win, and you can't without knocking stuff over and going off the road and drifting on the turns." She tips her head to one side, looking into the middle distance, then she tips to the other side. "And you know what? You didn't lose any points for that necessarily, and actually, I wouldn't change a thing. No notes. Ten out of ten."

She gives me two thumbs up and walks into the booth.

What the fuck just happened there? She fell back when I told her I was into it, and of course I was. But I'm not *supposed* to be. We agreed we shouldn't be into it, but I mean, come on. We were both there and it wasn't fake.

I'm not sure demanding the critique proved anything to her or even myself, but I smile at my board for a minute.

I like her.

Skye and I have only worked together that one time, but today it's like a meeting of the minds. She's all over it. The anxiety that kept her from getting a decent take is either gone or under control. Maybe she's working through it right now, but you'd never know it. We get "Like Love" in the can, and before I can even lay a bass track to make it easier to judge, she comes out to listen on the headphones, standing behind my chair.

"Totally worth it," she says on the second playback,

putting a hand on my shoulder. "To do it all those times."

When an artist is as excited as this, the best thing you can do is get the fuck out of the way, but I've been looking at her through glass for hours and the way she leans into the mic as if she's approaching a tiger, and the businesslike way she flips the pages, and everything has just been making me bonkers. In a good way.

So that hand on my shoulder? The little flash of skin on skin?

Yeah. It's not sisterly.

"Pizza," I say, jumping out of my chair. I take out my phone.

She takes off the headphones. "To eat?"

"No, for the album cover." My phone is in my hand. Why? What am I doing? "I'm joking. Yes, to eat. We haven't had shit since I opened up a can of olives for lunch."

"Okay." She drops into my chair, and I start to think I was imagining her leaning on my shoulder after hours on her feet was for anything but plain comfort. "What do you want on it?"

"Whatever. Olives."

"You really like olives." She takes out her phone. Wait, she's ordering? "What else?"

"I have it." I show her my phone and slap hers down.

"You got it last time." She reaches for me to get my phone out of the way.

"That's my job." I turn away to pull up the pizza place on Larchmont. "You want sausage or nah?"

She reaches over my shoulder for my phone. I turn. She ducks under my arm. Now her back is against my chest and my face is in her hair. She seems to realize we're too close.

"What's going on?" I ask even though I'm supposed to be the one saying what's what.

"I'm ordering pizza."

"Don't. Okay? Just quit it. You're sitting there like that. With that..." That body. Those legs. That face. I sit on the couch across the room and lean my elbows on my knees. My hands droop between my legs. LIVE FREE upside down.

I can't be free without being honest.

"We didn't finish talking about last night," I say.

"We didn't?"

"You did. If we're going to keep all the rules, I need another one." I run my fingers through my hair. "I can't... I don't know." I look at my phone. "Olives and sausage, yeah?"

"Colton?"

I can hear her, but I give the phone my full and complete attention, and we don't say another word to each other until I press ORDER.

"Thing is." I fling the phone onto the couch. "I need physical distance or I'm gonna want to fuck you."

She thinks about it by deepening the 11 between her brows, tilting her head back and forth.

"When we're out?" she says finally. "And you know, having this 'relationship' people are 'talking' about?"

Fuck, she's cute without the anxiety weighing her down. She's snarky and funny and at her most fuckable.

Which, obviously, is the problem. I like a girl who doesn't get up in her head if you tell her you want to fuck her. And she doesn't have her sexuality all locked up. She's *together*, and the more comfortable she gets with me, the more I'm finding out just how together she is.

"When we're alone, I need you over there," I say.

"This is totally doable if you're feeling a certain way."

"I'm not feeling anything, all right?" Too snippy. I gotta take it down a notch. "It's just... whatever. If there's glass in the middle, it's fine... but this kind of proximity all day? It's working for me, so it's not gonna work, if you know what I mean."

"Okay." She stands. "So, like this much? You think this is enough?"

No, it's not enough. She needs to be somewhere in Castaic. But if we're both in the damn garage, we don't have to have our backs to the wall.

"That's eight feet, give or take." I stand and take a step to her. "Here. Let's make it six." I point at a spot on the floor in front of me. "I'll show you."

"You'd think we'd know six feet from the pandemic."

We come together in the center of the room.

"This is a foot, right?" I put my toe against her toe. "So, six."

I step back toe to heel twice, two feet. She puts a heel forward to her toe, coming ten inches closer to me, but pausing before doing it again. We're too close, and she presses her lips tight together, because she knows it.

"Don't you have a ruler?" she asks, and yeah, she's got a point.

There's a tape measure right in the drawer. We can put those big dots on the floor and put our arms out to measure the distance between us whenever we're in the same room. It's a damn circus.

"A ruler." I repeat her last words as if her tongue is in my mouth. "For the rules."

"Ruler. Rules." She laughs nervously, looking away but not moving away.

"What if I said..."

Nothing. What if I said nothing? What if I kept my stupid mouth closed.

"What if you said... what?"

"What if I said fuck the rules?"

My body moves faster than my brain.

20

SKYE

I've kissed Colton Crowne before. Four times, exactly, and I was tipsy for two of them. Now I'm sober, and I know what I was missing. His kiss is lightning—pure electricity, reaching down from the sky like a hand made of light and grabbing me between the legs to pull me up to heaven. I'm levitating, then I'm really off my feet with my legs wrapped around him and my back to the wall. When he separates his lips from mine to speak, I still feel his connection.

"Just once," he says.

Tightening my legs, I pull him against me. "One time. Today."

"I don't want to hurt you."

"Are you flattering yourself or me?" My hands can't touch enough of him. His shirt is infuriating.

"I mean—"

"I know what you mean." I try not to sound impatient and fail. "I used to fuck Fátima. We're best friends now. Roommates. I can handle it if you can."

His answer is a kiss and a jolt against me. Pinning me to the wall with his hips, he reaches under my shirt and pushes his hands under my bra.

"Jesus, Skye." He cups and squeezes my breasts, finding my hard nipples.

I push his head down to them, and he takes the hint, mouthing the pebbled tip before sucking so hard I groan and arch, forcing him to step back. I almost drop off the wall, but he catches me and pulls me back against him. I put my arms around his shoulders. He puts his hands under my ass and carried me out the garage, into the kitchen.

"How long before the pizza comes?" I ask.

"They can leave it out front." He kicks open a door and sets me on my feet.

We're so busy kissing and stripping, I have no idea if I'm in the bedroom or laundry room or on the fucking moon. Peeling off his shirt, I can finally feel his tight muscles and scratch at the hair on his chest. I barely feel it when he unhooks my bra because I'm tugging his belt open, reaching for the bolt-button of his Levis while he bends to suck a nipple again.

Geometry isn't working for us and he knows it, so he throws me back. I land on a mattress. Bedroom. Got it. I'd look around, but I can't take my eyes off Colton, standing over me as he opens his button and zipper in what seems like one move.

"Please say you have condoms because—"

"I have, I have," he interrupts, stepping out of his jeans and exposing the shape of a baseball bat under his shorts. Bending down, he peels off my jeans and underwear all at once, throwing them aside like a useless shell and crawling over me for a kiss.

"You still have your underwear on," I say.

"You in some kind of rush?" He kisses down my neck and chest.

"The pizza's coming."

"I'll hurry." His lips run inside my thighs. "I can make you come four times before the cheese gets cold."

"Four?" When his mouth makes contact with my pussy, I stretch my arms over my head. "Oh, God."

"Put him on speed dial."

With a suck and a flick of his tongue, an electrical storm lands across my whole body and passes with a final jolt. Colton gets up on his knees and wipes his mouth with the back of his wrist.

"That was…" Words fail me. I reach for his waistband.

"One." Arching his body over mine, he opens a night table drawer and roots around. "That was one."

Pulling his briefs down as far as I can reach, I scoot down to get them off. He's still digging around in the drawer and sits at the head of the bed to get a good look at what he's doing.

"If you don't have protection, I swear to God, Colton."

"Got it."

I snap the condom out of his hands and check the expiration. "It's fine." Putting it to the side, I keep my eyes on his while I strip his briefs. "Lucky for you or I would have eaten all the pizza while you went to get a new box. Now I can eat something else."

"Come here." Before I can get my mouth on his dick, he pulls me in to straddle him. "I want to feel how wet you are first." He pushes my hips down over his erection, lining it up in the space at my very center, and pulls toward him, sliding us together laterally so there's direct contact on my clit.

"That's good," I groan.

"You're so fucking wet." He increases the pace, then shifts his hands to my chest. "Make yourself come on my cock."

I put my hands on the headboard behind him, sliding back and forth. It's not long before I'm close, but it's not quite enough.

"I don't know if I can because I just did."

"Come on, Skye." He pushes up hard against me and the sensation breaks through. "Do what feels good. Use me."

"Okay. Yes." I go faster and harder, with a ferocity I've never felt before, rubbing my clit on his shaft with shorter and shorter strokes until I throw my head back and come with a cry.

"Very nice." He pulls me down for a kiss, then rolls me onto my back, kneeling between my spread legs. "That's two."

He rips the side off the packet with his teeth.

I grab it. "You're not going to do all the work here."

I slide the condom over him while he lifts my leg and kisses the inside of my ankle. When it's on, he lays that leg over his shoulder.

"You ready?"

"Been ready."

He lines himself up and enters me. I stiffen so he can thrust harder. The position allows him to go down to the root and push up against pain.

"That's okay?" he asks.

"Deeper."

He shifts and hits deeper than I thought possible. He closes his eyes and stretches his neck, sucking in a breath.

"You okay?" I ask.

"Too good." He looks as if he might let go, which is fine. A guy sometimes can't help it, but I stay still in case he can manage to keep it together. Then he looks at me and smiles. "Thank fuck for the condom."

"They're multipurpose."

I let my leg fall off his shoulder so he can be fully on top as he slowly fucks me.

"I want to fuck you in every position, Skye. I want to see you on top. I want your knees over your ears." He rolls us over until he's sitting with his back to the wall and I'm facing him. "I want to fuck your sweet cunt from behind, against the wall, bent over the couch. I want to taste myself on your tongue." He reaches between us and presses my center toward him so that my clit rubs against his shaft as he enters me over and over. "I want make you come on my cock until you cry."

"Colton." By Colton, I mean we can't do all that today. The pizza will get cold, and the sun will set and rise and set again. But that's the only word I have. The slide of his shaft on my clit is reaching the breaking point. "Colton."

He speeds up and I follow, but he's holding on by a thread, just like me. "Come, Skye. Please."

I don't need to be told twice. He fucks me while I stiffen, frozen in place as I'm engulfed by the most powerful orgasm yet.

"Yes," he whispers, eyes on me. "Skye."

I push his hand away and shift myself to give him friction so he can come while inside me. He takes me by the hair, gripping tight, as if holding our faces together for dear life. His lips part and his mouth falls open, and after an overture of *ahhs*, he lets out a long groan. This—what he's feeling—is mine.

Finally, he pulls me close and strokes the hair he just pulled. "You're fucking beautiful."

In a post-coital haze, people say all kinds of goopy things. Sometimes they say it because they think as a woman, I'm supposed to feel bad, or dirty, or guilty, and the goopy words are like a salve I don't need. Sometimes they do it for their own wounds. Mostly, of course, intentionally or otherwise, it's bullshit.

Colton believes it. He believes I'm not just beautiful, which may be true in a strictly physical sense, but *fucking* beautiful, which is a completely different thing without boundaries, disclaimers, or a door the fuck out.

Knowing all this, my immediate reaction is goopier than it should be. It's an inner expansion of feeling that's kind of a cross between the warmth of seeing a kitten yawn, the awe of the vastness of the universe, and the same awe turned to something as small and intimate as the connection with another human being. Not just another human being, but him. I want to take care of him. Smooth down the lick of hair that's sticking up. Care for his body. Take responsibility for his happiness. Invest in his life.

It's a forbidden feeling and I don't like it. I'm not supposed to have it. It ruins the afterglow of the best sex I've ever had.

"I have to get off you," I say.

"Cool, yeah."

We manage the condom, and I stand naked in the middle of his bedroom while he sits on the edge of the bed.

Talk about fucking beautiful.

"Thank you, Colton." Turning away, I get dressed before I can give in to the desire to crawl back into bed with him.

"That was fun. A good valve. Right? Now it won't be so tense, you know?"

He doesn't reply. When I'm buttoning my jeans, I finally turn back to him. He's got his back to the headboard and one leg straight on the sheets while the other foot is crooked on the floor. Half a room away, the feeling doesn't seem any less impossible. It's bigger. It pulls me tighter. I should be terrified of what's happening to me, but this is the exact opposite of fear.

"I still owe you one," he says, holding up a finger tattooed with an E.

"One what?"

"I promised you four." He holds up four lazy, languid fingers.

I don't need him to keep his promise. I don't need a fourth orgasm. I need everything that leads up to it.

We can't do this again. We've already smashed the no-fucking rule into a million pieces. I can't claim that matters at all anymore, and I assured him I'm perfectly capable of having a good time with a friend without getting attached.

But his hair is still a little mussed, and the soreness between my legs doesn't hurt as much as it makes me think of how close I feel to him.

He doesn't feel anything. I'm breaking this rule on my own. Shit. I have to get out of here.

"I'll check on that pizza."

21

COLTON

I can't do this.

I can't live on some fucking razor's edge, waiting to fall on either side. I can't walk this line between being with her and being without her based on no more than the whims of Eugene fucking Testarossa. I can't let myself want her this badly if I fall on one side and let myself say goodbye if I fall over the other.

Not that it's my choice to make. I'll never mean anything to her. Clearly she's capable of keeping her emotions where they're supposed to be. She might have an anxiety attack when she has to sing in front of strangers, but when it comes to people she's comfortable around—like me, I guess—she's cool as shit.

What am I supposed to do with my own mess? I had all my emotions fenced in. Not locked tight or anything—because that's the Crowne way, and I'm not doing shit the Crowne way—but just milling around the pen, bumping against the railing once in a while.

It got too easy. The shepherd was busy while a fox reached inside the gate and unlocked it. The sheep are getting out, and yeah, I'm lying in my bed, watching her go get the pizza and thinking this metaphor's getting stretched a little thin. But it's not a stampede. It's just a wooly mess and I don't know where to start because the fox never wanted the sheep at all.

"Fuck this." I jump out of bed, put on a pair of pants, and grab my phone.

When I peek out into the living room, the kitchen door's just been shut. I need to go outside, but she's there and she'll be back in thirty seconds. Dialing Liam, I go out the back door to a narrow space between the back of the house and the back gate. Logan's groundspeople roll the garbage cans through here on Thursdays.

"Great timing," Liam says. "I just hung up with the stupidest record exec in LA."

Liam isn't the hardest logic puzzle I've ever solved. I don't need a cross-referenced index to know who he's talking about.

"He said no about Shooting Star?"

"It's better for him to leave the slot empty than to risk it."

"She's fine. I'm fucking telling you!" I lower my voice. "We just recorded two songs that... I swear to God..." I hear Skye come in and duck under the window like a burglar outside my own house.

"That leads me to my next point. They want your plug-in."

"What? Why?"

"It's a good sound, Colton. You can't mistake it for anything else. They want it to be proprietary for one of their indie sublabels. My guess? They need an original sound for a band that sounds ten percent too generic."

From the other side of frosted glass, the bathroom light goes on, illuminating the garbage cans. Skye came back with the pizza and didn't see me. I won't be able to hide out for long.

"I can't think about that right now," I whisper.

"It's a chunk of money, but I think they'll license, which in the long run—"

"Liam, please stop. Fuck." I'm hunched against the wall, my butt six inches from the concrete. The garbage cans are taller than I am right now.

"What am I telling him?"

"Tell him to ask me during Skye's set at Shooting Star."

Behind the little window above my head, the shower goes on.

"I told you already. It's a no."

"Then he can wait until I'm ready."

"He needs it now."

I rub my eyes, which clears nothing. It's still dark. I still don't know what to do about Skye, which makes me want to obstruct everything else in my life until I've figured out how to have her.

"He can't have it. It's for shit I produce. If he wants it for a sublabel, he knows what he's got to do."

"Sharky. I like it. I'm not sure he'll go for it, but—"

"Are you telling her?"

"Who? Skye?"

I lean the back of my head against the wall. He really expects me to answer that.

Fine. I'll answer. "Yes, Skye. We have one song left to do, and if she hears about the stupidest executive in LA rejecting her, she's skipping the performative breakup. She's getting in her car and going home. So, are you telling her?"

Silence on the other end of the line. For almost a full minute, Liam just breathes.

"This isn't about giving you another day to finish the EP," he says finally. "Is it?"

"No. It's not."

"Look, even if I got him to change his mind, which I doubt I can do, I can't make her stay the next time there's a setback."

"I know."

He lets the silence hang for less than a minute before he shatters my illusion that I have this all buttoned up. "Does she know?"

His question is based on growing up with me, slapping me in the back of the head, teaching me how to dress with my waistband at my waist, how to talk to people without being too intense, how to stop being a nerd and just be a dude. It's based on who I became after I threw away all his lessons. I'm not the hardest logic puzzle he's ever solved.

"No. We're fake. That's the rule."

"And you're afraid to break the rules? Who the fuck are you?"

I know a rhetorical question when I hear one, but I can't even answer it rhetorically. I am Colton Crowne. The lowest of a family high. The squanderer. The disappointment. The one they sigh over and shake their heads with pity. Their lamentations say more about them than about me. There are sons who cause far more suffering, but a family gets the black sheep they get, and they all tsk the same.

No. They don't. I should know by now... all those voices belong to me.

"When I met Malin," Liam says, "she was pretty shy. I know that's hard to believe, but the ballsy, no-bullshit Malin you remember... she wasn't that way at first. If I hadn't told her how I felt, we wouldn't have Matt."

The shower stops, which is when I realize how loud it was.

"You wouldn't know the difference either," I whisper. "She'd just be a girl in your past you got over."

He scoffs but doesn't argue. He does much worse.

"Tell her, Colton. Just tell her you love her."

I shoot to standing. This is not what I want to be talking about right now. These are not the words I want to be using.

"I'll tell her," I say. "About Gene. I'll do it."

"It's my job."

I cut the call before he can talk some professionalism into me.

22

SKYE

The pizza was outside in the dark, on the little table just outside the gate—and not as cold as I'd feared.

Colton, however, was gone when I brought it in. So I got in the shower, and by the time I get to the kitchen, he's as icy as the pizza. Though it's a little off-putting at first, I get why standing on the other side of the kitchen island makes sense. Minimizing eye contact is the wise move. Cool courtesy— giving me the first slice, making sure I have a plate, getting me the ice water I ask for—is the way to go.

The urge to ask him if he's all right creeps up on me, but I resist it. He's sending me the loudest signals I've ever gotten, and I'm not pretending I can't hear them just so I can be a clingy, needy girl with uncontrolled emotions.

Business. We need to talk business.

"You said I needed to do a cover," I say. "I want to do 'Someone to Watch Over Me' and I don't want a whole ensemble. Just me on piano."

He looks at the clock. It's late. Nighttime even. Anyone who isn't already out is settled in for the night. "Tonight?"

"Tomorrow." I don't elaborate immediately, but though the silence that follows is short, it's unbearably hollow. "I'll call Fátima to cover the shift for me. She owes me."

"Let's do it." He tears the crust in two and rips off the end of one with his back teeth.

More silence. When he chews, I can see the muscles of his jaw work. Something's on his mind. Is he feeling the same things I am? It hadn't occurred to me... but is it possible at all?

I'm staring. I have to stop that.

"So," he says. "You and Fátima."

"Mm-hm." I take another slice, leaving the strip of crust from my first. So much for business.

"You guys were a thing."

"A 'thing'? No." I bite into the pause and let myself chew while I decide whether or not to say more. "More of a diversion."

Colton's not entitled to a play by play, but when people you fuck ask for your life story, they're trying to gauge relationship potential based on past history. Third-date-worthy men often use the answer to either plan the wedding or rule out a tenth date, though their dicks will eagerly show up for four through nine. Right about date seven is when I break it off. Saves everyone a lot of stress.

Colton and I won't have a second date since our first was fake, and this isn't a date. But is he asking to gauge our future?

"It was great," I say. "She's great. Like you."

"Like me?"

"Like you and me."

"A diversion?"

No. Not like that. He's not a diversion the way Fátima was. But what am I supposed to tell him? What if he's just making conversation and I'm reading into it? Not knowing is unbearable, but the risk of heartbreak—and yes, there will be some kind of break if I've developed feelings he hasn't—is even more unbearable.

"Just great." I pass the ball to him, hoping he commits to something, anything more than accepting being a diversion. All he does is avert his gaze.

"You need more water?" he asks.

"Sure."

He fills my glass, and while his back is to me, the pressure of the untold story weighs on me.

"She put the room up on Craigslist and I answered," I say. "We hit it off. I moved in. Met her family. We fucked for a month or so, but we knew it wasn't a long-term thing. Then there was an opening at her store. So we stopped."

"You just stopped?"

"She's the manager. It would have been unethical to keep on."

"Wow." He shakes his head and soaks up rust-colored grease with the last nugget of crust. "That's something." He pops the bread in his mouth. "That you could just... stop and still live with her. Didn't miss a beat."

"First few weeks, we missed a few beats." I shrug, biting the last bit of sauce off the crust. "Sometimes I'd catch myself touching her, just, like, when we're talking, or I'd turn around and she's looking at me, you know, that way." I reach for a third slice. Cold is better than hungry. "But we got over it."

"Are you not eating any of that crust?"

"Yeah, no." I toss the twisted columns of bread onto his plate.

"You're missing out." He reaches up into a cabinet for a bottle of olive oil. Will I read the tattoo inside his arm as if it's new every time I see it?

Everything. Now.

"You're friends with all your exes?" He pours a puddle of olive oil into his plate and spins the cap back on.

"Yeah. You're not?"

"Sometimes it's not a choice. Sometimes they just don't want anything to do with you."

If I ask him if he's talking about Tamika, I'm not just asking about an anonymous woman he's mentioned before. I'm gossiping about a household name.

My curiosity's a pit bull though. Courtesy needs a minute to wrestle it down and duct tape its mouth shut. There's no room in my head to construct a reasonable change of subject. In a thoughtless trance, I watch him soak his crusts in olive oil. The way his hand swipes at it, fingers pressed against the bread.

"What?" he asks after I've spent too much time deciding what not to say.

"What?"

"You're spacing out. You getting tired? You can stay here if you want."

"No. I was just... I'm not asking because it's not my business... but who would want nothing to do with you? I can't imagine that kind of dynamic with you."

"That's sweet."

"I'm not trying to be sweet."

He huffs a little laugh then rips off a piece of crust. "Tamika thought we could stay together while she scrubbed me from her music. Screw me with one hand and keep fucking me with the other."

"Why did she want you off the music?"

"Control freak, I guess. Or she was listening to Gavin McCormick, who wanted his fingers in it and her. Or maybe I suck at this."

"You don't."

He shrugs. "Sure. But I want you to know, you're good. Okay? No matter what happens or whatever industry douchebag says no to you."

"Sure." I try to sound like him when he shrugs, but I don't have any "live free everything now I don't give a shit" in my core.

"You are. You have to believe it. You don't need me or anyone. And you can't give up when I tell you—"

"I am going to break up with you." I can't stop saying it once I start. He freezes mid-chew, and who can blame him? "I... it's not that there's even a thing to break... but I don't want you to worry. I'm going to... you know... get everything mixed up."

"Skye. If there's anything I'm worried about, it's getting you set up, getting my brother to pay me, moving on to Halley, and getting her done before I throw another party and get kicked out... I mean, look at me." He spreads his arms at the borrowed house. "Am I the guy looking for a thing?"

"No. Okay." I exhale and slide another slice out of the box. "It's not that I thought you were, because we already have an agreement. And yeah, we broke a rule, but just once."

"So far." He drinks his water, looking at me over the edge of the glass. "I still owe you one."

Coagulating cheese has never stopped me before. I take

two massive bites, make a few perfunctory chews, and wash it down with half the ice water.

"Just once." I put down the glass, suddenly unafraid of ruining everything. The anxiety has a life and logic of its own. Without it, I'm either braver or stupider. "I think within, like, a twenty-four-hour period, it counts as one session."

He looks at the clock, nods as if he's considering it, then gulps the last of his water. "Makes sense."

Scooping up his plate and glass, he turns to the counter. The leftover ice clinks against the bottom of the sink. I close the pizza box, grab my plate and glass, and stand next to him. He moves away, and I figure he wants to finish cleaning up before he gives me what he insists he owes me, so I rinse my plate and put it to the side.

When I look behind me, he's gone. Bathroom maybe. I step back to find the dishwasher, which is exactly where it's supposed to be, and empty.

I put the dishes inside and close the dishwasher, and I'm about to step away when I feel him behind me. I gasp with surprise and try to turn, but he pins me against the counter, puts his phone on the granite next to me, and reaches around me to shove down the sweatpants without so much as a how-do-you-do.

"You really want that fourth," I say.

Still without a word, he puts his hand between my shoulder blades and pushes me forward, bending me over the sink. It happens so fast I shouldn't have enough time to get aroused, but by the time he kicks my feet apart, the rest of my body has caught up. I look over my shoulder, discovering why he hasn't said anything. He's got condom packet in his teeth.

"I keep my promises," he says around it while undoing his jeans.

"I can see that."

Keeping his teeth clamped, he rips open the foil and spits the strip so he can dig out the rubber.

"If I knew this was a twenty-four-hour deal"—he looks down and I assume he's putting it on—"I wouldn't have promised to make you come four times."

"You don't have to—" I lose the rest of the sentence in a gasp when he enters me. My head almost hits the faucet.

"I would have said ten." He slaps the faucet to the side.

I leverage myself against the far side of the sink, knocking down the sponge. The detergent bottle follows.

"No, I mean, God, Jesus. Let's say it's twenty-four total..." Our bodies snap together like puzzle pieces. He spreads my ass and thighs apart and shoves deeper. "Not including... yes." His strokes get short and fast. "Like that. Ah."

"Not including what?"

"Sleeping. Twenty-four total. Hours. That feels..." I have no words for the deep, churning pressure inside me. His dick fills me and his hand wraps around me for the nub of my greatest need.

"No matter what happens," he murmurs in my ear, "I want you to say you won't give up."

"Give up what?"

The knot of pleasure under his finger expands into a ball of heat.

"Your work."

"I won't."

"Say you won't leave."

"I won't leave." Where am I going? Why? I don't have the bandwidth for the question or the answer.

"Say you'll never stop trying." He buries himself deep and makes short, intense thrusts angled toward the bundle of nerves inside me. "No matter how unfair it is. No matter how hard. You'll stay here and keep trying."

With the next wave of pleasure, I know what he's talking about.

"I can't..." My denial lapses into a moan. "I'm going to..."

"Stay."

"I don't know."

"Promise." His free hand has me by the jaw and the back of the neck, pressing my cheek to his lips.

"Why..."

"Say it now."

"It now."

"Fuck, Skye. Please." He takes a handful of hair and pulls back my head. "My God, please."

If he's pleading for me to come, he gets his wish. Every muscle in my body clenches. He slams into me then stays there with a groan, shoves deeper, releasing my hair as he lets himself go. He kisses my neck, pulling me to standing but keeping me pressed against him.

"Promise." His whisper has both the power of a command and the cloy of a plea. His phone buzzes, shaking hard enough to move a quarter inch against the counter. He puts his hand over it. "Or I'll fuck you until you do."

He doesn't get it. I don't know how else to explain that I can't live without knowing who I am. I try to turn, but he has me pinned. The phone buzzes again.

He turns it around, and in that split second, I see the text preview.

—Did you tell her?—

He shuts off the phone, but it's too late. I push him away

and turn around. His arms are up and his dick is out with the stupid, saggy condom hanging from the end of it.

"Tell me what?" I ask.

"Promise me first."

"Fuck off."

"Just give me a minute." He steps back against the kitchen island, looks at his dick, starts to put the phone down but stops himself as if he doesn't know whether or not to get the condom off and button up or deal with the text.

"No." I grab the phone out of his hand. Locked. I hold it up to his face to unlock it.

He tries to get the phone back, but he's too slow. I face the sink to look at the phone, and I see it all.

"Skye."

The texts are from Liam. The first one from today says, "That was a mistake. I should do it." The second asks if he told her yet. Before that is a cute picture of Matt. There's nothing else.

"I'm her," I say.

Behind me, the trash can squeaks open and slaps closed. I look back to find him buttoning his jeans.

"Let's sit down." He makes it halfway to the living room.

Fuck this. I'm not sitting down. I'm not going to a bunch of cushions where he can get me on my back.

"I don't need to sit."

"Well, I do." He throws himself onto the couch and pats the seat next to him, drapes his arms over the back and leans his feet far apart against the table's edge.

Fine. I go into the living room and toss the phone between his legs before sitting in a chair across from him.

"All right," he says faux-casually. "So, it's really not that big a deal but—"

"No showcase," I say before he can convince me that something is nothing. "I'm out."

"You're not *out* but—"

"Am I on the schedule or not?"

He tightens his mouth and rocks his head back and forth, which I can tell is him looking for another way of saying "out."

"I'm not."

"Not this time, but—"

"Why?" I demand an answer assuming he knows.

His hands flip palm-upward, then down before he takes his arms off the back of the couch and his feet off the table. I guess this is where he decides to become a serious person. That hurts me and I don't know why.

"He saw you freeze at Fountain." He plants his elbows on his knees. "So here's the plan."

"The plan?" I lean forward so hard my butt comes off the chair. "There is no plan, Colton."

"We finish the EP."

"That's not a plan."

"Listen."

"No!" I pound the table.

He blinks in shock. Good. He needs to wake the fuck up.

"There's no plan without an achievable goal. It's all just an endless circle jerk." I stand. "I had a plan. It failed. Again."

He stands. "You cannot give up."

"I'm not. Because I still have to live this life. The one I have, not the one I can't get. I still have to get up in the morning and do things and know what my future is. I will not give up, and that's why I'm going back to school."

"You're not leaving, Skye."

"Oh, I am. I'm going to pack up, get in the car, and drive back in time for registration."

"You shouldn't. Okay? That's all I'm saying. It's a mistake."

"It's my mistake to make."

"You're going to come back, you know. We worked too hard."

"We—"

"You!" He rushes to fill a breach that isn't open.

I'm not looking for credit or possession. I don't give a shit about the pronoun. I do give a lot of shits about the person behind the other half of "we," and the only reason I can admit that is because I'm leaving.

"No, Colton. You were right the first time. We. You and me. These three songs, they're as much yours as mine."

He snaps up the napkins and wax paper, throwing them in the trash. "Whatever."

"You promised Liam four. You were right. We need to finish."

"What's the point?"

"There is no point." I put my hand on his forearm, feeling the taut skin over hard muscle. He's warm and real, right here in front of me. Maybe I'll come back. Maybe I'll continue to make music in Michigan and find a reason to feel this arm again. "Let's just do what we said we would."

"Now then." He puts his hand over mine before I can take it away. "Not tomorrow. Now."

"Don't you sleep?"

"Not when I'm in the middle of a project."

"I can't." I pull my hand from under his. I'm pretty sure I'm too close to tears to try to sing a song Ella Fitzgerald already perfected. "I don't have anything inside me. I'm tired.

I'm sad. I'm just empty. Can it wait until tomorrow? I'm going to have to leave in a few days, so it's not like—"

"Fine," he snaps. "It's cool. You tell me when."

"I will." I sling my bag over my shoulder. The pizza's turning into a sticky mass in my stomach. I want to throw up more than I've ever wanted to do anything in my life. But I won't be able to do that any more than I've been able to do any of the things I've wanted to.

"Do you need a lift?"

"I'll get an Uber." I hold up my phone to illustrate how easy and accessible this method of getting away from him is.

"Cool." He flings the last two slices of pizza in the fridge without even wrapping them.

"We're still friends, right?"

"Sure. I can do it your way."

He closes the empty pizza box and takes it out the back door. I call the cab while he's folding the box and stuffing it in the bin. When he gets back, my app says the cab is two minutes away.

"You know what?" he asks without a question in his voice. "No. Not your way. Three is fine. We don't need the cover song. You're leaving. You don't have to come back. And friends? Friends isn't some agreement. It's earned. So we'll see."

"You're mad."

"Yeah. I'm mad."

"Don't be."

"I'm supposed to be the one quitting. I'm the one who runs from city to city before I can find a reason to stay. I'm the one who couldn't be bothered with college. I'm the one who says my way or the highway hoping to fuck it's highway. That's me."

My phone beeps. I don't have to look at it. The Uber's here.

"Just go," he says. "Do what you have to do."

I can't leave him here seething, unable to look at me. "Will I see you before I leave?"

"I don't know. That's all I got. I don't know." He leverages his arm against the counter, exposing the inside.

Everything. Now.

My phone beeps again.

"I have—"

"Yeah."

"I want to—"

Before I can finish, he gathers me in his arms. I want to see him again, and his embrace—the way he buries his face in my hair and takes a long breath, the way he pulls me into him, wrapping the whole length of his arms around me—it tells me he knows what I want. He's just not sure he can give it to me.

23

COLTON

Once she's gone, I don't get any less pissed off.

This is not going to stand. Not on my watch. It's a fucking shame that Gene Testarossa—who was an asshole while he was at WME and is now an even bigger asshole at Glendora—is the one who gets to determine whether or not Skye Phillips gets to succeed. But that's what it is, and if it wasn't him, it would be another asshole with an iced-out Rolex.

Skye's not giving up because of him. She's not leaving so she can become Grosse Pointe's one and only singing doctor. Not on my watch. No. She needs to be the world's voice.

She may accept her defeat, but I reject it.

With Tamika, it didn't matter what I wanted. She wanted another producer, so that was that. I could stew in my own shit or move on. I did one, then the other.

This is different. This isn't me. This is worse, because I want her more.

With my headphones on and my attention totally in the

game, I can hear explicitly what was implied with Skye in the room. The layering. The tonal inaccuracies that make her sound so genuine. She comes in early a lot. I can fix that, but when I do, it's flat. Her instincts are flawless. So are Liam's. Gotta give him credit where it's due. He found something real.

The first pass at the easiest song is done by midnight. I nap on the orange couch and dream of her voice coming from the next room. When I follow it, I hear it from behind the walls. Punching a hole in the sheetrock doesn't release her, and I wake up with my fist clenched so tightly it aches.

Without windows, the hands moving around my watch face mean nothing. I drink water from the little fridge, go into the kitchen for the leftover pizza, my last can of olives, and expired cups of ramen noodles. When that runs out, I order in, opening the door to find blasting sunlight when I expected twilight.

I haven't felt this good since Memphis, when I had a hard drive full of some of the best shit I'd ever heard. My girlfriend's shit. The flow was so intense that I forgot she was my girlfriend. When she put her hand on my shoulder, I practically jumped into the ceiling like a cartoon.

How do I sound? This was before she was a superstar. She wanted notes on her performance, not the microphone's.

Good. I was too busy to get into it.

Can I listen?

I wouldn't let Tamika hear what I was doing to her song, to her voice, and remembering it brings up other shit I haven't thought about since I drove out of Texas.

Come on, let me hear it. She sat on my lap and tried to get my headphones off.

I was a billionaire's kid who didn't care about shit, and

she was a middle-class daughter of two teachers who'd taught her that she had to be twice as good to get half of what she was owed.

Seriously. Tam.

She got off me and walked out. I continued working as if nothing had happened. Months later, when the shit hit the fan, she said I didn't respect her. I thought she'd lost her fucking mind, because I respected her a fucking lot.

Sure, the problem had been our personal relationship, but on the professional side, I wasn't exactly laid-back about how I wanted her to sound and who I was working for.

Myself. I wanted to impress whoever heard the work. I wanted my voice to be heard.

The focus now is different. I'm not programming a new plug-in so the song will sound like nothing anyone's ever heard before. I'm not trying to distinguish nerd loser Colton Crowne from party animal Colton Crowne from the casually proficient professional I want to be. I'm distinguishing Skye Phillips from every artist she's not. It's not about me. It's one hundred percent about her. When I adjust the song through my plug-in, I'm dialing into her rough edges. She feels shitty. I can hear it. I turn it up.

My phone's silenced and face down, but it's dark enough to catch the outlined flash of a notification. It's Liam calling at... holy shit, five thirty in the morning.

"Why would you get up so early?" I ask.

"I want the rest of those songs, like now. Today. An hour ago."

"We don't have the cover yet."

"Why not?"

"I just got more done with her in two sessions than every other studio in Los Angeles. Lay off."

"The other two by lunch."

"I'll do what I can."

"And I need you to be seen breaking up."

"No, no." I'm out of my chair, pacing, head out of the zone I've been in for hours. "No fucking way." Hungry, I go into the kitchen.

"Why not?"

The cupboard is bare. Way in the back, I find an emergency jar of kalamata with pits.

"Why? How about that? Why?" After I smack the bottom, the top twists open with a *thwup*.

"Because I have to start over with every other record company and not every exec's going to care if she's dating you. Some won't like it and I... *she* doesn't need any encumbrances."

My jaw works around the pit, chewing off the meat until it's as bare as a knuckle.

"This was your idea." I spit the pit into my fist and toss it in the sink. "Now I'm an encumbrance?"

"Yes, Colton. It was a good idea, but now it's not."

Two olives takes some concentration. Pits suck, but I'm so mad at Liam that the chewing is cathartic.

"No fucking way." I can barely understand myself with two rocks in my mouth. I spit them out. "No breakup."

"Colton. If you want to date her, just date her, but keep it under wraps." There's a beep from his side and the churn of a motor. He's on the treadmill at the crack of dawn. Fuck him for that too. I fill a Solo cup with water.

"I don't want—" I stop myself. I don't want what? To date her? We're past that, and also not even close to it. "If you give up on the showcase in Mojave, she's going to leave."

The point makes itself. Skye leaving is a bad thing. It's a

tsunami. An earthquake. A financial crisis. It's a disaster no one wants.

"I have clients from all over."

"No!" Is he fucking blind? How could he not see how bad it would be for her to leave? Or does he want the tsunami?

"What's with you, Colton?"

"You want to get rid of her, is that it? You don't want to let her go, because she might make a dollar before she's done, but right now she's a burden. She's a failure to you. A dud."

"That's not how this works…" He's huffing now. He must have that thing set at a run already.

"Skye's not a failure." If I could get through this fucking phone and throttle the motherfucker, I would. "She's not…"

I bite back putting the word loser in the same sentence as her name. I'm shaking like a fucking dryer on spin. With the rest of the sentence dead on my lips, I hang up.

Fuck. Fuck this shit. We're not having the amicable breakup. We're not letting that asshole Gene make her decisions and we're not letting her drive off into the sunrise. She's not leaving as long as I have a card to play, and I have a really fucking good card.

I drain the Solo cup in four gulps.

Liam texts. I'll apologize to him later.

Smashing the cup into the garbage, I make a plan. First, I gotta clean up. Shower and shave. Then—

Another text from Liam.

—**You love her. I know it. You know it**—

—**We can work with that**—

Another one comes as I'm typing out a firm fucking denial.

—**Does she know?**—

"Shut the fuck up. There's nothing to know."

Enough. I have a few hours to fix this before my brother tells her it's okay to leave.

———————

Doing a deep search while the sound renders, I find out Gene Testarossa is lactose intolerant. He's from Florida. His first job was as an operator at an amusement park. He doesn't think talent waits in the wings or needs to be developed. It's either there or it's not. You're a star or you're no one.

He tried to rep Tamika when he was at the WME Agency but couldn't get his boss's support. That's why he left for Glendora with a contract that says he signs who he wants, when he wants, to the terms he wants.

I find a five-year-old interview he did with *Variety*. He bragged that he got into the office at seven in the morning, no matter how hard he partied the night before.

I believe the spirit of the claim, but not the specifics, so I get to the Glendora building with two coffees in a cardboard tray at seven thirty. At the back service entrance, I act as though I belong there and get on the elevator to the fifth floor. The early morning receptionist is just getting in. I go right past her.

"Excuse me, sir?"

I wave and keep walking, sticking to the outer ring of offices—where the windows are. His voice chops through the hall.

"—for *Brooklyn*? I said, 'Man, you're killing me here.'"

I find him right next to a corner space with his sock feet on his desk. He barely bats an eye when I show up in the open door.

"Yeah, still bought it," he says into the phone.

By the time he waves me in, I'm already halfway to sitting across his desk.

The receptionist appears in his doorway. "He's not on your chart."

Gene puts his hand over the phone and whispers to her, "It's fine. Close the door." Then he takes his hand off the phone so he can laugh into it. "You don't wanna know."

I put the coffee holder on his desk. He bends down to look at the stickers and chooses the one with oat milk.

"Agree hundo percent. Hey listen, I got someone in my office... yeah... okay... catch you later... okay." He takes the phone away from his ear. "Jesus Christ, I don't know what they got in the water on the sunrise side."

"It's ten thirty in New York." I take the remaining cup with the black drip. "They're on their third gallon of coffee."

"Ain't that right. So. To what do I owe, et cetera?"

This part of it—the business, the negotiations, seeing around a contract's blind corners—isn't what I'm good at. That's how I ended up in a situation with Tamika.

"Liam says you want the plug-in."

"Yep, yep, we're ready to make an offer, provided you—"

"No."

"You haven't heard the number."

"There is no number."

"You want to license it? Of course you do. Word of advice? Your job isn't to make your agent's life easy, okay? Even your brother. If he's taking his ten percent, he should be the one sitting in that chair breaking my balls."

"Sure." I take a thumb drive from my pocket and flick it to him. He catches it. "You listen to that and tell me what you think."

"Am I getting a hint of what's on it?"

"Skye Phillips. Three songs."

"That's not an EP." He flicks it back.

I don't react in time and end up swatting it onto the floor.

"Three is enough." I lean over the side of the chair to pick it up. "Either you're a star...or you're no one." I click the drive onto the surface of his desk.

"Either you can do the job or you can't, bro."

"She can. We're fixing it."

"Word of advice?" He folds his hands in front of him, getting serious.

"Another one?"

"You're producing her. Maybe you're banging her. Neither of those things makes you her therapist."

An electric mass of rage shakes inside my rib cage. The hair on my arms stands up. I don't know if I'm reacting to the idea that I'm "banging" her or that I'm not responsible for her, but it doesn't matter. It takes every bit of self-control I have—and then some—to keep my shit together. This is why I get screwed. Gene's right. Liam should be on this side of the table. I'm chill, but my brother's calm. There's a difference. He'd never try to appeal to Gene Testarossa's sympathies, as I'm about to do.

"She's going to go back to Michigan," I say.

"Let me check my list of problems and see if... nope, where Skye Phillips lives is not on it."

"She's giving up. We both know that's not right."

"She can't sing east of the 15? Come on, man. I know you're some rich LA kid, but you're being a real snob."

"I've been all over. I've been to Nashville, Austin, Memphis, Detroit. Every scene has a different sound, and if you don't fit, you fail." I pause a moment to check his reaction, because if he denies it, he's profoundly stupid. But he nods slightly, conceding the point. All right, maybe I don't suck that bad at this. "She fits here, in Los Angeles, and she's going to outshine, outperform, and out... whatever every other act up there."

"Nice try." He leans back. "And sure, maybe she will. So don't take this the wrong way—the deer in headlights thing is bad, yeah. But there's the other baggage."

"Baggage?" I ask from the near-falling-off edge of the chair.

"Nothing personal."

"What baggage?"

"You."

"Me?"

"Come on. How we gonna market her when she's already attached to Tamika's man? It's going to take a ton of time and treasure to unscrew that bolt."

Me?

I'm the baggage?

We started faking for this fucker's benefit.

"You took that picture," I say. "On Serrano and Wilshire. It was you."

"Dash cam."

"And you sent it to DMZ."

He shrugs. "I was asking if they had any backup intel, because yeah, it was interesting. It was a slow night, so they published it. What can I tell you? It was interesting for five minutes, but now I'm thinking... nah."

"Why is she taking the hit when I'm the problem?"

"Because it's not your day to get hit. You're a fucking operator, I have a relationship with your brother, and we want the plug-in. We'll pay for exclusivity, but a license is gonna be a tough sell to finance. They don't mind buying shit, but regular expenses... the VP makes a face."

Unbelievable, and completely expected. He wouldn't dream of cutting off Liam and his entire stable of talent, and as long as I have something he wants, I'm excused as an industry operator.

"She's in the showcase."

"It's not even eight in the morning. Don't make this into a full-length ball-breaking session."

I stand and drive my finger at him. "She's in."

"Dude. No."

"Design your own plug-in, you no-talent starfucking fuck."

I walk out before he can claim I'm the no-talent starfucker, which is at least half true.

24

SKYE

Pulling the box out from under the bed brings a snowdrift of dust along with it. I really need to vacuum before I move.

I'm moving.

Part of me can't believe it. The forms and leaflets Mom sent seem like messages from a time that's dissolving from memory. I can do all of this online, but I stay on the floor, unfolding pages and ripping open envelopes. I need the physicality of the paper. It takes more time to stack these than to scroll through a website. I need that time, but I don't want it. I'm tired of waiting. Sick of the false starts and childish dreams. I don't want to be one thing in the world and another in my hopes. I just want to *be*.

And there's Colton. Cocky, vulnerable, brilliant Colton, with his swagger and smile, his easy confidence and casual devotion. Of all the men I've known intimately and otherwise, he's the only one I've wanted to want, and the only one I've wanted who I won't let myself keep.

We did too much, he and I. We shouldn't have touched or kissed in private. From letting him give me so much pleasure to revealing my deepest self, I made mistakes. I'm not one hundred percent sure I can leave him behind, and I'm one hundred percent sure that if I do, it'll hurt. We'll be friends in name. We'll smile when we remember our hours in the studio and never speak a harsh word about one another, but we'll be strangers. Maybe I'll invite him to see me play Eponine at the Grosse Pointe Community Theatre, but he won't come.

The catalog for the University of Michigan Medical School sits open on my lap. I flip through to the page where they tell prospective students what to expect the first year. Morning classes and at least four hours of lab work and assignments in the afternoon. Twelve to twenty hours of studying on the weekend, depending on the exam schedule.

I can hack it, but there won't be any time to come back to Los Angeles to hang out with a busy music producer.

The book closes. The cover is shiny cardboard with a block of blue at the top and bottom. White lettering. In the center, a handful of students in lab coats smile. Some look at the camera. The rest look at each other and laugh as if sharing a joke only med students would understand.

The picture asks, "Don't you want to be one of us?"

I don't. I really don't. I'll be out of the frame while they laugh, wishing I was in a garage in Los Angeles with Colton.

Splat. A teardrop falls onto the cover, crowning and dropping into the shape of a flattened spider. I wipe it away, streaking a wet line across a smiling face.

"Sorry, lady. Also fuck you."

I'm not even anxious. The punitive voice that tells me I

was always going to fail and my mother's loving voice that knew the world would fail me have both been proven right.

My phone rings. It's Mom calling from the house phone. Whelp, might as well tell her to clear her shit out of my room, since I'll be staying there a few weeks.

I clear my throat, hum a clear note, and answer with a chipper, "Hello!"

"Skyebird!"

"Daddy?" Of course it's my father. I know his voice. And who else calls me Skyebird? "Is everything all right?"

"Yes. Why wouldn't it be?"

"You don't usually call." I'm crying for real. "It's Mom and sometimes you're in the background."

If he asks me why I'm sobbing, I won't be able to answer, so I take a deep breath, but I sound like a car that won't start.

"She said you were coming back to school, and I wanted to tell you I spoke to the dean about you."

I try to thank him, but I can't get my tongue between my teeth long enough to make a *th-* sound.

"'Kay." He deserves thanks, but an agreement is all I can choke out. My vision's blurred with thick tears and my mouth is flooded with spit.

"Skye." He sounds concerned. I sniff to speak, revealing that I'm drowning in tears. "Are you crying because you're leaving?"

Not really. There's context and nuance. There's feeling alive all day. There are my friends. I came to depend on the hope that I can someday be everything I ever wanted to be. And there's Colton, who I can count on even if he can't count on me. Of the things I'm leaving unfinished, ending my time with him is the most painful.

So, no. I'm not bawling just because I'm leaving, but yes is close enough.

"Yeh-yeh-yeh—" My breath refuses to get under control.

"Sweetheart."

All I can make a *nnhh* sound.

"Listen to me." From his side, I hear the squeak and clap of him closing his recliner. "Are you listening?"

"*Nnhh-hh*," I affirm, dragging my sleeve across my face to wipe off an impossible amount of gunk so a flood of new gunk can take its place.

"Don't push this." I know he's standing and pointing his finger just from his tone, and I cry harder. "No school. No nothing. Nobody wants a sad doctor. What are you going to do, cry on the patient's gown?"

"No."

"No. Damn right. You'll be on rateyourdoc dot com in two minutes flat. 'She cried through the entire exam. I felt much better in comparison. Five stars.'"

In the middle of a hitched breath, I laugh so hard I nearly choke.

"What's that therapist you have there doing for you? What's her cure? Is it crystals? Organic food? Some people talk about turmeric. I don't know. I'm just a brain surgeon."

"There's no cure." I rip a page out of the school catalog and wipe my nose with it. "I'm just an anxious person. I can only learn to manage it."

"What's the point of digging around people's brains if I can't take away what hurts them? That's what I say."

"Being a brain surgeon's pretty badass, Dad."

"Sure, sure. But you? When you sing a song, I forget my troubles. A scalpel can't bring that much joy."

"There aren't a lot of openings for that job, and too many

people want it. I need more than a nice voice. I need to be bigger. I need presence, and confidence, and I need to be able to perform in front of people without turning into a sweaty ice cube."

"Do ice cubes sweat over there?"

"I freeze and… forget it." I stand. My knees are stiff from sitting cross-legged for so long. "I'll be there in time for registration on the fifteenth. I didn't get picked for a big deal thing, so I can drive and get there in time for registration."

"What is this Big Deal Thing?" He pronounces each word as if it's worthy of its own capital.

"Nothing. It would have been another drop of encouragement in a big empty bucket. It would have dried out before the next one came just in time to keep me here and it's like the way you can split the number one in half an infinite number of times and never get to zero."

"So, you lost hope?"

Yes. Mostly. Not really.

I haven't lost hope as much as run out of rope.

I could write that into a song, but there's no point.

"I'm coming home. I'm going to med school. The end." I snap two tissues from the box and sit on the bed like a dead weight. "I'll still sing with Mom at Christmas or whatever. I'll sing 'Someone to Watch Over Me' when you're in the OR."

"That's one of my favorites. But I can play it myself. You don't need to come here and sing it. Wait. Erase what I just said. I never want you to doubt yourself."

"Thank you." I sigh and crumple the tissues. I stopped crying at some point, but I don't know why. "I can't pretend anymore. I just need to come home."

"Are you sure?"

"I am, Dad. But thank you."

"I believe in you, sweetheart. Whatever you set your mind to. I believe in you."

I say goodbye and hang up, because I don't share his belief.

Colton is fine. He did what he had to do, and I helped him. He's going to get out of his brother's house, build his own studio or rent one, whatever. Maybe he'll still use his brother's place. It's not my problem.

We're still friends and it's not my problem.

So why are there flutters of anxiety in my chest?

"Skye!" Fátima calls from the living room. The door closes right after. "I brought back tamales!"

Well, at least one good thing is going to happen today.

A foil-covered tray sits on the counter. One side is peeled open to expose corn-leaf-wrapped treats. Half are tied with a bow of leaf fibers—those are the sweet ones. The untied will be the spicy. I like those too. Fátima's grandmother could fill a *tamal* with horse hooves and onions and I'd beg for more, but the dulce are enough to make me forget all my problems for a hot minute.

Plucking out a sweet one, I drop it onto a plate.

"It's warm enough?" Fátima asks, holding her hand over the tray, looking doubtful.

Cold tamales are sacrilege. And you can't just pop them in the microwave or they'll dry out. It's a process, and I'm hungry. She pulls her hand back with a nod. Good enough.

"Do you want to work on the ad with me?" she asks, flipping open her laptop.

"Sure." I trash the corn husk.

"Hancock Park adjacent." Fátima stands by the kitchen counter, typing. "Large sunny bedroom-slash-bath. That's the title."

The sweet tamale sits on my plate, steaming and fresh. I twist the fork in my hands, unsure if I can get any food down. "Skip adjacent."

"Large sunny bedroom-slash-bath in Hancock Park, exclamation point."

"I'd click it." I take a corner of the tamale and chew it. It's the same as any other perfect tamale Fátima's grandmother has ever made, but when I swallow, it sticks there.

"Bedroom and private bath in luxury home. Shared kitchen. Blah blah. Okay, this is the important part." She clears her throat. "'I can be real nice and easygoing, but it's my name on the lease, so I'll need all your socials to make sure you're not an asshole. If you're into forced birth or don't believe gay-slash-trans people should exist, federal law says I can't discriminate against you, but I can be a real spiteful bitch. Don't expect me to share shit or be forgiving of your dishes or your laundry. Take that into consideration when you call. Street parking. First and last month's, blah blah. Done.'"

"I'd move in all over again."

"Cool." She clicks around to post the ad.

My stomach feels too small for the tiny bite of tamale I'm trying to get into it. I can't bear the thought of leaving Los Angeles. Fátima. Becca. Stupid David. Colton. Colton. Colton.

"*Mija?*" Fátima says right before the first teardrop splats on my plate.

"It's cold." I push it away.

"Hey." She takes me by the shoulders, but I keep my head

down for another drop to fall on the IKEA porcelain. "You don't have to go, you know."

"I promised."

"Okay? So? You can't tell your parents, 'Sorry, I'm going to hang here for another while.'"

"I don't have your family, Fátima!" I'm too loud. Too sharp. She doesn't deserve my worst. "I'm sorry."

"Don't be." She lets her arms drop away and takes my tamale. "You want this?"

"You have it."

"Never thought I'd see you give up a sweet one." She rips a paper towel off the roll and runs it under water.

"Giving up is what I do."

"Good job, making it so you can't win either way. That's like some superstar shit." Having covered the tamale with the wet towel, she claps the microwave door closed.

"Hey, so maybe Becca could move in? Then you wouldn't have to put up the ad?"

Fátima sighs. "We had our first date, like, a week ago."

"You want to come to Michigan with me?"

"You got pretty lesbians out there?"

"Sure, but they're all in puffer coats half the year."

"Hard pass." The microwave beeps. "I'll visit in summer though."

She's joking around, but the thought makes me happy anyway.

25

COLTON

Fuck Eugene Testarossa. He wants to reject Skye based on what *might* happen? Well, I *accept* her based on what might happen.

"That's right!" I shout into my windshield when the light turns green. "I have this. I'm going to solve this fucker."

I'm talking to myself because I have no choice. I'm blocked. There has to be something I can do to save Skye from med school, but tying her up is illegal, and calling the school to cancel her registration isn't going to win me any fans in the Phillips' household.

Which doesn't matter. I don't know them.

I want to though.

"Nope!" I drown out the thought, turning up the radio. It immediately goes to a commercial. I flip the station, and Tamika comes on like a fucking bulldozer on La Brea Ave.

She's good. She was always better than I gave her credit for.

I blast my ex-girlfriend's voice.

The windows are rolled up, no one's around to hear me, and I know the words.

Your life stole your storeeeeey…

Ah, shit, I sound like a wet cat. I can't even listen to myself.

Skye would eat this song for lunch, but she never will. She's not just giving up her geography, she's giving up on herself.

"Nah, nah, nah." I turn onto Logan's stupid block, leaving the music up. "This ain't happening."

If I say *nope-nope-nope* enough times, I'll believe it. Then I'll be able to figure out how to convince someone to get Skye into the showcase.

It doesn't work. I pull into the driveway optimistic, but planless.

When I get back to the back of the house, Ella's pacing her veranda.

"Colton!"

"Yeah?" I look up at her, shading my eyes against the sun. She's wearing a teal satin shift with a low neck.

"Is this too tight?" She points at her midsection, which looks as if it's doubled in the past few days.

"I can't really see it from here."

"Well, then come up. Please?"

I've never heard her sound so desperate, so I go into the big house and up to the dressing room attached to the master bedroom.

"Well?" She demands a yes or no, but how should I know? She's a literal fashion designer.

"Isn't this what you do for a living?"

"I'm biased and hormonal. Logan's working and you're going to have to figure it out. Tell me."

Staring at a pregnant woman's belly is shit manners, so I have to overcome that, but once I do, I can't lie. "Too tight."

"Goddamnit! How do people do this?" She storms to her racks of dresses and flicks through violently. "I literally had this made last week."

"Get it fixed." Figuring she'll ask again about some other dress and unwilling to go to the back house where I'll have to deal with the fact that I can't do a thing about Skye leaving, I sit on the chair by the patio doors. "Don't you have a warehouse full of women sewing?"

"Men sew too." Her voice comes from deep in the closet. "And they're all busy doing November deliveries and spring samples."

"Uh-huh." I put my feet up on a suitcase in the middle of the floor. "Where you going?"

"Greece next week and I figured I'd pack while I got a dress together but no. Here we are." She's so deep in the closet she sounds as if she's talking to me from another timeline. "And I'm not buying another thing when I'm just going to get bigger next week. I'm giving birth to Godzilla at this rate."

Out the window, I can see the house I'm going to have to leave soon.

"Cute Godzilla," I add, opening Craigslist on my phone.

She pops out of the dressing room and holds up a flowy lavender thing with a high waist. "What about this?"

"What was that show with the four old ladies living together?"

"*Golden Girls?*"

"Yeah." I wave my hand at the dress. "That."

"Fuck." She gets eaten by the closet again.

"What's the event?" I scroll through the listings, tapping

on anything that seems mildly interesting, only to find out I'm not interested.

"Music For All Foundation fundraiser. 'Bringing new music to Los Angeles,' blah blah. Whole family's going." She pops her head out. "You do know you're invited, right?"

"Yeah, sure." I know like I know my social security number. With effort, and only when asked.

"You going?" She's back in the closet.

"Nah."

"Why not? You're a music guy. It's a music thing."

"It's a music *industry* thing. I don't need an agent. My brother already went to the dark side."

"Is it because Tamika's going to be there?" She holds a long blue shirt against herself, then throws it on the bed.

Yes. Now it is.

"No."

I'm about to close another uninteresting apartment listing when I see the name at the bottom of the description.

~Call Fátima

There's a number under it. Is this Skye's apartment? Is this real? How did this happen? How have I been sitting here shooting the shit with my sister-in-law when she's leaving?

"Could be good for Skye," Ella says, turning in front of the mirror in a lace and black pinstripe dress that goes to the floor.

"What's good for Skye?"

"The fundraiser. You can take her, introduce her around."

I could. And if she's on my arm, someone besides Gene might assume my magic touch is creating the next big thing.

Or maybe Gene will realize the error of his ways when Skye gives him a radiant smile. She could get the showcase spot and stay in Los Angeles. We could do a full album or just say we are and spend days fucking instead.

Or I could just be baggage.

"This way when they hear her next week at the showcase—"

"She didn't get in."

~Call Fátima

"Oh, bummer. So Mom and Dad didn't end up helping?"

"She said she didn't want them pulling strings. You heard her."

"I figured you'd tell her that's just how it works."

"Nothing breaks solid Midwestern values."

~Call Fátima

Skye's leaving. She really meant it. Or not. Maybe this is a different Fátima. I don't even know if I'm going to see her again. That hurts more than anything.

"Colton?"

"I need a dress for her. She said something about a red shiny thing?"

"Sparkly. And that's in the archives at work." Ella goes back into the closet. "But I have something close, I think. What size is she? Like an eight?"

"How the fuck should I know?"

~Call Fátima

I'm going to call this number and ask Skye to come to this thing. I could just call her directly, but first I want to know if this is her roommate. I have to find out how close I am to losing her for real and forever.

"Here." Ella drapes a long dress covered in red beads over my lap. "That's bias cut. It'll fit unless she's carrying Godzilla."

"She's not." I put away the phone, throw the dress over my shoulder, and stand. "Thanks for this."

"So, you're going?"

"Yeah." I kiss her cheek. "And this one?" I wave from the bottom of the black dress to the top. "Fits. Works. Five stars."

She spins back to the mirror and nods. Before she says a word, I'm gone. Hustling down the stairs, I tap the link to call Fátima about the apartment in Hancock Park.

It rings twice, then picks up.

"Hello?"

"Fátima, hey, I was calling about the room."

"Yeah so, hey it's—"

"Not really about the room." I burst into the backyard. "I need to ask you a question."

"Okay, if you're some weirdo stalker, I have a black belt and will not hesitate to kick your incel ass."

"Do you have a roommate named Skye? Skye Phillips?"

Silence. The question is too much. Any woman knows that even saying no, there's no Skye there could open someone else up to a weirdo stalker. She should reasonably hang up right now, and I want to prevent that.

"It's Colton. I saw your ad on Craigslist and I know this is probably not the right place and I'm sorry."

There's a muffled shuffle on the other side.

"Colton?" It's Skye. She should also reasonably hang up.

"Hey, I—"

"You have my number."

What do I want? Why did I call this number instead of the one I have?

"Fátima's looking for a new roommate?"

"Yes. She is. What do you want?"

"Nothing. Forget it. I don't..."

211

... care. But I do care. We're friends, officially, and friends are allowed to call. I didn't have to sneak through an anonymized Craigslist number. What I don't have is the right to demand Skye stay when she doesn't want to. Only a guy who admits he gives a shit about her and also being with her, beside her, behind her—that guy gets to ask why the fuck her roommate's looking to replace her.

"You're really leaving."

"Colton," she starts with a sigh. "I told you."

"It's fine. I was just looking for a place."

"You are? He's really kicking you out?"

"Probably maybe? I don't know. It's just time, you know? I got paid and I… uh, it's really close to the studio, if Logan lets me keep it."

"I could put in a good word for you if you want my old room."

I never saw her room. I never knew if she was living in some generic shithole or if she'd thrown her personality all over the walls. If I'm being reasonable with myself, gotta say, that's kind of a red flag for not really knowing her. How can you catch feelings for someone if you haven't seen their space?

"It's probably not…" I sit on an arm of my U of patio couches. "I just came across her name and figured…" I rub my face so hard the skin feels as if it's going to come off. What am I doing? I'm telling the truth, but my living arrangements aren't important. We agreed no feelings. I told her with fucking words that I didn't catch feelings. I'm moving out of my brother's place. That's it. The end. "You know what, it doesn't matter. When are you leaving?"

"Maybe in a few days. This is all happening so fast."

"Yeah. Life comes at you." I didn't call for dime-store

philosophy. I called to ask her to the fundraiser, gala, party, event—what should I call it? "Hey, so I was wondering if—"

"Fátima needs the pho—"

Muffled voices. Murmurs. A giggle.

"Colton," Fátima's voice comes through the speaker, "Skye just vouched for you not being a latent rapist, so if you want the room and whatever tamales I bring home, it's yours."

"Tamales? Homemade?"

"My grandmother makes them every other week."

"I ain't made of stone."

"He hasn't even seen the room!" Skye calls from somewhere far away.

"That's true," I agree.

And also, I don't want the apartment. It probably smells like the ozone in the air before it rains and, between tamales, I'll spend all day jerking off thinking about her.

"I'm going to work," Fátima says. "If you can come today, Skye's home because she's *not working*."

The last two words are a playful accusation that tell me I'm not the only one with the rug torn out from under them.

"I haven't showered or anything!" Skye says.

"I'll be there in an hour."

Before Skye can weasel out of it or I can change my mind, I hang up. Just like that. My thumb does stuff my brain doesn't have time to fill out a permission slip for.

Smart thumb. Fuck my brain. My brain is fucking stupid. One hundred percent fuck me for ever listening when it said I had no feelings, and fuck my dick for screaming that it wants her, and fuck my heart's squeaky little voice for speaking a language I can't understand.

26

SKYE

The apartment's in pretty good shape and it's not like Colton's going to care whether or not it's one hundred percent tidy, but I straighten up because one, Fátima wants to make a good impression without being late for her shift. Second, I want it to be nice for him, and as inexplicable as that desire is, a clean apartment shouldn't be something a girl has to parse out.

So I dust, vacuum, unload the dishes and put the dirties in, wipe the counters, swish the toilet.

The tub doesn't need to be cleaned, but I need a shower, so I do both at the same time. When I get out, I only have my everyday moisturizer. The good stuff is packed and the mostly-but-not-quite-empty stuff is in the trash.

Colton's coming. He's going to see the packed boxes.

There's not much I can do about them except shove them against the wall. Books, clothes, music notes, a hundred handheld things that failed to relax me in front of strangers. Ninety-nine failures and packing ain't one.

I'm still in my towel, unmoisturized, when there's a knock on the door. Shit. Has it been an hour?

"Coming!"

My hair is dripping wet and there's no time for makeup, but none of that matters. I throw on sweatpants and a raglan shirt. He and I are cool. We have a professional relationship. We're friends who fucked. Pick one or both. Neither is a big deal. Hundred percent non-issue.

I open the door and melt. Under a black leather jacket, he's wearing Levis that are perfectly worn in all the right places and a tight black T-shirt with a neck that's stretched out past his collarbones. He looks like a Jet on his way to rumble with the Sharks but who stopped by to do a little tough guy song and dance first.

We're cool.

We're former colleagues. Friends now. It's fine.

"Come on in." I step out of the way.

He comes into the living room, checking out the place. This guy, raised by billionaires in one of the most status-hungry cities in the world, is looking at my dinky apartment as if he could ever live here.

Then he looks at me as if he could live in me too. I'm not wearing a bra, so when my nipples twist and tighten, they must be the most visible things in the room. He manages to only glance down for a split second before meeting my gaze.

"It's nice. The place, I mean."

"It's smaller than your brother's guest house." I close the door. "But whatever."

"You vacuumed." He points at the tonal lines crisscrossing the carpet to show me that if you read carefully between them, you can make out the words *I CARE*.

"Fátima wanted to make a nice impression, so I straightened up a little."

"Cool. Hey, I brought you something for the trip home." He pulls something out of his jacket pocket and holds out his fist, then opens it.

"It's a Pez!" Garfield the Cat's head sits on a plastic orange pillar with the letters P-E-Z raised on the sides. The sound and feel of my nail clicking against them is very satisfying. "Will Logan notice it's gone?"

"He gave them to me. He said the baby could choke so..." He shrugs off the thought of a Pez-asphyxiated baby. I push the head back and a yellow brick comes from under the fat cat's neck. "I filled it up, so you can make lots of mistakes before you run out."

"Thank you." I put the head down and the wafer slips back. I don't want to waste a mistake. "Liam said he's going to bring the songs around town once you send them."

"He believes in you."

"That's the hard part. Disappointing him. And you. You both worked so hard and I just... I can't cut it."

"Nah. I'm getting what I need out of it."

"Good. I'm glad to hear it." I straighten up. The sad sack routine is a drag. "Hey, so come look at the room. It's not much really."

Bouncing down the hall as if I don't have a care in the world, I open my door, spin around and spread my arms as if I'm showing him a stunning, three-sixty view of the Swiss Alps. When he comes in, he takes a deep breath through his nose, as if savoring the mountain air.

"Here it is."

"That's a lot of baggage," he says about the black garbage bags full of clothes I couldn't part with.

"Yeah. Um, the dresser and stuff, I wouldn't mind leaving behind if someone I liked was taking it."

"Oh, such as... me?" He fingers the edge of the mirror as if everything in this room isn't entirely beneath the social status hidden under his sexy *West Side Story* getup.

"Yeah. Such as you. Dork." I sit on the bed. "But the stuff you got from Jab's grandfather is nicer. Older, but nicer."

"How many days are you going to be around?"

"It's, like, a four-day drive and I should be at the school in X days, so..."

"X-4 days." He takes off his jacket and throws it next to me.

"Why haven't you sent Liam the songs?"

He shrugs, hands in his pockets. I wait, but that's all I get.

"There's a little balcony." I pull the string to open the vertical blinds. "It overlooks basically the little alley between us and the next building, but are they bad?"

"Cool." The sunlight blasts all the detail out of his face. "Wait. What?"

"Are the songs bad? Is that why you haven't sent them?"

"No, Skye. The songs are not bad."

"Is it bad that they're three and not four?"

"Liam doesn't give a shit at this point."

Of course he doesn't. Who would? I've got my stuff boxed away. It's over. Three songs. Four. Doesn't matter.

"What about the bed?" Colton asks.

"Um, I was going to have it sent, but..."

"I mean, what about you and me. On the bed."

"Colton."

"I'm just saying, if you're leaving, then it's game over. The rules aren't really a thing anymore, right?"

The rules fenced in a relationship that didn't exist. The

gate opened and nothing real escaped, only the things we imagined and hoped for.

"True," I say. "I'm not saying no, necessarily."

"What are you saying necessarily, then?" Behind me, he puts one knee on the mattress.

I twist around to face him. "Not no, per se."

With his knuckles on the duvet, he's a torso-length closer.

"Per what then?" He's fully on the bed now, leaning toward me until his breath warms my lips.

"Per our last conversation, when you told me, and I quote, 'Friends isn't some agreement. It's earned.' So let's earn some friend points."

"And stay friends."

That shouldn't be like a knife in my chest. We stuck to our agreement so that neither of us would feel the way I feel right now—stripped of defenses, skin, muscle, everything gone but the exposed heart with a blade sticking out of it.

I recognize when I'm being dramatic. He's right. I'm leaving, and being anything more than friends would hurt both of us.

"A few days of fucking could be fun," I agree, letting my nose touch his. "If we just keep that one rule. Friends. Not feelings."

"And one more."

Our faces dance together, choreographing something that's not a kiss by any measure. It's cheeks and chins, breaths and bones. It's a prelude, circling energy in a whirlwind around our lips.

"Which one?" I whisper.

"You're an alto."

I am that, and I'm foolish, and careless, and I've been so mature and sensible with whomever I've had sex with before that I truly believe I can be mature and sensible with Colton. So I kiss him, and more importantly, I let him kiss me.

The kiss is unlike any other we've shared. I attribute that to a different moment, a different space. His hands do more than touch me. They treasure every inch of skin. When he pulls my shirt over my head, his fingertips graze my ribs and the sides of my breasts with gentle appreciation. We undress each other in a slow, steady rhythm.

I kiss his neck. I kiss his chest. He finds my most tender places and loves them awake, buzzing, and ready. He pulls my legs apart as if he's opening a present and can't believe his luck at what he's received.

We don't fuck like friends. We fuck like two people who should have been more. Who have one last chance to crawl inside each other and feel everything without rules around what we're allowed.

He's on his knees. I'm straddling him. Face to face, angling my body to stimulate my clit along his length, I slide slowly down. He has one hand in my hair and one at my back, keeping my pace at controlled leisure. I feel everything. My whole body feels where we connect.

"Slow," he whispers to me, even as I reach climax. "So beautiful."

It lasts forever.

He's dressed. I embrace him as if it's the last time we'll ever part ways, which it probably is and which I'm trying to appreciate, but he stops himself mid-kiss with a burst of laughter, letting me go so he can rub his face.

"I totally forgot."

"What?"

He takes his hands away. "I brought you something."

Grabbing my hand, he pulls me to the front door. I shove my feet into sandals and let him take me through the courtyard and to the street where his car is parked. Officially, we live in the same neighborhood, but compared to his block, everything about this street is shoddy and worn. The gate to the courtyard doesn't close all the way. The sidewalk is uneven. He kicks an In-n-Out cup that spins into the uncut wild grass in the parkway.

"Okay, so listen." By his car, he stops and turns, taking both of my hands. "I should have opened with this but..." He glances back at his car, then at me. "Nothing's changed about the showcase. I tried but—"

"You tried?"

"Yeah, but whatever." He releases my hands and digs in his pocket. "There's this party Saturday to fundraise for next year's Shooting Star event. And I didn't think you'd be interested." Retrieving his car fob, he unlocks it. "But it could be fun." He opens the back door and reaches for the hook over the door, retrieving a garment bag. "And I figured you'd say you didn't have anything to wear so..." He unzips it to reveal a maxi dress. It's red with shades of red bugle beads twisting all around it like vines. "I got a loaner from Ella."

"Is it one of hers?" My hands go grabby, and I pull the bottom part out of the bag and toward me as if seeing it horizontal will change anything. The black label flicks in the breeze, revealing a little silver butterfly. "It is!"

"You like it?"

"God, yes. And you're really kind of a jerk."

"Because I'm trying to control you with a fucking dress?"

"Exactly." I tuck the skirt back in the bag.

"That doesn't make me a jerk. It makes me a gaslighting asshole."

"I don't think this rises to the level of gaslighting." I zip away the dress. "But." I take the hanger from him. "Consider me in your thrall."

"Yeah?" He seems slightly surprised and genuinely delighted.

"Pick me up Saturday."

"All right." He slaps the back door closed. "Yeah."

"Good." I take a few steps back, hitting a heaved ridge of sidewalk. Almost trip. Don't. But he's still got my arm, right there in a flash. He lets go.

"Sorry." He backs up into the street.

"It's fine."

"Okay."

"Thanks for the, um, spin around the old..." I'm in public, so I don't finish.

"Yeah. Also? I don't need the bed." He opens the driver's door.

"No good?"

"I mean, if you're not in it, it's kinda meh."

I smile. "Got it."

"Good."

"Okay, bye." I wave.

"Bye." He waves back, then shoos me. "Go."

Once I'm behind the broken gate, he gets in the car and leaves.

27

SKYE

"What's taking so long?" Becca cries from the other side the bathroom door. When I open it, she has her fist up, ready to pound. Her hand opens and covers her mouth. "Honey, look!" Fátima comes behind her, and they clasp hands. "Our little girl's all grown up."

"Oh, shut up." I turn my back to them. "Zip me."

Becca zips me and we all hustle into Fátima's room, which has mirrored closet doors. The neckline has a deep drop, but the halter is secure enough to keep me out of the danger zone. The halter and the bead pattern are the only complexities. Otherwise, it's a straight column down, with only enough flare at the skirt to let me walk unrestricted.

My roommate drops a pair of red Jimmy Choo stilettos in front of me. She got them after she was promoted to manager, and she's loaning them to me so I don't have to buy red shoes to wear once.

Once they're on, the skirt is lifted off the floor. They stand on each side of me and look in the mirror. Becca did my makeup and hair. Fátima slips me a little bright blue clutch. The contrast is apparently all the rage.

"Perfect," she says.

"You sure you don't want a party?" Becca whines. "I really, really, really want to throw a party."

"Then throw a party."

"Yay!"

"Just not for me."

"Boo."

"I want to slip off into the night."

"What do you think he's going to wear?" Fátima changes the subject. "One of those T-shirts with a tux printed on it?"

"Maybe," I answer. "Or a tux with a backward baseball cap."

"Dodgers or Yankees?" Fátima asks.

"*Loro Piana*," Becca calls back, on the way to the front of the apartment. We follow.

"I say rented tux," Fátima says. "Holding a corsage in a clear plastic clamshell. Roses or carnations."

"I'm not sure about these lashes," I say, blinking hard. "I can see them."

"You get used to it," Becca says, straddling a kitchen stool. She addresses Fátima, who's boiling water for tea. "So, he moving in?"

Becca lives right off Alameda, in a loft overlooking the 10 freeway. It was a dead, empty space when she moved in and it's now highly personalized in shades of pink and laid out for a DJ… yet she's looking at Fátima ruefully, as if she wants to be the one to move into this tiny dump.

"I'm not sure he's super reliable. He has no steady income whatsoever."

"I didn't have a job when I moved in," I say.

"You were hot, and I was horny."

"Aw, you guys," Becca says warmly, without a trace of jealousy, putting her hands on her heart. "Memories." She's being corny and over-the-top to play her true feelings as parody. "I'm going to miss you."

"She'll be back." Fátima shakes the jar of teabags until one she likes comes to the top. I'm about to say I'm not ruling it out, but that med school is really hard so it's not like I'll be able to take a weekend off until... "She's dick drunk."

"I am not!"

"She is not!" Becca defends me, or so I think. "She's in love."

"I am..." The *not* falls dead on my lips and gets swallowed by the doorbell.

Rescued from a lie, I jump to get it, but Fátima, who moves with the speed and grace of a cat, gets to the door before me, throwing it open but blocking the view of my date.

"I lost this one bad." She gets out of the way.

No part of me anticipated the guy standing there.

His black sneakers are the least surprising part of what he's wearing. His shirt has a traditional pleated front, but he's skipped the tie, leaving the neck open two buttons. The jacket's open, and the sleeves are pushed up below his elbows, with the shirt cuffs rolled over them enough to expose —ything. *Now.*

But the backward black baseball cap is perfect. Fátima declares me the winner. She sounds as if she's at the other end of a tunnel.

"You look nice." His voice is quiet. Not as if he's trying to tell me a secret, but maybe as if he's talking in a church, or if doesn't want to break a spell with too much noise.

We're the only two characters on stage. The scenery goes dark and rotates behind the curtain while two spotlights isolate us.

"Come here." He beckons me to him, and I step forward until our spotlights merge. "Yup. Nailed it."

Has he ever looked at anyone this way before? He could murder women with that look. Leave a trail of bodies he never touched and shrug in that way he does. "I didn't do nothing. I was just looking."

Why do I feel so alive then? I'm more alive when he looks at me as if every bit of attention and brain power is processing me from head to toe. He has to be using the energy reserved for breathing and swallowing. There can't be anything left to keep his heart beating.

"You look nice too." *Nice* doesn't really cover it, and "devastating" is undercut by the rolled-up cuffs and backward cap.

"Dude," Fátima says from next to me. "Let me see that cap." She snaps her fingers.

He takes it off and runs his fingers through his hair. "I couldn't get the hair right."

"*Loro Piana*," Fátima announces. "Good call, baby." There's a smooching sound behind me.

"I got it out of Logan's front closet."

"Your hair looks fine," I say. "You don't need it."

"We'll hang onto it." Fátima, again behind me.

"Oh, it looks good on you!" Becca cries.

"Keep it. My brother looks like a douche in it." He beckons me to follow him. "Let's go."

I take his arm and we walk out of the courtyard, side by side.

Colton pulls to the back of the line of black stretch limos that all look the same. A skinny guy with a clipboard approaches. Colton rolls down his window, gives our names, and Skinny checks us off.

"You've done this before," I say when the window's closed again.

"Since I was a kid. Just the youngest son of a really fucking rich guy. I know the deal."

"Good. Because I don't."

Another reason I should go home. I may really like Los Angeles, but I'll never fit in.

"You nervous?" His elbow is bent at the top of his door and his index finger rubs the space between his lower lip and chin. He looks serious, yet too confident to be anything but casual.

I'm not. I'm relaxed. Relieved. I'm the picture of calm and peace. I'm fine. I'm so fucking fine.

"Hell yes, I'm nervous. The minute I step foot out of this car, there are going to be so many people. I'm going to die. Bang. Right on the sidewalk. As a matter of fact..." I clutch my chest because now that I mention it, the usual tightness has twisted into something more painful, but the neck is cut so low there's nothing to grab. "I might not even make it out of the car."

"Okay, listen."

"This is a bad idea."

"That's not how this is going." He slaps the car into park and takes my hand. "You're not doing this."

"Doing what?"

226

"Sabotaging yourself." He leans so close his face is the only thing I see.

"You didn't want to come. You were right."

"Look at me."

"Take the win."

"This ain't a win. Focus on me right here. Yeah?"

In the shadows, I latch onto the one fleck of his eyes with enough light to look blue.

"You're going to have a great time."

"What if I don't?" I ask.

"I'll take you home."

"What if I want to go home now?"

"Same answer."

He'll take me home, away, out of this.

The car in front of us goes.

"There's space. Move up," I say.

"Let them go around."

He sits with me. When Skinny comes to the window, Colton puts his hand up and spins a finger while keeping his eyes on mine. Skinny directs the cars behind to go around us.

"I wish you had Garfield." Colton says. It takes me a second to realize what he's talking about.

"I brought him!" I dig around the clutch bag and find the orange cat. "Just in case I got anxious."

I tip back Garfield's head and offer the candy to Colton. He removes it and holds it to my mouth. When my lips part, he places it on my tongue.

"Lemon," I say.

"I got an orange." He pops his Pez and puts the dispenser back in my hand, closing my fingers over it.

I feel the edges. Run my finger over the letters. I give full

227

attention to its texture, temperature, calling up the exact shade of orange in my mind.

"It's no big thing to take you home," Colton says. "This event isn't shit. I just wanted to go out with you one last time."

"Me too."

"I thought it was the dress."

I laugh. "Kinda the dress."

I'm not sure if Colton's calm is the reason the shock of anxiety has worn down to a smooth nub, or the feeling of the cat-shaped plastic dispenser in my hand.

"I'm not ever going to see these people again," I say. "Except you. Maybe. Some time."

When he smiles, his left eyebrow rises slightly more than its partner. "What do you want to do tonight?" He brushes his thumb over my cheek as if removing a stray mascara fleck, then it slows into a lingering touch.

"I'm fine."

"You're fine." He breathes on my mouth.

I inch forward, eyes fluttering closed until everything's striped with vertical eyelashes. Anyone watching this movie can tell we're going to kiss. I don't want to muddle this. If I got control of the panic, it can't be about him, because he's not going to be around much longer.

"I'm fine." I sit straight. "I am."

He's caught bent at the hips with parted lips and corrects that promptly.

"Good." He drives, closing the gap with the car in front of us. The line moves, and we stop. "They don't care about us. No one's going to even look at us unless we're in a gap between, like, Jay-Z and Taylor Swift."

I gasp. "Is Taylor Swift here?"

"For real?"

"Is she?" I crane my neck to catch sight of her.

"I have no idea. I was just saying, for example. Those guys get clicks. You and me... they're not taking their cameras off anyone important for us. Okay?"

"That actually makes me feel better."

"You ready?"

"Yup." I slip Garfield back into my bag.

"If it starts again..." Making a V, he points two fingers at his eyes.

"I shall stab my eyes." I put my fingers to my eyes.

The door opens behind me. I gasp. His was supposed to open first.

"Stay there. I got it," he says.

The time it takes him to get out, go around the car, wave the valet away from me, hand over the keys, and bend down to meet my eyes... let's just say I'm pretty sure I could have sung every song from *Phantom of the Opera* with time for a curtain call.

"Come," he says, holding out his hand. There are so many people behind him, all doing their own thing. None of them care about me. "I have you."

Taking his hand, letting it enfold mine so he can pull me up without holding me up, I get out.

So many people. I hear his name once behind me. Businesslike. Normal tone. Security guy.

But Colton keeps his eyes on me. Half of his face flashes bright, but he doesn't lose focus. Not for light or sound. He smiles with approval when I'm standing next to him. All the distracting noises are muted. Contrasts are veiled.

He puts his arm around my shoulders. We walk toward the door. The inside of his elbow is behind my neck and his hand dangles loosely in front of us in a half-embrace of fully-confident ownership. There are flashes and voices, but I focus my attention on keeping pace with him, hip to hip, letting him guide me over the red carpet. A blonde woman with bright red lipstick approaches with a microphone, followed by a man in all black whose face is hidden by a huge camera. Colton turns away from them, pulls me to him, and kisses my head.

"Let me," he whispers.

But before I can let him do anything, the blonde's gaze flicks over my shoulder, the camera swivels, and deafening screams go up from the crowd. I turn to see Tamika herself, wearing a dazzling yellow satin dress, getting out of a limousine.

Colton pulls me forward.

"She's taller than I thought," I say in awe.

When he doesn't answer, I look at him. His permanent state of chill is broken, and suddenly I realize how uncomfortable his ex-girlfriend's presence makes him.

A guy with a headset opens the door for us. It's gorgeous inside. Flowers and glass and wool carpets, but I don't have time to take it all in with Colton's arm around my neck as we enter the ballroom.

We're at a music event, but I don't recognize most of the guests. They all look very dressed up and very rich. Acting normal as we pass Brad Sinclair and Michael Greydon is easy. Monica Faulkner is harder. It's only the way Colton wraps his arm around my neck that keeps my lungs working. He nods at people and keeps walking, sliding us into a bare spot at the bar. I don't recognize anyone else, but they all seem to recognize each other.

"Who are these people?" I murmur, tucking Garfield into

my palm. I drag my nail over the raised letters on the side, counting clicks to get my mind off all these people.

"Businesspeople. Shit-ass executives. I know some from school. Some from my parents. Those two over there?" He nods toward a couple so achingly hip they seem like otherworldly creatures. "Showed up to my parties for a month before introducing themselves."

From the way he looks at them and the way he smiles when the bartender approaches us, I can tell he respects the guy serving drinks more than the people who can make or break a career.

"Ginger ale and..." Colton turns to me. "What are you having?"

I shouldn't drink, but I point at the gold frame sitting on the bar. There's a printout of the drink special in it. California Mojito. Tequila and lime and some weird fruit I've never heard of. "This."

Colton nods to the bartender, and he goes to make the drinks.

"What do we do now?" I ask.

"Fucked if I know." He snaps a toothpick from the bartender's lineup of supplies and lodges it in the corner of his mouth. "I hate these things."

Tonight, I feel as if I'm seeing Colton for the first time. His slouchy confidence is part of his personality, but his tics and denials reveal a deep apprehension. A backward baseball cap with his tuxedo announces he doesn't care what anyone thinks—as long as they think he doesn't care what they think. Unless it's me, telling him to leave it with Fátima.

I have a responsibility here.

I'm going to make sure he leaves this party feeling like a king.

28

COLTON

Skye's looking at me as though she's got something on me. Everyone in here has something on me. They all know my story. Tamika. The lawsuits I paid a fortune to keep out of the media. The shit I said in front of lawyers. Maybe she thinks I'm some weakling who ruined his business over love. Maybe she's glad she's getting away from me before she gets tied up in the same bullshit.

"What?" I try to say it as if I'm just curious, but I'm not much of an actor.

"It's stuffier than I thought it would be."

Is that what the look was about? Knowing I'm uncomfortable in a tux? I flip my toothpick to the other side of my mouth. Nah. She knew that already. Her face says it's something new.

"Yeah." I look away. Our drinks arrive. I leave a five on the bar while she sips hers. "How is it?"

"Not bad. Sweet."

"Like you, baby."

She rolls her eyes. "Should we go around and... I don't know..." She offers a half shrug, scanning the room from behind her glass.

"Show everybody your pretty face?"

"These eyelashes are making me bananas."

"How are the nerves?" I ask.

"Not bad enough to leave."

I laugh, and for a split second, I forget to scan around for Tamika. Then I do, so I can avoid her. I don't see her or any of the throng that usually follows her around.

Fine, then. Let's do this. I'm about to walk off with Skye when I feel a hand on my back. It's my father.

"Hey, Dad."

"You clean up right." He shakes my hand as if I'm an equal, not the mailroom guy. "No cap, huh? Just letting the hair fly free?"

"He tried," Skye breaks in. "I thought he looked better without it."

"Well done."

"I'm Skye, by the way." She offers her hand, and he shakes it.

"Doreen told me all about you. Said you had a little tingle in your touch."

He laughs, putting his other hand over hers, but this shit is not funny. I don't want her to know about this tingle thing Mom has, and Skye already thinks my parents shake hands too long.

Ella steers Skye away to meet Byron and Olivia just as Mom approaches and does that thing where she kisses my face as if it's the only one in the world. She caresses my cheek, and though her hand shakes, it's honestly not that bad tonight.

"Hey, Ma."

"It's so nice to see you dressed up." She pulls away so she can look at me from sneakers to hair flying free. "Is this the suit I got you for Byron's wedding?"

Yes. My mother bought me a fucking suit. I'd just gotten back and I had nothing. I glance at Skye to see if she heard, but she's talking to Ella, who's wearing a blue gown that's definitely made for a pregnant lady.

"Yeah. Still fits."

She's admiring me as if she created me, which she did, but I'm also not a work of art. Definitely not a finished one.

The photographer comes by, requesting a family shot. We oblige.

"Liam said you were coming," Dad says through his photo-smile. "It's good to see you back in business."

"It's a party, Dad."

The photographer thanks us and folds back into the crowd.

"They've missed you in the mailroom. Barry says you were a lot of fun."

"Well, there's email."

"And I'm told you're lying about this girl?" he murmurs.

"Jesus, Dad," I whisper back. My father hates lying. I have no idea how he became so damn rich telling the truth all the time. "It was just a couple of dates for PR. It's nothing."

That's a lie.

The only truth is the past tense... because once she goes home, it'll be over. But nothing? No. It's not nothing anymore. Not when Skye's back's to me while she's laughing with Ella and all I can think about is kissing every inch of her spine. Taking her hair down. Untying the back of the halter so the whole thing falls and I can get one last taste of her breasts.

Before she's gone.

I'm so absorbed in my fantasy I don't register the shift in energy behind me. I should recognize it, because only one person I ever knew could cause it.

"Colton?"

Shit. Even when she talks, you can hear the music.

I'm not going to be rude in front of my family or Skye... especially Skye. So I plaster on a smile and turn around. Tamika's wearing a canary diamond necklace that matches the yellow dress. Her ebony skin is perfect, as always, and she doesn't seem uncomfortable in fake lashes.

"Tam. It's good to see you." I find Skye with a quick glance. Her back is to us. I need her to come here right now. I don't want her to see me talking to Tamika from afar and think she's anything but the only woman in the room I want.

"How formal, my God."

"There's been a lot between informal and now."

"Do you want me to not talk to you? You telling me to fuck off again? I can fuck off." She smiles to shave some of the edge off her words, but she's just edgy. That's how she is. I know better than to get cut up about this when her lawyers did so much worse.

"Nah. How's Gavin? Still trying to make you sound as good as I could?"

She rolls her eyes. "The egos on you men. I'm the one who makes me sound good."

"That's what they said about me. I did nothing. I was baggage."

"Did you not hear what they said about me? I was the whore of the month, and thanks to you walking out on me, I wasn't even getting laid for my trouble." She looks to the side. "Speak of the devil."

I follow her line of sight and all I see is Skye.

Tamika leans close to me. "You play nice, Colton Crowne."

I don't know what she means until Skye shifts a little. She's talking to none other than Gavin McCormick. Looks like Gene is introducing them. That motherfucker knows Gavin fucks anything that moves.

Now Gavin's getting in her ear, saying things that make her nod while she puts her hand behind her back so she can rub the corners of a Garfield Pez dispenser.

He thinks he's going to fuck her. I want to rip that thought right out of his head.

The state of raw, blood-pumping rage exposes me to myself. I want to take care of her. Give her whatever she needs. He will take her away from me. Turn her against me. He is a thief and he's stealing Skye. He wants to produce her. He wants to fuck her.

"Angel food?" Tamika calls me by the name she used to.

"Don't."

"You had to know he'd be here."

"I don't care about him."

She stands next to me, following my gaze to McCormick talking to Skye. "Is she yours?"

"She's mine."

"Whoa." In my peripheral vision, she turns to me. "Did you ever look like that when a man talked to me?"

"I don't know. Did I?"

Before she responds, McCormick puts his hand on Skye's back to guide her away, chattering the whole time as if he's going to slide a proposition or an assault under the constant deluge of words.

"I have to go. Nice seeing you." I start after them.

After two steps, Tamika has me by the arm.

"Don't." She hisses in my ear with words running together as fast as she sings them. "It took me a long time to work out that it was always business with us and I'd misplaced my personal. Now I don't know if you got something business or personal with that girl, but I know that look, angel food, and it's not business. Do not do what you're about to do here. You hear me? Do not let your personal fuck your business."

"Why do you care?"

"I may need you. Soon. Business."

Chatting like a man filling regrettable gaps in a woman's knowledge, McCormick leads Skye past a set of double doors, cutting her off from view. As if a rope's been yanked, I leap forward, but Tamika gets in front of me.

"Let me take care of it."

"Get the fuck out of my way, Tam."

She doesn't. No one ever made Tamika move one way or the other if she wanted to move in a third direction, but that doesn't make me her bitch right now either. I'll plow her down if I have to, but I take her by the shoulders and she doesn't fight when I move her to the side.

Once she's out of the way, I'm at the doors in ten steps, pushing between them to a kitchen service area with stainless steel counters. The second set of double doors on the other side of the room are still swinging. I smash through and wind up smacking McCormick into a wheeled table with silverware on it.

"Hey, what the—you?"

"You don't talk to her."

"Colton." Skye's next to me. "It's okay."

"It's arright." McCormick straightens his sleeves. "You're jist outte yer depth agin."

He's got a decade or so in the business on me. He loved patting me on the head and telling me to run and play. He can't insult me with that anymore. Not when Skye's at stake.

"The next time you want to speak to her, I'm there," I say.

"Colton." Skye's right in front of me, pushing me back. I could mow her down the same way I almost ran right over Tamika, but her voice cuts through the rage. "It wasn't anything."

I could look at her, but once I do, the fight's going right out of me. "Did you hear me, asshole?"

"Aye, the entire kitchen 'eard ye."

"And you don't touch her." I'm pushing at Skye, trying to get over her without hurting her, but she has her arms around my waist now.

"He wanted me to listen to something where it was quieter," she says.

"I bet he did."

Tamika's voice comes from behind me. "My God, you're both so cute when you're drunk on testosterone." She comes between us, but to the side so she's not in my way if I decide to launch.

"Oh my God," Skye whispers, grabbing my jacket lapels. "Is that…?"

"Tamika, baby." McCormick reaches for her, jutting his head forward for a kiss on her cheek. She holds him back by the shoulder. "I didnae know you'd be 'ere."

"I should let him tear you apart." She points at me while

she speaks to him. "Don't tell me you didn't know what you were doing."

"It *is* her," Skye squeaks into my chest.

I put my arm around her shoulder to keep her close. She calms me. I kiss her face and bury my nose in her hair.

"I'm sorry," I whisper. "I know I'm losing you but not tonight."

"Dinna you hear? The whole thing was fake."

"You and I were fake, Gav." Tamika points at Skye and me. "But this? Does this look fake?"

I look up from Skye's hair at the two people who ruined my life. In the fluorescent light, McCormick looks like a mannequin in a suit, not the heat-seeking missile I thought of him as. And Tamika... well, she's Tamika. She looks however she wants to look. I never had any hope of containing her.

"Could be fake," Gavin says. "Maybe."

I have the same chance of containment with Skye, who pushes me away to face them.

"It's not fake, okay? Nothing about this is fake. I love him. I love him so much I don't know how I fit it all inside myself, and I don't know how I'm ever, ever going to stop."

She looks shocked by what she just said. At least as shocked as I am.

She runs out.

29

SKYE

My doubts are real. They exist and I've earned them. I'm not giving them up just because he's behind me, calling my name, and I'm not stopping, except that my feet hurt and I want to sit while I cry.

So I run into the bathroom like a baby, thinking he won't follow me in the ladies' room.

Of course I'm wrong.

He snaps the bolt on the door, muting those doubts.

"Leave me alone!"

"You sure?" He takes half a step toward me in his black sneakers.

"No. I'm not sure about anything."

He lays his hand on each side of my jaw as if he wants me to stay still when he kisses me. I won't object to the touch. I won't move. With his lips on mine, the way his tongue pries between my teeth, and the strokes down my neck, I can almost forget this is different. I've said things I haven't even let myself think.

"Me neither." He speaks into my mouth because we can't stop kissing. It's physically impossible.

"I'm sorry." I put my hand on his chest and grab his shirt, drawing him closer.

"Don't be."

He lifts me onto the vanity, kissing my neck, my face, my ear. My legs wrap around him and pull him into me. He sucks in a breath and grinds forward. I don't know what I'm doing. A million reasons to stop fight for attention, but not a single one gets through. All I can focus on is the flood of urgency between my legs.

I open his belt. He pushes up my dress. We can't get at each other fast enough. Unzipping, unsnapping, pushing past yards and miles of fabric, he gets to my underwear and drives his fingers through the lace, shredding it. Two fingers slide right in. I gasp. My mouth stays open as a silent, blinding shout runs through me.

"Fuck." He curses with surrender and a little awe, removing his fingers and pulling me forward so he can get his cock inside me. "Oh, Jesus."

"Wait."

He pulls out, eyes half closed. I kiss his cheek while he comes onto the corner of the vanity.

We laugh together.

"That was almost—" I start.

"—really stupid. But just for a second it felt—"

"—really good."

"Yeah." He pushes me back. "I'm not done with you."

He opens my legs and dips down to get between them. He kisses lightly, then probes with his tongue, spreading me apart with gentle fingers. I arch. The chandelier above is too much for a bathroom, but it's as perfect as his mouth.

"Look at me." He puts two fingers to his eyes, pulling my underwear to my knees with his other hand.

I can't imagine looking away. Eyes on mine, the bottom half of his face disappears between my legs to flick my clit with his tongue. He runs it along me, top to bottom, and back up again, ending with a suck that takes my breath away. My arms flail, knocking over a pile of cloth napkins. The bottom half of my body is coming loose. I grab for something to keep myself steady as his mouth works me, finding the faucet. Its motion sensor turns it on. I don't care. I grab it harder as his tongue flicks my clit, then licks it, then flicks again.

"Look at me when you come, Skittles."

My agreement is a little whine. It's a promise I'm sure I can keep until he licks me with the flat of his tongue, then sucks hard, moving his head as if he's devouring me. Hands on either side of me, grabbing at anything, I turn on both faucets.

The door shakes.

"I'm coming!"

My hips rise into him and my eyes want to close so badly, but I watch him between my legs, eye to eye, as promised, trying to call to God but only making little squeaky sounds when I climax.

The door shakes again. I sit straight. His dick's already in his pants.

"Hold on." He snaps up a cloth towel from the floor and runs it under hot water. "They can wait."

He wrings it and cleans the counter he came on, then helps me to stand. I grab the rest of the towels and put them back on the vanity. We're a well-oiled machine.

"Ready?" he asks when I'm tucking my hair back in the clip.

"No, but yes."

He opens the door. No one's there. He steps to the side and lets me out first.

Back in the world, all the reasons I ran into the bathroom in the first place come back.

30

COLTON

I love fucking this girl. I could fuck her every day. I could make her come, towel her off, slide her underpants back up, pat the creases out of her dress every day for months. Maybe even years.

So of course, when we're face to face in the hall, I expect her to have some kind of post-fuck glow. But she doesn't. She's making an eleven up there. Even when she smiles, the lines are hard to miss.

"Hang on." I lick my thumb and rub the 11 as if there's a spot between her eyebrows.

"What is it?" She touches her face and starts back for the bathroom mirror, but I stop her.

"You got something on your mind and I'm trying to get it off. Hold still."

When I rub her forehead again, she laughs. So I guess it works on some level, but not really. The goal wasn't a second of escape, but real relief.

"We should go back," she says. "I don't want your parents to think you pulled me into a public bathroom for a quickie."

"You kidding? My mother would throw a fucking party. For real. And you think I can party? She brings down the house."

"Because you're having a quickie?"

"Because I'm with you. She's likes you."

"She doesn't even know me."

"No, I know, but she does." I regret starting this conversation because I don't want her to think this is a big deal and I can't tell it without saying that to my mother, it's only exactly the biggest deal.

"What did she say to you?"

"Nothing." As we come to the lobby, a smaller service bar comes into view. "You thirsty?"

"She said, 'I like her' after I defended American cars or after I didn't wait to introduce myself to your father?"

"Not exactly." We get to the makeshift bar which has a row of short glasses full of drink garnishes. I pull out my last twenty. "What do you want?"

"Coke, please."

The bartender waves away the twenty. "It's an open bar, sir."

I put it in his hand and take the cup of olives from between the onions and the lemons. "Two Cokes." I put the olive glass between Skye and me. "Have some."

"They have peanuts." She takes one anyway.

"Here's the thing." I pop two to give myself a second to frame this in a way that isn't terrifying, but I'm not good at reframing shit on the fly, so she's going to have to deal with it.

Our Cokes come. The bartender walks away to wipe down glasses at the other end of the bar.

"Go ahead," she says. I should kiss her to change the subject. But as if I know her already, I can tell she's not open to it.

"All right." I say it as if I'm ready to launch into the explanation, but what I'm really doing is stalling. "So she's funny. She has this thing. She calls it the 'tingle,' and basically, it means she has a good *feeling* about a person."

"And she had a tingle about me?" Skye squeezes a lemon into her Coke.

"Yeah."

This is going fine. It's a three-olive pop-pop-pop kinda feeling. Skye sips her Coke through the stirring straw. Her lipstick is fresh, and she looks perfectly put together, but a strand of hair escaped when we went at it and never got put back. I could do it, but no one's watching and we're not alone enough to fuck. That kind of intermediate-level affection is probably out of bounds right now.

"So. Okay." She puts her drink down half empty. "That's what your dad meant by having 'a little tingle in my touch'?"

"Yeah. She gets the tingle sometimes when we bring a girl around." I shrug and tuck the straw behind my finger so I can feel the ice tap my upper lip when I drink. "Maybe a guy, but it's never happened for a guy."

"Does she tingle for every person you have over?"

"No." I shake my glass and drain it down to the ice.

"Is it good or bad?"

"Generally good." I line up my glass with the wet ring of the napkin.

"If she doesn't tingle, does that say something about the person like... they're an asshole?"

"No, it's not like that. It's just... hard to explain."

"Okay, but I'm not really dying to go back into that crowded room, so take your time."

I can't tell if she's trying to corner me or if she's doing it by accident, but the result is the same. I shrug, but that doesn't make me feel less trapped into telling her. Doesn't make me not care about scaring her away either.

"Gotta say, I think it's the Parkinson's talking," I say.

"It's not the same as Alzheimer's, you dork."

"No, no, I know. She has, like, her facilities. But... fuck." I take a bunch of olives in my fist and dispense them one by one. "She's seeing what she wants to see, you know. Because one day the disease is going to do what it does, and that's the end, and knowing I'm with the"—I pop the last olive to air quote—"the 'right' one will—"

"Whoa, there. I'm the 'right' one?"

"It's not real, Skittles."

"The tingle is, like, I'm your forever thing? But you told her we were fake. I was right there."

"What can I tell you? It's not up to me how she feels."

"You're right." Skye picks up her Coke and uses the straw to drain it down to the crushed ice. She shakes it to get another drop before putting it down. "Look, you heard what I said. I broke another rule. I have feelings." She doesn't even look at me when she says it. "But I don't want you to worry about that. I'm still leaving."

"Why?"

"I promised. Do I want to go? No, I don't, but I keep my promises."

"What if I felt the same way? What if I loved you?"

"Don't love me, Colton. That makes it harder."

"Well, too fucking late."

Why am I angry? She loves me. I love her. Nothing else has changed.

She sighs. "I don't think we should see each other again. It's too... it's intense. And it's just going to make things confusing for me."

She has to stay, and all she's doing is leaving. It's getting worse. It's an avalanche of bad and I'm at the bottom of the mountain, trying to hold it all up.

"For you? You're the one who's friends with all your exes."

"We're friends. It's just..." She's trying to make sense of something that makes no fucking sense. Or she doesn't want to say some even more hurtful thing.

I don't have time to watch her figure out which one. I fucking love her.

"It's just, fuck you, Skye. Really, bottom of my heart. Fuck you. It's one thing to run away from a city because shit's not going your way. But you're running away from me, and I never did anything but fall in love with you." I can't believe the words coming out of my mouth. The love part, yeah. And the fuck you part. And also the part that's halfway out before it's proofread. "You know what? I'm sorry, that was... not me. It's cool. It's fine. You and me. We're good. You do what you have to do."

It's not good, or fine, or cool. But I don't know what else to say, and I don't know what else to do but pop an olive in my mouth and shrug.

"You sure?" she says.

"Yeah. Life happens. And I shouldn't've talked to you like that." All nervous energy, I pick up my glass just to shake the ice at the bottom so I don't have to look at her.

"It's okay."

I put down the glass. "We should split."

31

FOUR DAYS LATER

SKYE

The dry cleaner hands me the dress. I hang it in my car and stare out the windshield.

My chest has been tight all week. The low hum of anxiety's just waiting to turn into a sonic boom. My brain's been looping the constant refrains of *I'm fine* and *It's okay* and *You're doing great!*

I want Colton. I want to know what he's doing right now, and ten minutes ago, and last night. If he's going to parties and laughing with his friends, I want to feel bad that he doesn't miss me. If he's heartbroken, I want to feel a little better at not being the only one.

Mostly, I want to talk to him so he can call me Skittles and I can soothe this pain behind my ribs. But I can't. It's not right to lead him on if I'm leaving. If he wants to talk to me, he'll call, but he doesn't.

So, there's that.

This dress still has to go back.

Ella hasn't responded to my texts and her email bounces back an Out of Office notice. She's apparently in Greece. I could drop the dress at the Papillion office Downtown. That would be clean and easy. It won't get lost. I'm sure if I could trust it with the dry cleaner, I can trust it with the office it came from.

But that's all the way Downtown, and I could skirt Dodger Stadium traffic, but traffic is everywhere until eight o'clock even without the game happening. And I have to see Dr. Solomon first, and she's on Wilshire. I wouldn't get to the Downtown office until after hours and someone will probably be there, but maybe not. And where will I put the car? It's not like you can park Downtown at all, ever. No. The only thing to do is to return the dress to her house. Ella may be away, but Colton's still in the back and it's on the way home from Dr. Solomon's.

It's a no-brainer I think about a little too hard.

In the dry cleaner parking lot, with the dress hanging on the back seat hook, I text Colton.

—Hey. What are you doing in the next couple of hours?—

No. He's going to think I'm coming over for sex, which... if it happens that's great, but there's too much pressure. I delete most of the text and retype it.

—Hey. You going to be around at 7pm?—

Too specific. Delete, delete. This isn't such a big deal. If I want a hookup, I should just ask if he'd like to hook up. If I want to drop the dress and leave, there's no reason I shouldn't say that.

What do you want, Skye? The question comes into my brain in Dr. Solomon's voice.

What do I want?

My life is now a series of achievable goals, but what do I want right now? Really want? If I'm being as honest with myself as I try to be with everyone else, I have to admit that I want to spend every minute of the next few days in bed with Colton Crowne, and I don't want that to scare him away.

I decide to start simple and see where the conversation takes us.

—You around?—

That's not scary. I guess he could assume I'm in some kind of emergency, but when he answers, I'll just say I'm fine. I'll gauge and assuage.

After I hit *Send*, I put the phone away and drive to Dr. Solomon's.

I park the car ten minutes before my appointment. I look at my phone. No answer.

I give it three more minutes.

Nothing.

Pulling the dress off of the back seat hook, I go up to the office and sit in the waiting room. When Dr. Solomon calls me in at the split second when my appointment starts, Colton still hasn't answered. I shut off the notifications.

Whatever.

What-the-fucking-fuck-ever.

I pull up the dry cleaning plastic to show Dr. Solomon the dress.

"Oh, I bet you looked wonderful in that." She touches the fabric. "Feels nice too."

"And it fit like it was made for me." I yank down the plastic and hang it on the doorframe. "I'm going to hate taking it back, honestly." Sitting in my usual chair, I take a deep breath before speaking. "So, I'm definitely going back to Michigan."

"Really? When?"

"I mean, there's no real reason to wait. If I go now, I can get settled in, make orientation, all that. There's probably time to get an apartment." I softly clap then fold my fingers together. "So, I think this is our last session."

"And do you have any feelings around that?"

"It's fine. Not a big deal."

"Really?"

"Why do you sound so surprised?" I ask.

She shrugs, and it kind of annoys me.

"What's the shrug about?" My voice turns aggressive, and my forehead gets tight. "Forget it. You're not going to explain. No. You're going to deflect it right back at me and I'm going to wind up explaining. So, okay. Fine. One thing I can tell you about shrugging therapists is that it's not a gesture that means 'whatever' or 'I don't care.' It's punctuation... like the period at the end of a sentence, but at the beginning, and it means, 'don't overthink what I'm about to say, but it's really important.' I'd appreciate it if we could just cut out the dance and get to the part where you tell me what you think. Because I can't do this alone, Dr. Solomon. I'm lost." With a burst of energy that makes sitting impossible, I shoot to my feet. "I'm onstage and it's my line, but I don't have the libretto. I don't know the music. Everyone's staring at me, and no one can tell me how this act ends. So if you've read the script, please, don't shrug."

Therapists don't take it personally when you're snappy, but I feel absolutely shitty for talking to her like that.

"I'm sorry." I drop into my chair in self-reproach.

"That's all right. But you know I don't have a script for your life, right?"

"You have to know something about something."

"Skye, what do you want?"

"I want to know what to do!"

"You seemed pretty set on a plan a minute ago."

"Shit!" I bury my face in my hands, because she's right. She sees me and I can't bear to see how right she is. "I did."

"How would you feel if I told you that you didn't have to go? You could stay here as long as you wanted and never go to medical school."

I look up. "I don't think that's true?"

"But before you told yourself a story about what was true, how did you feel?"

I can't think back that far. A few seconds or a few years. Before I told myself that it was impossible to stay because I hadn't fulfilled all the conditions I needed to, I believed what Dr. Solomon told me. I can stay here and have this life instead of the one that I'd run from. I can make some more songs with Colton. Stay in my apartment but maybe, sometimes—if I'm not working—sleep in with him after a night of pretending we're exactly what we are.

Dr. Solomon sees my hesitation and rephrases. "When you gave yourself permission to stay here, how did you react? What was your immediate feeling?"

"Relief."

"Ah." She straightens her skirt. That's her way of giving me a moment to absorb what I just said—that I was relieved. "What's the first thing you'd do if what I said was true? If you could stay here and pursue the career you want?"

"The one I don't have the talent or personality to succeed at?"

"I'm not sure we're talking about the same career, but let's say we are. What's the first thing you'd do?"

"I'd call Colton and tell him it's back on."

"Exactly what's back on, Skye?"

"It."

"The faking? The pretending?"

"No. Not that part."

"So you'd tell him you care about him?"

"I already told him." I clamp my mouth shut, because a denial is a lie, and lying to your therapist is like cheating at solitaire. Instead, I cheat by deflection, looking the other way while I pull an ace from under the stack. "It just doesn't change anything."

"Are you sure?"

"That was the deal. Those were the rules."

"And how many of those rules are meaningful when you broke most of them already?"

At first, I take it as an accusation. How dare I break a promise!

That's my mother's voice and it twists my rib cage like a dish towel.

"I'm fine," I say more to myself than the doctor.

"Skye, are you all right?"

"I am. Give me a second."

I'm fine. But I need to think about this without my

mother's voice telling me I need to be dependable and reliable or my own voice shouting her down.

"I broke my rules with him," I say. "The only one I kept was singing in alto." The unspoken facts behind what I admit I won't admit twist in my chest, tightening it, but there's more to say. "I'm not sure what I feel. I'm not sure if it's about him, or this career I'm fail—am trying."

The tension remains, but it loosens enough to let me think.

"Can you separate the two? Step back and look at what it is?"

"Yes, but in the end, it doesn't matter. He's going to stay here. He's fine. We'll be friends."

"Going to be really hard from Michigan."

I cross my arms to guard against the truth. It doesn't work.

———————

My phone stays silent in my pocket until I'm sitting in the car, ready to go. When I plug it into the charger, the screen lights up.

Colton called while I was in the office. He didn't text. He voice called. Well. Okay, then.

Since I'm parked, I might as well voice call back. Right? Or is that going to surprise him? No one just calls. That's weird. But he called me. But that was an hour ago and I sent a text first. He must want to talk if—

No. Stop.

It's dumb that I'm thinking about this so much. I put myself through a lot, but I've never put myself through this particular mental hell before. It's garbage and I hate hurting myself with it, so I just call him.

On the second ring, the call connects. I hear people. Laughter. Music.

I'm interrupting him at a party or something. Shit. This shouldn't suck, but it does.

"Skittles, hey." His *hey* is warm and inviting, even pleasantly surprised that I called.

"Hi, um, if it's a bad time?"

"No, it's fine." With the click of a door, the background noise cuts out. "I just had some people over for the game."

"Yeah. The Dodgers. There's traffic."

"Yeah."

"I didn't know you cared about baseball."

"I mean, they could clinch tonight." That's obvious to anyone who lives here, I guess, which I don't. "So. What's up? What are you doing?"

"I was just out running some errands."

"To leave?"

"Yeah."

"When are you going?"

"I'm heading out Friday, I think."

"Going east? There's a lot of traffic to Vegas," he says.

"Oh."

"Yeah."

"But anyway." I clear my throat. "I wanted to bring the dress back, but I can come tomorrow."

"All right."

"Okay, then."

That's that. It's fine. It doesn't matter if I return the dress today or tomorrow. Or if I see him, which I have to admit to myself I was looking forward to.

"You can come now if you want."

What do you want, Skye?

"Sure. If that's all right."

"Yeah, it's all right. You can stay and watch the game. Jab and Halley are here. You can say goodbye to them if you want."

I don't want to say goodbye to anyone, and that's the problem.

32

COLTON

Sitting on the edge of the orange couch, I hang up the phone and stare at it for a second in a beer-haze.

When I told Ella I was having people over to watch the game, did I say how many? That was almost a week ago, as she was out the door to the airport. It's all a fog. I've talked to a few friends since. I said they could bring someone or a couple of someones. I did more inviting than I thought, and by the time the Dodgers get their fifth run, the kitchen counters are piled with tumbling-over party trays, the fridge is full of beer, and now I could be a liar.

I can manage that with a mop and a few extra trash bags.

But I told Skye the same story I told Logan because it sounded better. Like responsible-guy better. The guy who's a loser for reasons that aren't so apparent. Now that she's coming, I'm a little concerned about what she's going to see.

I have no idea what she expects, but for the guy throwing the whatever-I-called-it, there are more people here than I expected.

Right. So what do I want, again?

I want to not feel like this. It's weird. It's uncomfortable. She'll think things or she won't. Who the fuck cares?

This could be the last time I see her, and I want it to be under better circumstances. That's what I want. A controlled environment.

This is still my house, and she's cool. It's all right. Maybe we can slip away for another last fuck.

That's the plan. Good. Done. I cross from the garage into the kitchen, locking the studio door behind me. I don't want any of these people in the studio. The sun's not even down all the way and it's already a little rowdy in here.

Back in the living room, cheers roll up. Pelton caught Huang looking and retired the side.

"We're gonna clinch this thing," I say, taking another pull of beer.

Logan gave me his old TV. It's so huge it goes over the doorway molding, and it's so clear a guy could convince himself he could walk though it and get transported to Elysian Park. I may not have a lot of money, but I have a lot of stuff money can buy.

"It's the second inning," Terrill says as though being a downer is his only job.

"Already up by four."

"Can they hold it is the question."

"Can you hold my dick?" Carmy shoots back.

These masters of deductive logic attended some of the most elite private schools in the country and make more money in a week than most people see in a lifetime. They're going to embarrass me in front of Skye.

"You coming to my skybox Friday?" Rog swings his arm

over the couch to face me. He means his father's skybox, but he's with a girl, so it's his now.

"Can't. I have a thing." I don't have a thing, but that's the day Skye's leaving and maybe she'll ask me to see her off.

He shakes his head, pulls his arm back, and turns to the Sprint commercial.

Outside, there's a splash and laughing. The party's spilled out into the pool. I'll probably need to do a stealth skim and chlorine shock.

Giving a shit whether Skye has an opinion of this shitshow? That's crept back up my spine like an itsy-bitsy spider after a rainstorm. She'll go home thinking she dodged a bullet. She'll remember me as a good fuck with a conga line of crumbs along the crease in the sofa cushion. She'll remember this damn chaos and think… why do I care what she thinks?

"Jason!" I yell from the living room. "Where do you live, fucker?"

Jason stands with his empty bottle over the garbage pail.

"In Agoura Hills, why?" He drops it.

"No." I walk over the couch, between Rog and Carmy, and step over the back. "Right now, you're in el-fucking-aye. Get that bottle out of there and put it in the recycling, you lazy shitbag." Affectionately, I swat him in the back of the head.

"What's with you, man?" Jason pulls out the bottle.

"Grab a couple more while you're in there."

I feel a tap at my shoulder. Turn. More people.

"Hey. Wesley!" I put down my beer to snap-shake my friend from high school.

He introduces me to his girlfriend, Gina. My beer's one of many in the garden of drinks on the table. I have no idea which one has my spit on the end.

Growing up, I had everything. Now, the loss of a beer feels like driving my Porsche into the Silver Lake Reservoir. Which didn't happen like that. I wasn't driving.

A splash from outside brings me to the pool. It's dark now. Jab and Halley are chilling on the couches, under a cloud, with a few of his finance crew. It smells like a cannabis dispensary out here. Number jockeys party really fucking hard.

Kelly's at the center of the waves, naked body lit by the underwater lighting. Jellybean's on the end of the diving board, also naked, pussy shaved smooth as an egg.

"Colton!" she calls. "I can do a flip!"

From the living room, a cheer goes up from the crew who came here for the game.

"She can't even," Kelly says.

"Just don't piss in—"

Jellybean jumps, turns midair, and lands flat on her back.

"—the pool."

She comes up laughing. "Ow, that fucking hurt!" Still laughing.

She's fine. It's fine.

Everything's going to be fine.

Is it only the fifth inning?

Of course it's going to be fine. It's always fine.

I left the driveway gate open so people can just come back, and I'm about to sit with Jab where I can keep an eye on the gate to intercept Skye.

"Colton's going to help me get out of accounting," Halley says to one of her friends. "My own personal savior."

"Give it a rest, Hale," I say. "I pity the guy who tries to save you."

Jab laughs and we click bottles, but half my attention's on the gate.

"I love you anyway, little man." She leans into me for a side hug.

"I happen to be medium-sized, statistically."

Jellybean splashes out of the pool, still laughing, as Skye finally comes down the driveway. She's not more than a shadow of a woman carrying a garment bag in the garage lights.

"Hey, is that Skye?" Halley cries. "Hey, honey, over here!"

I rush over to Skye, wiping sweaty palms on my pants.

"Hey," I say.

The game's been turned up to blasting so it can be heard over the music I never said anyone could start. A bottle drops somewhere. Jab bellows a laugh. I wish I could turn down the volume on all of it. I don't care that I live in a frat house right now, but I kind of do. A lot. I just don't know why.

"Hey," she says. "I didn't know this was a whole party."

She's dressed to run errands. Jeans. Keds. A shirt with froufy sleeves. My back's to the pool, but I can smell the funk of Jab's smoke and hear the splash of another naked girl going into water.

Fuck. I care. I don't want Skye here right now, and wherever else I want her to be, I want to be there.

"They still winning?" she asks.

"Of course. That's all they know how to do."

A cloud of boos come from inside with a bright bolt of "fuck you, Dan Dropper!"

"Oh," I say. "You mean the game? I have no idea, but I guess Dan Topper just dropped the ball."

Skye smiles and I can't take my eyes off her. Maybe it's

the beer. Maybe it's me, here, with all these guests who—besides a few—don't mean much to me and who act as though they don't give a shit about anything.

With that smile, Skye sees me—the reckless and irresponsible side I've hidden—and reveals herself. This is who she is. Vulnerable, smiling through it, and as magnetic as a neutron star. Under the anxiety and the need to make herself small, she's a thousand watts of light, and I'm a moth hurtling myself into her light.

If she keeps smiling like this, she's going to hold the world in her hands.

"I didn't see it," I say.

"See what?"

I need my beer. I need to think. I need a piece of her so badly I'm like a starving man grabbing for a sandwich.

"Colton!" a voice sings from the patio. It's Kelly in a pink robe she got from the pool house. I'm sure it belongs to my sister-in-law. She's holding a pitcher in one hand and a stack of red Solo cups in the other. "You have that lime tree." She walks forward, bare feet on the stone, referring to my brother's tree. I got nothing, least of all a place to put a tree. "And there was mint growing under the fence. Minnie made mojitos. Is that okay?"

It's a little late for permission, but whatever.

"Sure."

"You guys want some?" She comes closer, robe opening. "She makes, like, the absolute best."

I stall, waiting to see if Skye shows any sign of... anything. She doesn't. At least nothing bad, until she speaks.

"No, thanks," she says. "I'm not staying."

She's leaving. She already said she came to drop off the dress, because she has to pack up her life and go, and I want her out of this disaster, but getting what I want is worse than not getting it.

"We're good," I tell Kelly, who trots back to the patio with the pitcher and cups.

"Wow," Skye says when the half-naked girl in the pink robe is out of earshot.

"Wow, what?" Why am I asking when there's a naked girl on the diving board and the smell of pot and how many beers have I had? I clear my throat and focus on the most obvious thing. "That's just... Kelly and Jellybean."

"Yeah. I guess it's one thing to hear about your parties. Being here is another."

"You want to come in and stay for the whole experience?"

Say no.

Say yes.

"It looks like fun." She looks at the patio couches.

Halley waves to her. She waves back. Fuck. This is bad. If she stays, I'm going to want to kick everyone out.

"But..." Skye turns back to me, and I'm crushed that she's about to tell me she's leaving. "I don't think... me and parties... the people. When there are a lot... I get... that way." She puts her hand on her chest.

I was bound to lose no matter what she did.

"Right." There's no word for the feeling of being disappointed and relieved at the same time... probably because it's not fucking normal.

"If I could make a pit stop, though?" She crosses her ankles and bends her knees, making an "emergency" face.

I'm about to tell her to just go, she knows the guest house as well as anyone, but the little frosted bathroom window is lit and shadows move against the ceiling. Either someone's rowing a boat in there or she's going to walk in on a cheap porno.

"The one in the big house is cleaner." Not a lie, if you think about it, because Logan and Ella's house is always in better shape. Actually, this works out fine. She'll be away from the crowd and I'll have a minute with her. "Here." I hold out my hand for the garment bag. "I'll take that."

She hands it over in a way that ensures our fingers don't touch, which is one hundred percent fine.

I lead her past the garden, the patio for the big house, and inside. The kitchen is lit above the counters for late-night trips downstairs. I slide the glass door closed behind her, shutting out the noise from the party.

"Wow." She looks around, up and down, as if she's thinking of buying the place. "It's nice."

"It is." I point through the coat room. "Just around that way."

33

SKYE

Colton told me he was having a few friends over. I don't know what I expected, but it wasn't this many. And it's not as if they're all milling around, overdressed, looking at their watches. These people are comfortable here with him. They make drinks in his kitchen out of fruit picked from his tree and wild herbs from under his fence.

If I invited all of my friends over, they'd fit in the kitchen. Maybe I could scrape together another handful, but they'd be true guests who came on time and left before it got too late.

The guy in my courtyard, putting dumplings on my plate with chopsticks, the rule-maker and rule-breaker, the ears and mind who could make me sound better than I thought possible isn't Colton. He's not the genius at the smart-kid school. He ran from that for a reason.

He's a man who can bring people to him.

LIVE FREE

Everything. Now.

He put those words on his body because he meant them. I

met him in a space where he was trying so hard to be different, but he's failed to change. This party is who he is.

In the deepest, darkest corner of my heart, I envy him. The rest of my heart is just wistful. I like the way he's been with me in the studio, in bed, everywhere. I came here for more of it, but the guy I love isn't the whole story.

This Colton, talking to a half-naked woman hoisting a pitcher of mojitos? Inviting so much uninhibited joy into his home? I don't love this guy in the same way.

I love him more.

Then he takes the garment bag, and he's as tangible as he's always been, but bigger somehow. As if the only way someone so huge could appear so human-sized is to be miles away.

Sure, I can love him. But he exists on a planet I can only see through a telescope.

Why would he love me?

He points me toward a bathroom situated right off the mudroom. There's a little nightlight over the sink, making it easy to find my way in the dark. When I close the bathroom door, I lean against it and breathe. The sounds of the party come through the little window. The mirror's right in front of me. I flick on the light. My clothes are in place. My hair is behaving, and my skin is clear.

I've always believed I'm pretty and the reflection doesn't change that, but pretty doesn't mean anything. I need to be more dynamic if I want to stay in Los Angeles—like Mojito Kelly with the open pink robe, and Halley from accounting, and especially Colton. Tender and respectful Colton, the secret genius who's not as careless with my heart or body as he is with his own life. I need the natural, inborn power they walk around with every day, and I don't have it.

I do my business and wash my hands. The bathroom off the mudroom in my parents' house is beige with a white toilet and sink. Not like Logan and Ella Crowne's. Three walls are covered in a sepia-green-blue wallpaper of old-timey fashion magazines. The last wall is the darkest version of sepia-green-blue in the print the same color as the embroidery in the linen hand towels, which are the same deep chartreuse as the curtains and every fifth matte tile in the floor. The shower has a thick glass door, and the sink counter is dark blue stone finished to the texture of baby powder. It works. If I tell myself what it is, it's terrible, but when I look at it, it works.

Who takes this kind of care with the bathroom off the mudroom?

The house my parents raised me in is really nice, with all new things and a handful of people to keep it clean, but it's not this daringly tasteful.

It's a deep blue confirmation that I just don't belong here.

Colton's leaning on the kitchen sink, poking and swiping at his phone in the dark.

"Thanks," I say.

"Cool." He puts away his phone but doesn't move a muscle to show me out.

"We should." I make a clicking noise with my tongue against my teeth and jerk both thumbs outside.

"Nah."

"Nah?"

"I want to talk to you."

"Okay." I lean on the counter across from him, arms crossed loosely over my waist.

"You shouldn't go."

I sigh and look away. The refrigerator has two side-by-side doors. Between them, a narrow glass door reveals tilted wine bottles. I've never seen that before.

"I probably should," I say.

"Listen. Hear me out. You stay, we pursue labels. Maybe do another couple of songs."

"How many years am I supposed to put it off? My graduation money's gone."

"Hey, for real, I know how that feels. We'll figure it out."

We.

He's got to be kidding me. Mr. Popularity. The captain of Team Party with the backward cap, the rich family, and the IQ hiding behind douchebag lingo isn't going to take time out of his life to figure out my life when he can't figure out his own.

"Colton, you don't understand."

"I do." He puts his hands on my arms and I like it, but I also I wish he wouldn't. "I know what it's like to have family pressure. I know what it's like to want to run away."

"You came back." I don't mean to growl, but his comparison sucks.

"I did." He squeezes my shoulders. "But you don't have to. Skye, you're so good. Don't give up."

"I'm not giving up." I shrug his hands off me. "I'll graduate. Do community theater. Sing at birthday parties. I'll go around the neighborhood and sing fucking Christmas carols on doorsteps with my mother. Once in a while I'll go into Detroit to a show, with a few hundred or a thousand people staring at one person, just to remind myself why I couldn't cut it. And that will be my life. Eventually, I'll forget this was even a thing. It won't feel like giving up. This entire city will just be something I did."

"Nah." He shakes his head. "Nah-nah that's bullshit. You're staying."

"I don't feel safe here!" My shout forces him to lean back. I don't want to scare him. "I mean I feel safe with you. When I'm with you, it's like... I'm home and I belong... but I know this thing..." I move my hands between us. "It's not real for you." He starts to say something, and I can't bear the vulnerability of what I haven't said. "Or me. There are feelings, but look, it was a casual thing for both of us. So that's fine, but I can't depend on you."

He steps back against the counter as if I slapped him.

Was that a terrible thing to say? Does terribleness make it less true?

The party seems to have gotten louder, or maybe the kitchen's gotten that much quieter.

"Fine," he says, finally. "You want to make a mistake so bad? Go for it."

That's it. I should walk out. I don't.

He can't go before me because it's his brother's house. So. I should leave. I can't.

"I want..." I drift off. "I want to stay friends."

"Who said we wouldn't be?"

"No one."

"Okay."

"Okay. But I feel like I hurt your feelings."

"Nah." He waves off the suggestion that I have any power to do that. "We're cool." He holds out his arm to guide me out. "Come on. Let me go see what they're doing to my house."

I go outside ahead of him and wait while he slides the door closed. He has to go straight to get to his party. I have to go left to get to my car.

"Okay, so," I say. "I'll see you around."

"Call me if you need anything."

"I will." How can I say that and mean it? I just told him I couldn't trust him. "I'm sorry I said that. About not being able to depend on you."

"I know what you meant, and gotta say, you're not wrong."

"You've been very dependable."

"It is what it is." He backs up toward the pool. "I'll see you around."

He spins on his heel and heads to the house, hands in his jean pockets. I watch him, memorizing the way he walks with such a slouch and such confidence.

When he turns his back on me and walks to his friends, he dislodges a feeling I didn't know was inside me, leaving a narrow, endless hole. I feel empty. Floating in space with nothing but my own thoughts. I have never felt so lonely in my life.

We aren't leaving it like this. He's not turning his back on me as if he's not going to think about me again. I can't accept the isolation of being cut off from him.

Rushing forward, I get to him in the center of the patio—before he's close enough to talk to anyone but too late to get him alone—and grab his shoulder. He turns around, leaving his party in the background.

"Just say it," I demand.

"Say what?"

"What you're not saying because it's too hurtful or too vulnerable. Whatever it is. Just say it."

He presses his lips tightly, shakes his head, looks back at the party, then at me, as if he's battling to not say what I need him to. In the end, he loses and speaks every word as if he wants to take it back as soon as it comes out of his mouth. "You are so. Fucking. Blind."

"Okay. Go ahead."

"You push for something. You leave home to get it. You get this close, and the closer you get, the more you want to run. And don't point at me like I did the same thing, cos I didn't. I really, really fucking failed big before I gave up. You're not even close to how in the shitter I was. And look..." He twists his whole body without moving his feet to present his brother's guest house, and his voice goes up. "I'm doing it again. I have an entire rager going because I need to paint myself into a corner. It's win or die trying. And yeah, that's a problem. But you. You want to lose. Even when it's easy, you can't handle winning."

Halley and Jab are behind him. And Jellybean. Rog. There are so many eyes. Everyone's looking at me. Strangers, all with their own agenda.

Not just strangers. Friends of Colton, who's angry at me. Publicly, in front of them, and no one here wants to know my side of it. They're squeezing my heart into a pebble. I can't breathe. I clutch for the Garfield Pez, describing the familiar forms to myself, the click of the raised letters under my fingernail.

It isn't mine. It's his, and they all know it.

I can't break down in front of all these strangers. I will die. I can't imagine a life after that.

I drop the Pez and run down the driveway. My car is parked so far away.

"Skye!"

No. He's chasing me, and I won't be caught. Not this time. I'm not going to sit in the driver's seat without going anywhere. I'm going to start the car and leave before he can say a word.

I open the car door without looking at him. Get in. Start it, flooding him in the headlights. He's stopped because he thinks I'm just going to sit here and do mindfulness exercises.

Not today. I take off, leaving him behind, and I don't stop until I'm home.

It's not until I realize Fátima isn't in the apartment that the loneliness turns to devastation. My stuff's in boxes. I barely live here anymore. These rooms are the furthest thing from home.

34

COLTON

How the fuck did this happen?

How did I end up with a backyard full of people and Skye walking away mad? Not just walking away, but packing up and staying away with a belief that she doesn't matter here?

The beer's through my system. I'm a little nauseated, but sober. Crystal clear actually.

This party isn't any fun.

"Hey, man," Jab says on the approach. "You all right? That was—"

I walk right by him and stand on the patio table.

"Everybody!" I shout once, then again, finally doing a two-fingered whistle. The music goes off. The TV inside stays on to the game. "Listen up!" I yell to get the attention of the last few stragglers. "Party's over. Get. The. Fuck. Out."

They seem baffled. As though they heard me say words in the English language but can't figure out what they mean.

"Get your shit and go! Please."

Please must be the key to unlock minds, because Jellybean puts down her drink and Kelly blows me a kiss.

"You all right, bro?" Carmy asks.

I jump off the table. "I'm fine," I reply to him, then make a broader statement. "I'm fine, just… you gotta clear out."

Jab holds up his hands. "You all heard the man." Then he looks down at me. "I'll take care of this."

I decide to let him do what he says he's going to, because I don't want to talk to anyone right now. I don't want to make excuses, and more than anything I ever didn't want, I don't want to explain myself.

Passing through a confused group of baseball fans and their many friends, I cross the kitchen and go into the garage. The studio is always off-limits, so once the door is closed, it's quiet. It's just me, my second-hand furniture, and all the equipment I kept. I could have sold it and stayed away from LA another few months. Instead, I kept it and came home broke. I could have stayed with Tamika instead of mixing up business and love.

With my back against the door, I slide down to a crouch. The sound studio is dark. The board is covered. The standing lamp doesn't light more than its little corner. This is everything I have.

Getting my feet from under me, I sit with my back to the door.

Selling the equipment would have meant no Skye.

Staying away from LA? No Skye.

Tamika in my life would have left no room for Skye.

If I'd sold it all, stayed with the superstar and come home with a hundred grand in my pocket, Skye wouldn't have come into my life. I wouldn't have needed the money or the place to stay. But then… no Skye.

And now what? All those choices led me to her, and here I am without Skye.

Was I a loser after all those mistakes and miscalculations? Or am I a loser now—throwing away what those failures gained me?

I put on Ella Fitzgerald and lie on the orange couch, listening to her comfort in three vocal ranges, wondering what Skye could have done, given the chance to explore the octaves between who she is and who I told her she was.

Before the light rap on the door, I barely notice the sounds of the party diminishing on the other side of the wall. They're nearly gone now.

"You in there?" It's Jab.

"Yeah, come on in. It's unlocked."

He enters, looks around, settles back on me. "It's just me and Halley."

"Thanks, man." I sit up. "I appreciate it."

"It was fun." He sits in the green chair across from me. "And my girl takes no shit." He laughs to himself, shaking his head. "When she says leave, you get the fuck out."

"Jabari, I don't think I'm going to be able to work with her."

He nods, looks around, knee bouncing. "Had a feeling."

"It's not..." I stop myself from a variation of the classic, *It's not you, it's me.* Jab and Halley deserve better than that. "Skye's going back to Michigan. I can't stop her, so I'm going there to be with her."

"Skye? The girl you just yelled at in front of everybody?"

"Yeah. Maybe I can fit in a few songs with Halley before Logan finds out I had people over."

From the doorway, Halley says, "I won't be shoved in a time pocket like a leprechaun."

"He's medium-sized," Jab objects.

"That's not what I meant, Hale," I say as she comes into the room.

"Did I say I was offended?" She sits in the other green chair.

"It's me that was offended," her boyfriend says.

"Look." I lean forward toward her. "I know you trust me, but there are more reliable producers who'd love to work with you. Between this asshole and me"—I jerk my thumb toward Jab—"we know enough people to get you someone really good. Really committed."

"Mm-hm." She looks at Jab, then me. "Maybe you're right. You do lack commitment."

"I lack... what?"

"The way you left it all to Eugene Testarossa?" She says his name as I've been asking a child to do a man's job. "You know he's not going to chase her down until someone else is bidding for her. And if Liam can't pull that off, you could make some calls. But you didn't."

"Where were you last week when I needed that advice?"

"Sitting in accounting, watching him and Brian Milpas bid up some rock band from Idaho."

"Who got them?" Jab asks while I flop back on the couch in defeat.

"Victor Wallace."

"Allybird Records, Victor Wallace?"

"Same. Swooped in at the last minute. Him and Geraldine Krause. It was a feeding frenzy. The entire neighborhood was on the phone."

The neighborhood isn't geographic. It's just *around*, and if I put my head to it, we know far more industry people than we can count. I really could have done more, but I felt like too much of a loser to try.

"Too late now." I get up to change the record. Ella Fitzgerald is finished. The needle hisses and pops against the center label. "She's leaving any day now. And I fucked up. I'm lucky if she lets me follow her around like a puppy."

"Colton Crowne," Halley scolds. She's twisted around with her arm over the back of the chair. "What is wrong with you? Why are you giving up?"

"I'm not giving up on her. I'm giving up on staying here."

"Did she even ask you to follow her to..." Halley turns to Jab. "Where is it, babe?"

"Michigan."

"She wouldn't." I put on a Tom Waits record. "She hates it there."

Halley spins to Jab while pointing at me. "This is the most dehydrated motherfucking horse I have ever led to water."

Jab laughs.

She turns back to me. "Throw her a fucking party, you dumb fuck. Invite everyone. Your lab partner at Mirman. Your old neighbors from Malibu. Your parents' friends. Whoever. Most of them are industry. Invite everyone except Eugene Testarossa."

I'm about to object that I can't do anything in this house. I've hosted one too many parties. But if I'm not limiting who comes, why limit where it can be?

It's a terrible idea. She'll never go for it. There are a million reasons it will fail.

But why avoid failure when failure's already been so successful?

35

SKYE

"Who are you talking to?"

Fátima's been giggling and smiling at the phone for half an hour. She's already sworn it's not Becca, but now I'm getting a little worried, because she's way too delighted to be talking to the landlord. A little too whispery for a normal friendly conversation. She's making a bunch of calls. Tapping out texts. She's popular, no doubt, but she's acting as if it's her birthday and she's throwing herself a surprise party.

She comes out of her room and leans in my doorway with a grin so big, I'm a little put off.

"Why are you smiling like you just ate the last cookie?" I bag a handful of old underwear I found in the back of my drawer.

"You're leaving when?"

"Well, I was going to leave tomorrow, but Friday's traffic-into-Vegas day so..."

"Saturday?"

"I was wondering, if you could help me get some stuff to Goodwill, maybe I should go tonight?"

"Mm, no. That's not gonna work."

"Is Becca moving in or something?" More underwear. Old socks. Stockings. The plastic is stretching thin. "I can get this all out the door real quick."

"No," she sulks. "She might not since her place is pretty cool and this is... you know... not."

"She's a free spirit." I drag the bag to my out pile. "But love will find a way."

I hope I sound overwhelmed and tired instead of unconvinced. Love finds a way, but sometimes it gets lost. Most of the cream rises to the top. Karma is really not a thing, but sometimes justice is served.

"But that's not why I was smiling."

"Okay. Do you want this bag?" I hold up a teal purse I thrifted last summer. "Coach. It's leather."

She takes it, checks inside for a pocket, finds one, and holds it to her chest. "Sold."

"And the pots and pans? I'll be at my parents' for a bit, so..."

"I'll keep them, but hello? Are you going to let me tell you why I was smiling?"

"Sure. Yes. Sorry, I'm distracted." I prove my own point by remembering I have a night table drawer that hasn't been emptied since I brought it home.

"There's a party."

"Okay." I open the drawer and rummage right to the back.

"For you."

"For me?" I'm holding a gas station flashlight I never would've found in the drawer if the earthquake I'd put it there for had ever arrived.

"A goodbye party." She sits next to me on the bed. I cringe, thinking of all those people in one place, all focused on me—and she reads my mind as she always does. "It's all friends. Okay?"

"For real?"

"Yes. And if you don't want to be there, you don't have to come. We're having it with or without you. But it's Friday, so you can't leave until Saturday."

I was hoping to get out of here without anyone noticing, but a party could be fun. Sad—which I was trying to avoid— but maybe a little sad will be all right. What's the harm in indulging for a night?

"I can make it."

Fátima throws her arm around me for a moment, then jumps up. "You don't have to do a thing. We're taking care of it."

"But where? Here?"

"Starsong Karaoke. Liam got the big room on the fourth floor."

Wow. My agent, who I did nothing but disappoint the entire time he represented me, is helping to throw me a quitting party in a room that fits a hundred people.

"Is Colton coming?"

"It's his party. I mean, I'm doing the inviting, but it was his idea."

I look away when I smile to spare her the sight of a joy that—for only a moment—wipes away all my regrets.

There's too much going on to sleep. For no reason whatsoever, I write some lyrics about the emptiness of my drawers and closet. The forgotten things I gave away. Their physical weight in my mind. It's bad, but I write down the words hoping they'll stop bugging me.

The party is something to look forward to, but after that, the next few years are a void. All my college friends are gone. Med students aren't known for being much fun unless you count the end-of-semester decompression parties that seem like frat house antics by people terrified of a little chill.

Los Angeles is terrible. It's dirty. It's crowded. The very rich and the very poor are crowded together and separated, broken beyond repair. It has a terrible reputation.

In the dark, I send Colton a text.

—Thank you for my party—

I figure he'll get it in the morning, but he shoots a text right back.

—Just an excuse to see you again before you leave—

I sigh like a little girl looking at a picture of her crush. I'd be embarrassed if I wasn't in a dark room by myself.

—So we're not mad at each other?—

—You should be mad. I was a dick—

—you were—
—but I guess we all have a dick inside us—
—haha—

—speak for yourself—

—What are you doing now?—

282

I'm just curious, but I realize too late that that particular question in this exact circumstance usually means a hookup. He takes so long to answer I start to think maybe I've overstepped. The last time we saw each other didn't end well.

—*Wondering if I should put on my other shoe*—

—*You're wearing one shoe?*—

—**Figured in the middle that you maybe didn't mean to come over**—

My body comes alive. I sit up in bed, hand to chest.

There's nothing I intended less and nothing I want more.

—*Put on the other shoe*—

Fátima is at Becca's place, so it's okay that when there's a knock at the door, I don't have time to dry off. It's also fine to answer the door in a fuzzy blue robe that's sticking to my wet places.

"Hey." He's leaning to one side, hands in his pockets. Hoodie. No hat this time.

"Come in." I get out of the way and close the door behind him. He looks around, down the hall, then at me. "It's just us. Fátima's with Becca for the night."

"They're really hitting it off."

"Yeah, I'm thinking she'll move in here... hm... give it three months. So... sorry. I'd advise against taking my room."

"At least someone gets to keep who they want." He languidly pulls the end of the fuzzy belt. It comes loose and the robe falls open.

"I'm sorry," I say, letting him slide the robe off my shoulders, my body shuddering at his touch.

"For what?" His lips graze the backs of my shoulders. I hear him unzip his hoodie, dropping it to the floor.

"For not letting you keep what you want."

"Life. Not your fault." His arms creep around my body and bend my hard nipples. "And I'm sorry." I try to face him, but he holds me still. "For being the worst."

"I told you to just say it, and you did."

"All I could think about was nailing you to the floor with my cock." His left hand drifts between my legs, where the pleasure of the hand pinching my nipple lands. "So you can't leave." One of his feet wedges between mine. "Put your feet apart so I can feel you."

"I'm sorry, Colton. That I'm leaving."

I'm scratching the surface of my regret. Because I'm sorry for asking him to come over. It's only prolonging the agony of our separation. But when his fingers flatten and press between my legs, I stop feeling sorry. I stop feeling anything but his slow, circling pressure and the hardness against my bare bottom.

"I'm sorry for making you tired in the morning," he says.

"No, you're not."

He lets me go. Behind me, I hear him undoing his pants. He turns me to face him, cock out in all its gorgeous glory. When we kiss, he takes me by the back of the head, crashing us together, then he does something so shocking an explosion of heat flashes in my blood. He pushes me to my knees.

I look up at him to see if it was some kind of accident or if there's an apology coming.

No. There isn't. He grabs the base of his cock and points it at my mouth.

I open my lips and take him. He exhales, groaning as my mouths works the smooth skin of his head and my hands slide his pants down his legs.

How many days and years of learning out what he likes am I missing? Gripping him at the base, I open my throat and slowly push him deep. He sucks in a breath, whispering *yes, yes*.

I'm abdicating this to another woman. It's mine and I'm letting it go. For what?

I don't know. All I know is he's pushing my head against him. He's coming and every drop is for me. This one's mine.

Swallowing, I wipe my chin with the back of my wrist, then shift to stand, but he gets on his knees right in front of me. He brushes the hair away from my face.

"You're so fucking sexy."

"And you still have clothes on." My hands slide under his shirt, then force it up and off.

He kisses me. I run my fingers all over his body. He's hard everywhere, taut, awake, flexed as he grips the back of my neck to kiss me.

I push him away until he falls back onto the carpet and I can grab his boot by the front and heel. "Pull."

By the time his boots and jeans are in a pile, he's hard again and we're writhing on the floor like two animals fighting for dominance. Getting one of my legs over his shoulder, he reaches between my legs. As soon as he touches me, I explode in an orgasm so sharp and unexpected, I'm nearly blinded by it.

"Sorry," I say with a heaving chest. "Little sensitive."

"Holy shit, Skittles."

"Fuck me," I beg, grabbing for his cock. "Just fuck—"

He pins my wrists over my head, but when he lets them go to touch my breast, I move my hand to touch him. That's apparently unacceptable. He stops.

"What?" I ask.

He scans the room and gets up when he finds what he's looking for.

"You need to hold still." He picks up corner of the belt from my robe, unwinding the ampersand into a long, baby blue line.

"I'm going to keep you still, Skye." He kneels between my legs.

"Are you, now?"

"Hands over your head."

I reach above me. My knuckles hit the leg of the armchair.

"Good." He puts the belt in his teeth, bends forward, and straightens my arms until my wrists are on the far side of the leg, then he loops my wrists together on the far side of the heavy chair.

"Arrighty. Now I've got you where I want you." He casts around for his jeans, finds them, and plucks out a condom. He puts it on. "Now, your job is to not go anywhere. And my job is to make sure you have a pleasant stay."

"I won't go anywhere." I tug at the fuzzy belt.

"You can't come either." He enters me with no resistance. I am frictionless for him. "Not until I say. You got it?"

"Yes."

"You stay still and hold it. No matter how much you want to go."

"You mean come."

"Sure."

He pushes deep, pressing against my clit over and over. I can't hold him. I can't touch him. I can't pull him close and kiss him, and right now, I need to come.

"Don't." He's reading my mind.

It's as if he can feel the orgasm pushing its way to the surface. The inability to move while he fucks me loosens all the screws in my brain, and I fall apart. Forget everything I'm pissed about. All my disappointments. All the worry. Under him, the days and months and years without him stretch out into a band so thin it disappears.

"I can't." I'm nearly sobbing with the effort to hold it together.

"You can. You will. For me. You won't go without me."

"Soon?"

"Yes. Come with me."

He drives deep, circling his hips until the band snaps, and the future separates from the eternal present.

And then reality returns, and tomorrow is my last day here.

"Will you stay tonight?" I whisper.

36

COLTON

Of all the things I should be doing right now, lying in bed with Skye while the sun rises isn't on the list. I have a party to throw, a guest house to move out of, a career to start for real this time. But of all the things I need to be doing—the things I can't help *but* do—there's no list. This is it. One thing. I need to hold her while she sleeps. The end.

Well, besides the last-ditch effort of a party I'm throwing her tonight, this is the end. Sleep shortens the time I have with her.

If tonight succeeds and she stays, I'm going to sleep for a week.

If it fails, I'll look back on this morning and be glad I managed to fuck her when she woke up. With that decision made, I stay awake until the sun's just about up and then lose time.

The door buzzer blasts like a nuclear bomb.

"Holy shit!" I yell.

The sun's fully up, hanging from the top of the window

frame. Skye groans and turns out of my arms. Fuck. I fell asleep.

"Hey," I say in her ear.

"Hmmm."

"The door—" I'm interrupted by a second buzz which seems half as loud and is only half as shocking.

I wriggle out from under her and get out of bed. No need to wake her. Probably a package or something. I peer out the window. Her car is parked right below. I grab my pants off the living room carpet and shake them out.

Do I check out the window? I do not, because the only window on that side of the bungalow is over the kitchen sink, one room over. Quicker to just get my jeans on.

Buzz number three rattles the room as I'm buttoning up. What the fuck? Are delivery guys always this persistent?

Opening the door reveals the irrelevance of the question, because on the other side stands two people about twenty or thirty years older than me. The man is in a five-panel cap and has a long face and eyes the same shade of brown as Skye's. The woman is significantly shorter, with a smile that looks like... well... Skye's, if my Skittles ever smiled when she didn't mean it.

"Shit," I say by way of greeting.

"Hi there!" The woman's holding flowers and her grin is stretched so wide it has to hurt.

"I think we have the wrong address," the man says with a wave, stepping back to look at the number above the door. "Is this 341?"

"It... uh... yeah. It's..."

"Mom?" Skye's holding her fuzzy blue robe closed, since the belt's who-knows-where, which makes it look even more like we spent the night fucking. Which we did. But her dad is right here and I'm supposed to act as if I respect his daughter too much to tie her to the furniture.

"Skysong!" Mom slaps the flowers against my chest and practically knocks me over to envelop her daughter in a hug.

I feel more naked with the flowers covering me, but my shirt's half-under the coffee table, and getting it out to put it on would be like announcing that I started fucking their baby girl in the living room before moving to the actual bed.

"What are you doing here?" Skye asks.

"Your father." She lets Skye go. "He said no daughter of his was packing up her car alone."

"We didn't realize you had help." Dad cocks his head toward me.

"Yeah, I'm—"

"Don't worry kid." He slaps my arm. "That your shirt?" He points under the coffee table.

"Yeah." I head for it.

Mom grabs the flowers from me as I pass. I pluck up the shirt and pull it over my head. It's inside out.

"I'm almost all packed," Skye says. "You should have called."

"We decided late and figured you were asleep or... busy." She smiles at me with that gotta-hurt grin. "So, do you have a name?"

"Oh my God," Skye says, wrapping her robe tighter. "I'm so sorry."

"I'm Colton." I hold my hand out to Mom and she grips it loosely. I barely hold it any tighter.

"Pleased to meet you, but my, aren't you strong?"

I let go and offer my hand to Skye's dad, reminding myself to take it easy. He has a tighter grasp.

"Doctor Phillips," I say. "Nice to meet you."

"I don't know about you," Mom says to everyone, "but I am absolutely starving. Why don't we get a bite to eat before we let these men pack you up?"

Skye and I exchange a glance. She's asking if I want to come along and saying that I don't have to if I don't want to, and I'm asking if I should, because I want to be near her, but she can say no if she has to.

With a nod, the question is settled.

"Let me go change." Skye holds up a single finger for me —the exact number of minutes she's going to leave me alone with her parents—then she's gone behind the door.

"Did you guys fly?" I ask.

"We did." Mom's in the kitchen, opening and closing cabinets. "The only flight we could get was Southwest."

"Open seating," the doctor grumbles, looking at every corner of the apartment the way Skye looked at Logan's place.

"Do not recommend." She steps back and points at a top shelf. "Is that a vase?"

"Sure looks like it," Dad says with authority, somehow not actually understanding why she had to ask.

I rush to the kitchen and reach up to the top shelf to get the vase.

"Thank you," she says brightly, looking inside my elbow.
Everything. Now.

Fantastic. Great impression. Back in the living room, I try to locate my long-sleeve hoodie before Skye's dad—the literal brain surgeon—sees my life philosophy and decides, rightly, that I'm not a good fit for his daughter.

Mom fills the vase in the sink. "So, Colton, are you from Los Angeles?"

"Yeah." The hoodie's in the corner of the couch. I shake it

loose. "Born and raised." The arms are inside out, which is what happens when you strip it off like a wild animal.

"I'm back!" Skye bounds in. "Let's go eat!"

We walk to the diner around the corner. Her parents hold hands the whole way.

No pressure.

It's crowded, but we get seated in a booth without a wait. Skye and I on one side. Parents on the other. I hide behind the huge menu and kick her under the table.

When I have her attention, I mouth, "You okay?"

She nods and goes back to reading her menu. I don't believe her. Something's up and I'm not sure if it's her parents being here or me.

She orders her omelet, and for the first time, I wonder what will happen if the party convinces her to stay in Los Angeles. Why am I assuming she'll stay with me? She might keep her address and cast off her fake/real boyfriend.

The parents showing up is definitely not going to make this any easier. Who knows what kind of advice they're going to drop on her besides "come home"?

Once the menus are gone, it's time to talk about her trip, school, and living in a place with an actual winter. I'm not ready.

Skye starts. "I know you guys came to help me and stuff, but I'm not leaving until tomorrow." She waits for a reaction.

Dad smooths down his shirt. Mom smiles.

"Your father has surgery tomorrow."

"Okay. I mean, I have a party tonight. I know it's not

brain surgery, but it's my friends and Colton." She holds my hand, right there on the table, in front of her parents.

Shit. This feels more public than any face-sucking we've done for cameras. We've fucked and laughed and fought, but this may be the first time I know for sure she loves me.

"I'll stay," her mother says. "I'll change flights and stay in a hotel. By myself."

"Over my dead body," Dad says gruffly. "I can miss surgery."

Her mother spins practically one hundred eighty degrees. "Since when?!"

Dad shrugs. "It's elective. Freddie can do it."

"Elective brain surgery?" Skye says with disbelief, letting go of my hand so she can drink her coffee.

"I've heard of it," I add. "Parietal lift. Just pinch the cerebral cortex at the... uhh... central sulcus. Makes the entire frontal lobe think, like, ten years younger."

Her dad spit-laughs, and I'm sure it's more from surprise that I made the joke than the joke itself, which isn't that funny.

Our food comes as he's explaining that there is such a thing as elective brain surgery, that it is—his exact word— "easy," and that Freddie's usually the lead on these anyway.

"And what are you going to do when Skye's gone, Colton?" Mom asks, pushing her eggs into a forkable pile.

What am I going to do? How can I answer that when I'm busy making sure she has reasons to stay?

I got Eddie Milpas from SOS Records. I got a full-throated maybe from Trina Flores at A&V, who was in my class at Mirman. Jab called in a favor with the promise of an open bar. Liam's totally into it—even the sneaky part—and spent the day on the phone with his entire contact list.

So what am I going to do when she's gone? I'm going to wait for her to come back once the calls start coming in. And the calls are going to come in.

"You guys should come to the party tonight," I say instead of answering the question.

"Yeah." Skye jabs at her food with gusto. "Definitely. Get settled and come to the party. Let Freddie do the lift."

Her mother's smile gets even wider. "It's going to be so good to have you home, starting your life!" She reaches across the table and squeezes Skye's arm. "You can do the Christmas Revue at the hospital with me, like you used to."

"I was eleven," Skye grumbles.

"Well, you're even better now."

"You should come see it, Colton," Dad says. "It's quite a party. And it'd give you an excuse to come visit. Maybe stay awhile."

"Sure." I'm not sure if I mean it because right now, I can't see more than two hours into the future.

My phone rings. It's Liam. I excuse myself and answer it in the parking lot.

"Hey."

Why does my heart feel as if it's turning into a stone? I'm stiff, and tight, and no, it's not that my heart is getting heavier at all. It's actually lighter. Full of air and pushing up my throat like a balloon, bouncing against my esophagus.

"I got a licensing number from Glendora. It's pretty good, but I think I can get them higher. Can you make more of these plug-ins? It's a tight business."

"Her parents are here." Did the air turn solid? It's getting difficult to breathe.

"Are you feeling all right?"

"This just got really hard." I grip the edge of a planter to steady myself. "She's not going to tell them she's staying in LA right to their face."

"Whoa whoa, Colton. Brian Milpas or Trina from A&V could love her like a stack of money, they still got to talk to their people on Monday."

"Monday? No. Liam. You're the agent. Make it urgent. Whoever wants her needs to decide right away."

"No. We let them bid."

"I can't breathe." I sit on the planter, my fist to my chest as if I want to punch my stupid heart.

"What's going on? Where are you?"

"A Denny's parking lot." I can't be in cardiac arrest. It happens to men my age. Not often, but statistically... all the time.

"Which Denny's? I'm coming to get you."

"I can't let her leave. She. Can't. Go."

In broad, bright, California sunlight, a dark tunnel closes in. What's happening to me? Am I dying? My skin tingles. I'm cold and hot at the same time as my mind repeats, *She. Can't. Go.* over and over as fast as my clattering heartbeat.

"Are you there?" Liam asks.

"Yeah."

"I can hear the traffic, but I can't hear you. You're not breathing."

Breathe. When I pull air in, my lungs resist. They think they're too small for everything I need.

She can't go. But she might.

"Colton?" It's not Liam saying my name. It's Skye, standing over me, blocking the sun.

"Yeah." I stand and hang up on Liam.

"I'm going to take my parents to find a hotel and figure out how to move their flights."

"Good. Okay. Yeah." I spot her parents at a respectful distance, right outside the restaurant.

Mom waves with a smile. I wave back. I smile back. It hurts my face.

"Are you all right?" Skye takes my hands and threads her fingers into mine, regarding me with her head tilted and a deep 11 holding up the lines on her forehead.

"I'm fine. Just... I didn't sleep."

"Strange bed." She waggles her brows and fist-taps my arm. She's amazing and she's slipping out of my grasp.

"I'm going to catch a nap."

"I'll see you at Starsong then."

"The big room with the bar."

"Yup." She lets go of my hands.

I take her face and—with her parents right there to see—I kiss her longer than I should.

37

SKYE

After rejecting the Line as too hip, the Normandie as too old, the W as too expensive, and the Hyatt as too far away, Mom and Dad are safely ensconced in the Loews, which is too noisy, but fine for Dad, who's had just about enough of this.

Mom always does what Dad wants, so that's where they end up. It's only a block from a Gap, where they can get a change of clothes, and there's a little store downstairs where they can get seven-dollar toothbrushes. I don't bother telling them they don't have to go to the trouble or expense of any of this, because Mom would go to twice the trouble and ten times the expense to physically make sure I get in the car and go to med school.

They don't bring up Colton until we're at the hotel's front desk, waiting for the key.

"He seemed nice," Mom says.

"He is."

"Handsome too," Dad adds. Mom looks at him as if he's

lost his ever-loving mind. "What? I'm heterosexual. I'm not *blind*."

Mom turns back to me. "So, you like him?"

"I don't just kiss random guys I don't like."

"Maybe he can follow you. Move close to us."

"To Grosse Pointe?"

"Sure. It's lovely, don't you think? So quiet and..." She waves at the humanity swarming in and out of the lobby. "Not so messy."

"He's not moving, Ma."

"Why not? He doesn't like you back?"

"Kim," Dad warns. "Leave it, would you?"

She ignores him. He may get to pick the hotel, but when it comes to the children, she's the boss. "Have you asked him?"

"No. That's not a thing. He's not coming. He already moved all over the country and came home. He has a life here. His family and friends are here. His entire career is in his brother's garage, so there's no way he's moving anywhere just to be with me."

"Well, don't you worry, sweetheart." She cups one side of my face like she did when I was a foot shorter. "You'll find someone back home."

I can't stand there for another second under the shadow of her kindness, because it's all so misguided. I don't know where it's supposed to go or how she's supposed to act, but not like this. I don't feel any better. I feel a million times worse, and I can't explain it.

"No!" is the only word I have to describe what I want. I reject. I deny. I spit out whatever I'm being forced to swallow. "I'm already doing what you want. Don't make it worse."

"But—"

"But nothing!" My shout echoes off the high ceilings.

People turn to look at me. I don't know them, but they're making a judgment about me. I can't be here. I don't have a Garfield Pez and I don't have Colton. I don't have anything.

"But it's all going to be fine," Mom says. "It's fine."

"You guys." I step back. "Just call me when you're settled in, all right?"

The concierge comes to help them as I slip out the revolving doors. When I'm outside in the sun, I finally exhale.

Fátima and I take stock of all the boxes and bags stacked in the living room. I got rid of most everything, and she'll ship whatever won't fit in the Toyota tomorrow.

"I don't think any of this is going to fit."

"Boxes go in first," she says. She's going to the party early to set up, so she's ready with her makeup perfect and her hair strung into a dozen little ponytails all over her head. That's Becca's influence. "Bags of clothes can shape around them. You just jam them between stuff."

"My dad's not going to go for jamming anything."

"We'll get Colton to distract him." She fluffs her hair in the mirror.

"I don't know if he'll come tomorrow." It hurts me to consider that I might not see Colton in my rearview mirror, but he's not an early morning person, and my mom and dad will be knocking on the door with coffee and smiles no later than six thirty.

"Hm." She acknowledges me, but neither agrees nor disagrees. "Let's all just let loose tonight."

"In front of my parents?"

"Right in front of them." She snaps up her bag. "I'll see you in an hour."

"Thank you," I say before she leaves. "For the party. If I'm too busy letting loose later and I forget to tell you. Thank you for being my friend. And getting me a job. And for... everything."

"You forgot the tamales."

"Especially for the tamales."

"I'll thank my *abuela* for you." She kisses my cheek gently so she won't ruin her makeup. "She's going to miss making the sweet ones."

"She'll stop?"

"You're the only one who eats them." She stops halfway out the door.

"Fátima! I only met her once and I don't even speak Spanish."

"You said *dulce tamale*, which is backward, but anyway she made *dulce*."

"They take a lot of time, and she made extra just for me." My eyes sting with hot, fresh tears. "I'm not even family."

"You big stupid." She comes back in and takes me by the shoulders. "Of course you are."

"I didn't know."

"I'm going to cry and I just did my face." Delicately, she presses her finger under her eye to catch whatever moisture threatens to gather, sniffing back a wet one.

"Your eyes look beautiful. Don't ruin it." I clear my throat and remove any and all tension from my face. "Done. I have no feelings."

"Good. I'm going. I'll see you there."

She heads for the door, but I have one more question.

"*Dulce* doesn't mean delicious?"

"Oh, girl. Girl, girl, girl."

I'm an idiot, but even an idiot can find something they love by mistake.

"Can we sing 'Wind Beneath My Wings' tonight?" I ask.

"Late. Toward the end, when I can ruin my face. We have the room all night."

She blows me a kiss and leaves. We've sung that song together before, but I'm kind of excited to try it as an alto.

––––––––––––

Driving down Western Ave, I stop at the crosswalk and look for a slouchy, careless guy in a backward baseball cap. That was the first time I saw Colton and the first time he heard me.

The radio's on the news. That won't do. My voice needs to call him out of the ether and stop him in his tracks in the middle of the street. But I didn't plug in my phone, and the first station has commercials. The next one has Stone Temple Pilots. Then Ed Sheeran. Nothing I can stick. The light turns green before I challenge Colton Crowne to appear in the crosswalk, with the casually confident stride of a man who knows who he is, what he cares about, and what he doesn't.

The horn of the SUV behind me shouts and the fog lights flash.

Stopping at the Wilshire light, I don't see Colton anywhere, and why should I? How could I expect another freak occurrence to give me hope that my trajectory could change, when it won't?

Of everything I'm going to miss—sweet tamales, constant noise, the feeling of opportunity waiting around every corner, watching TV with Fátima, doing weird vocals once a week behind Becca—I'm going to miss my fake boyfriend the most.

"Have fun tonight, Skye." I grip the wheel tightly, commanding away the worry. "Just forget it and have a good time."

The yellow dude stands straight and still. I poke him, and when he bounces back and forth, the smile makes sense.

"Gotta walk the walk, little guy."

The light changes and I turn onto Wilshire, convinced I can make this my best night in Los Angeles.

When I get to Serrano, Colton's on the corner, hands in his pockets.

He sees me.

38

COLTON

I look up the symptoms of a heart attack in a young guy. I don't have them, but I learned more about cardiomyopathy, heart rhythms, and all the cardiums in ten minutes than I ever wanted to. Knowing I'm not gonna die tonight isn't much help.

The bar is staffed up, the bottles are full, and the music has been turned low. People are coming. Skye's not here yet.

There's a shiny black baby grand piano in the corner where two walls of windows meet. The karaoke screen is in front and to the side, so everyone can sing along. Becca is flipping through the playlist with Fátima over her shoulder. Becca's in charge of the song order again, and the deal is, she assigns Skye songs that show off her voice.

"She'll come in to a full house," Liam says, rolling his ice around the bottom of his glass. "It'll be great."

The Garfield Pez dispenser's in my pocket. She can use it if she wants. It'll calm her. She'll be able to sing, no matter how many make-or-break fuckers are here to assess whether or not they can turn a dime on her talent. I should tell her the guest list before she gets here. It may make it worse, but it may make it better.

"She's going to freak out," I tell him, even as I'm standing here hoping to God she won't.

But I'm the one freaking out. That heart-attack feeling has morphed from a jabbing terror to a kind of low tightness I can forget about for a few seconds at a time.

"She knows she's coming to a party." Liam puts down his drink to greet our parents, and I fucking can't deal with them right now.

I slip into the back, into a little room stacked with boxes of liquor. Alone, I can breathe into the uncomfortable tightness that's stuck in my chest. That makes it better and worse. Once Skye is gone, I'll go to the doctor. If he tells me I'm going to die, then whatever. I'll drive out of here right behind her. Gone. Me and her instead of just her.

"Colton?" It's my mother. There was never any hiding from her.

"Hey, I'll be right out."

"What's wrong?" She comes into the storeroom and puts her hand on my cheek. I press it to my face so she can feel it steadily.

"Just a little indigestion. Really. I'll be out in a minute."

She looks into my eyes and wrinkles them the way Skye does, making a much finer number 11. "You should stay back here as long as you need, but you have to tell me you're all right one more time... but you can't lie or minimize. I'll know."

She will too. She'll call me right out.

"I just..." I swallow and take her hand off my face. "I feel like I can't breathe all the way and there's this pain in my chest. I'm sure it's not a heart attack or anything."

"Oh, sweet Colton!" She laughs.

"What?" I'm both insulted and happy she's not freaked out.

"You were never a hypochondriac."

"I know."

"You broke your ankle in soccer because that other boy knocked into you on purpose."

"Harry Hawkins."

"And you shrugged. You didn't keep playing like your brothers would have. No. You acted like, yes, you were hurt, but you knew you'd be fine."

"A broken ankle isn't that big a deal. This is... so heavy."

"You were right, and you told the orthopedist exactly which bone was broken and how."

"So this... *feeling*? It's not like that."

"Do you feel like you have to run out of the room?" she asks.

"Yeah."

"Can't concentrate? Don't know what you're worried about but worried anyway?"

"Yes."

"World closing in?"

"Ma, yes. How do you know?" I ask.

"Are you saying things to yourself? Bad things about who you are?"

"No. I know the shit I say in my head, and it doesn't make me feel like this. I'm a loser and a fuckup yeah, yeah, yeah. And don't tell me I'm not. That's just not what's on my mind right now, okay? It's not about me. None of this is about me. I just want Skye to have a good time. I want her to know she's good. She didn't fail. She still has opportunities, and she has people here who love her, so she'll..." My breath hitches. "So she'll come back... Ma." Another hitch. Fuck.

"It's okay."

"I don't... I don't know what to do."

"You're having an anxiety attack. It's fine."

"Jesus. This is how she feels all the time? This is *terrible*."

"You get used to it, and for most of us, it goes away."

For most of us. That means not Skye. What have I done with this party? Trying to satisfy my own needs, what the fuck did I do to hers?

I fling my arm toward the wall as if I'm pointing out a huge room full of people. "I set up this whole thing. I told her it was only friends. I thought if she knew all these big assholes would be here, she wouldn't come, but now, she's in this situation. Walking right into it like *bam*. Because of me. Because I can't just let her go."

"Don't."

"I have no choice. I mean, we'll be friends and I'll call her and maybe... maybe we'll visit? But I can't force her to stay here with me."

"Don't."

"Mom! If you know the answer, just say it!"

"What do you want, Colton?" She creases her brow and repeats the question more softly. "What do you want?"

There's only ever been one answer.

"Everything. I want everything. Now."

"Go get it."

39

SKYE

As I come closer, he waves to me, alone on the corner where Gene Testarossa almost hit me. When I pull up next to him and open the window, he ducks to talk to me. He's always given off a quiet confidence in who he is, even if he was unhappy with his own actions. Now, he's a ball of tension. I've never seen him so wound up.

"Hey," I say. "What's going on?"

"I need to talk to you before you go up."

That's weird, but I hope talking to me just means a pre-party quickie.

"Okay. Let me park."

He points out a street spot near the corner I can pull into instead of going into the garage, so I do that and get out. He's kissing me before the door's closed and I'm thinking yeah. Quickie. That works for me. It'll stretch time until the moment I have to drive out seems like a week away. Maybe we can stay in whatever hotel room or little corner he's set aside for a few hours and he can make me feel forever.

"I need to talk to you," he says, holding my face still.

"You mentioned that."

"Okay, first of all, two things."

When he says that out of order, I take a serious look at him and notice he's agitated. There's an insistence about him that—coupled with what may be confusion—makes him seem like a man ready to shatter into confetti. He's never been like this in front of me.

"One." He points up at the building. "There are a fuck-lot of people up there. And what the... the bad thing I want to... I'm an asshole. Okay? Just accept that before I tell you why."

He waits for me to accept nonsense, which I won't. He may be agitated and acting weird, but that doesn't make him an asshole.

"No." I cross my arms. "Absolutely not."

A Wilshire bus blasts by us, flicking the tips of his hair in its wake.

"Fine." He crosses his arms so we're mirror images of each other. "Your friends are up there, like I told you. But I didn't tell Fátima I was inviting some other people."

"Other people?" That doesn't seem like such a big deal. There are always more people who show up at any given party. Is Liam going to ask me to pay for the extras? That seems unlikely.

"People who..." He shakes off his original thought and starts over with more force. "I wanted..." He stops and starts again. "I want you to stay and... hold on." He lays his hands on me before I can get out my objection. "I want you to stay and I am an asshole because I was trying to give you a reason to. It was a bad plan, it's not going to work because of the timing and also because you need to do what you need to do and that's hard enough. You don't need me trying to push you into a corner." He steps away and digs into his jeans pocket. "I thought, cool, I'll bring this." He extracts the Garfield Pez dispenser. "And I'll give it to you, so when you sing in front of a bunch of idiots who... you know, are low-rung record executives or assistants who'll come out for an open bar, or the one or two really big assholes who owed Liam a favor... I figured whatever, you'll be okay. It would keep you from freezing up."

He puts Garfield in my hand and closes my fist around it.

"Wait, wait. I think something got lost in there."

"I invited industry people." He lets me go as if he's too ashamed to keep touching me, but I'm still too confused to know what he's feeling bad about.

"Why?"

"So you'd sing! Karaoke!" he shouts toward the top of the building. "And they'd hear you and fall in love with you the way I did."

"Ah."

He loves me. I'm ecstatic and shocked—and I have so much to say besides that one breathy syllable, but he's not done.

"And you'd stay here, with me." He shakes his head, looking down. "I'm sorry I put you in this position."

I can be mad at him, but what would be the point?

"I might not sing, but..." I lay my palms on his crossed forearms, Garfield tucked under my thumb. "Can I still go to my party?"

"It's up to you."

Drawing him into me, I kiss him, but he doesn't kiss me back. He just returns the embrace, pulling me tightly into him.

"What?" I ask.

"Let me come with you."

My arms loosen and I lean away to get a wider view of his face. "Duh. Were you not coming up?"

He looks as confused as I am, then his face breaks out into a laugh. "No, I mean, let me settle a few things here, and then meet you in Michigan."

"Wait. No." The impossibility of it fills me with the need to be more emphatic, because he's not joking, and he really has to be. "Absolutely not. No fucking way."

"Ah." He fits a world of disappointment into the breathy syllable that just held my surprised delight.

"No! I mean, do I want you to? Yes. Hell yes, but Colton... it's a mistake. It's terrible."

"Well, no. Listen—"

"You can't!"

"I like Detroit. There's a music scene. I just—"

"I said no! You're not destroying everything you've earned here, leaving your family, your friends, this place... Los Angeles... which is so nice, and cool, and so alive. Like it speaks to me and...."

A car screeches to a stop at the light. I stretch my arm out toward the driver who miscalculated the yellow, who's now a symbol of this gorgeous chaos.

"You're going to leave Wilshire Blvd? And this park?" I point across the street. "I don't even know what it's called, but here it is. And how are you going to leave a sun that always shines? Do you know how cold it gets where I'm from?"

"I'll buy a coat."

"It's not realistic."

"What's not realistic about it?" He shrugs, his shoulders drop a little, and the disorganized tension when I first saw him on the corner is gone. "I sell the equipment. I license the plug-in. Then I'll go to Michigan. I'll work so you have everything you need. I'll make you sandwiches when you're studying. I'll drive you to school so you can read in the passenger seat. I'll carry your books. You'll become a doctor, which is so fucking cool. And when you're ready, if you're ever ready, you'll sing. The world may notice. Or only the ones who come to the doorstep to hear Christmas carols. Whatever makes you happy."

"It's not what you want."

"I know what I want, and it's not forever summer."

He means it. All of it. He loves me, but not just that, he loves me enough to change his entire life. It's a weight, and it's a lightness. The tensions between the earth and sky are too taut to bear. I look away from him at the light-flooded sky and its hidden stars. The bright signs of the closed businesses, the muck of unidentifiable garbage in the street, waiting for the sweeper to churn it away. The unknowns, the dangers, the surprises around every corner.

I shake my head. It doesn't make sense. "I started loving you back when I thought we were possible. I don't want you to think I don't love you. But what you're suggesting? It's not worth it."

He steps away from me so I can see the whole of his body as he spreads his arms to talk about the entirety of what we can perceive.

"Take the city. Take the music. The silicone injections. The spinning lights. The marine layer, el niño, the flash floods, the dry heat and the blue skies and golden sunshine all along the way. Delete the stupid earthquake app off my fucking phone. Take the mountains, the valleys... all of them. Take the coke-snorting Hugo Boss executives, the fake dreams, the soul-sucking jobs, the luxury stores, and multi-million-dollar McMansions an underpass away from a block of tents. Take the 101, the 5, the 110, and God please, please take the 405. Take the fucking stars. Just give me the Skye they hang in."

He seems so happy with this commitment, all I can do is kiss him. I don't know what to say to a love so sincere, so overwhelming. There's no way I'll let him do this. I love him too much, but he won't be convinced now. He'll sleep on it, wake up regretting it, and I'll release him from his promise.

Until then, I'll accept his love in whatever form it comes.

40

COLTON

A kiss isn't an answer. It's a delay tactic, but I did just dump this on her. She'll sleep on it and see it my way. Maybe she'll come around on the freeway out of here. It's okay. I'm patient. I know what I have to do.

"Let's go tell Becca to take you off the playlist."

I'm not sure when the anxiety Mom identified stopped, but it melted off me and I feel right again.

I take her hand and pull her into the building lobby, where the elevator's waiting. The doors are about to close when three people slide in. Though two of them are built like industrial cabinets, the third attracts attention like blinking lights on a dark night.

Skye sucks in a breath and squeezes my hand.

"Colton," Tamika greets me.

"Hey. I didn't know you were coming."

One of her bodyguards blocks two others from getting in, though there's plenty of room.

"My schedule's my own, angel food. Is this Skye?"

"Oh, yeah. Skye Phillips, this is—"

"I am *such a fan*," Skye says, then glances at me as if checking that it's okay to be a fan of my ex.

"She's a fan." The doors close and we start upward.

"So nice to meet you." Tamika's known for her graciousness, and it doesn't fail her.

"Also a singer," I add.

"I heard. And I listened to an EP making the rounds, produced by our own Colton Crowne."

Skye covers her mouth. There's a joyful excitement in the news, but her 11 is also grooved deep between her eyebrows. I have other concerns.

"Making the rounds?" I ask. "It's not ready."

"It's not. But they want to hear the talent, not the production. You know that from experience."

The doors open. The bodyguards stand on either side of the exit to let Tamika through. Once she's out, they follow and I have to hold the doors open for Skye, who looks too confused to move.

"Don't worry about her," I say. "You have this."

She takes Garfield from her pocket. I'm about to tell her that if I'm wrong and she doesn't have it, we can take the elevator right back down, when she tilts her chin up and pushes her shoulders back. Her nail clicking along the P-E-Z is the only difference between her posture and Tamika's.

"I have this." She kisses me before she walks out.

I follow as if I'm her biggest fan.

Tamika entering the room took some of the wind from Skye's arrival, but not amongst her friends, who treat her as if she's the only person in the room. Her mother's on her second glass of wine as her father nurses a gin and tonic. The pianist accompanies the karaoke machine. It's goofy and fun and a sideshow to the party itself.

"You seem back to your old self." My mother's crept up behind me as Skye talks to Brian Milpas's assistant.

"I decided what I want," I say.

"What would that be?" Her eyes twinkle as if she knows, but I don't think she understands that it's more than a woman I want. It's a life with her.

"I'm leaving again. Sorry, Ma, but I have to go where she is."

She takes my arm, gripping as tightly as she can, which is getting looser and looser. "I'm not losing you this time."

"This is different."

"Good. Good. I think I need to have your father take me home."

When I hug her good night, I realize the terrible weight in my chest is gone.

My Skittles meets everyone she ever dreamed of meeting when she lived here. In different conversations, I reach for her hand and find it, pulling her back to me.

"It's a crowded room. Are you doing all right?" I ask.

"I am." She clicks her Garfield Pez dispenser when I kiss her. "I'm going to get the nicest apartment overlooking the river. You'll love it... when you visit."

Fátima pulls Skye away and she's engulfed by her friends.

Liam approaches me looking just this side of smug. "I have a meeting with acquisitions at Bamboozle Records."

"In my entire life, Liam"—I clap my hand on his shoulder—"I have never heard of them."

"They think you're magic together, like Lucas and Madonna, Visconti and Bowie."

"We are, but not like those guys."

"Can you get her to stay?"

"Liam, I can do you one better. I'm going to get my ass to Detroit and produce her there whenever she's ready."

"You still owe me a song. I only have three."

"Aye-SAP."

He smiles. "It's been great working with you, Colton. Really. I thought I was doing you a favor, but you really did all right. Better than I expected."

He grabs me into a back-slapping hug so I can't tell him I had a feeling he'd hired me more from brotherly love than professionalism.

"I'm getting you a nice number for the plug-in," he says when he's done. "How many do you think you have in you?"

I watch Skye from across the room as she goes into the hallway. Bathrooms.

"One. Four. Ten. Fucked if I know."

A flow of attention follows her. A handful of people. It's Tamika's bodyguards clearing the way for her to go to the back hallway. If she's going to give Skye a hard time about that shit with Gavin or say some shit to hurt her feelings... I can't let that happen.

I make my way through the crowd—how many people did Liam invite, for fuck's sake?—and hit the hallway with the light up restroom signs. The two bodyguards stand at the ladies' room door like lions in front of a library.

41

SKYE

The bathroom has three stalls. Someone's in the one to my right. The one to my left is empty. I step out of the middle stall, check myself in the mirror. As I'm laying on fresh lipstick, the occupied stall opens and Tamika herself comes out.

Shit.

And yay.

"Hi," I squeak. "I'm sorry about the elevator, if it made you uncomfortable."

"It didn't."

"It's just that I'm in kind of the same situation with Colton as you were and it's weird for me, at least, besides the general fangirling which must get boring." I can't help but go on as though my brakes on my mouth stopped working and I'm careening for a cliff. "Except on 'Don't Be' when you say, 'Don't be my friend, don't be my,' but then you don't finish it, it's epic and that note is just right to the heart."

She looks at me in the mirror. Besides the part of me that

317

notices that she's a superstar, and human, and fallibly non-magical—I realize what those lyrics are about. How have I sung along to them this whole time without knowing they're about Colton?

Shit. The bottom drops out of the market for stupid babbling. I'm broke. I've got no words in the bank.

"I hear you're leaving to go to med school?" she asks.

"Yeah. I like living here, but it's not happening." I assume she'll know what I mean by *it*.

She nods as if she does, then shakes her head as she fixes her hair. "Poor Colton." She tsks. "Keeps on losing."

"No." My denial is quick and strong. He's better than what he thinks of himself. Better than any man alive and my face gets hot with offense. "He's wonderful. If you want to know, he's too good for me. I've been a waste of his time."

"How much of his solid gold time have you wasted? Come on, girl."

I've had enough. This isn't going anywhere I want to go and I'm not standing in front of this mirror to insult the man I love who just offered to give everything up for me.

"It's been nice meeting you." I start to leave.

"The day I graduated from high school, I started packing to move to Memphis." She says it as if I don't have my hand on the door. "Then spent five years working and meeting people and making music. My momma thought I was throwing my life away."

"You weren't, obviously."

"No way to know that." She takes out her lipstick. "Can I give you a piece of advice you didn't ask for?"

I can tell her no, but I'm too curious by far. "Sure."

"Our situations are not the same." She dabs lipstick on already perfectly-painted lips. "On the surface, maybe. But I knew the sacrifices going in. I had to say 'no' more than I had to say 'yes' and I had to say 'yes' a lot. Now." She puts her lipstick in her bag and pops it closed. "I don't know you, Skye Phillips, but I heard your songs. You have almost everything you need to make it... just about almost." She presses her lips together and pops them free. "Except patience. I'm not sure you understand how long this all takes or how hard it is. I can make a guess as to why you have the privilege of thinking it's easy, but it's not. It's a damn struggle from day one to death. If you're too weak to make it through, it's good you know that now."

I've been clutching the Pez dispenser in my pocket, and it's not until the sound of my nail clicking along the ridges that I realize how well I've been taking this whole conversation.

"I'm not too weak." Except I am. Even the denial lacks the most basic conviction.

"The world needs more doctors," she says, picking up her bag. "I wish you luck."

She brushes past me to leave. I'm alone with all my failings, and all the things I haven't failed at yet.

So many things to fail at, and I haven't even scratched the surface.

42

COLTON

Tamika comes out first. She's never let anyone leave a conversation before her, and judging from what I can see of Skye's expression, there was a conversation.

"Tam," I say, getting in front of her. She holds up her hand to keep the bodyguards from throwing me out a window. "What the fuck did you just do?"

"I came here to talk to you."

"You could have called."

"You have no idea how complicated my life is."

"Sure. Whatever. When you figure out how to make a simple phone call, you have my number." I try to get past her, to Skye, but there's a wall of black suit between me and the ladies' room.

"I need to get back to my roots," Tam says. "It's getting too slick. All of it. I'm losing that raw energy I had with you."

"If you mean 'with me'—"

"I do *not* mean it like that. But I needed to talk face to

face. On a professional level, I'm aware there's a lot of water under that particular bridge."

"And a drought. The river's dry," I say.

"I think we can make it rain again."

Can we? Do I even care? The offer isn't bad, but I know what I want and this deal has no effect on it whatsoever.

"If you get this wall out of my way, I'll think about it."

With the tiniest nod of her head, the mountain moves. I start to push open the bathroom door.

"She loves you, angel food."

"Call me that again and you can stay slick."

Without agreeing or disagreeing, she and her industrial cabinets walk down the hall.

Skye pulls the door open just as I push, and inertia propels me into her. We land against the vanity counter and I hold her there with my hips.

"What did she say?" My lips can't help but kiss her face.

"She's very direct. It's a nightmare sometimes."

"Nothing bad." When I hitch her onto the counter, she wraps her legs around me. "Hey." She pushes away my face. "If you want to meet me there and make me sandwiches... well, I like sandwiches. No. I love sandwiches... but—"

"That's a yes?"

"Only if you swear that if you're unhappy, you'll come home."

"I told you already." Her neck. The smell of ozone-soaked air before a rain, with all the promise and peril of clouds exploding. There's no living without it. "I won't be happy without you."

"So you're swearing?"

"Swear." My hands can't keep off her body, feeling for openings in her clothes.

I've found a zipper on her left side and I'm about to slide it down when the door opens and we part, remembering we're in a public ladies' room. We're laughing, but Fátima is not happy.

"Are you serious?" she asks with her hands on her hips.

"We're just leaving." I help Skye off the vanity.

"We're waiting for you!"

"Yeah." Skye grabs my hand. "I have a song to sing you."

She pulls me back out to the party.

"Skye!" Becca is at the microphone. The karaoke screens are blue with the song title in white. She spots us coming her way. "It's your turn!"

"Someone to Watch Over Me."

"Okay!" Skye gets up on the low stage as if nothing about it terrifies her. But I know what her anxiety feels like, and if she's having it and still sings through it, then she's a fucking goddess. "Hi, everyone. Thank you for coming... some of you, I know. The rest came for the open bar."

Scattered laughter.

"No shame. Enjoy it. It's courtesy of my agent, Liam Crowne." She shields her eyes, and when she finds him, she points in his direction. He raises his glass. "Say nice things about him tomorrow when you're hungover."

Applause for the guy funding the drinks. She's doing great. Without the pressure to be perfect, she's exactly that.

"Okay, so... oldie but a goodie. It was going to be on the EP a bunch of you apparently have." She pauses. Takes Garfield from her pocket. "Now you get it live instead."

I can feel her losing it a little. My fists clench at my sides. I don't know what made her suddenly tight. Maybe she saw someone she didn't know. Maybe it's nothing besides her own brain.

"Come on, Skye," I whisper.

Becca starts the music. Skye's part comes.

"There's a saying old..."

She's not singing. She's speaking the words, white-knuckling the microphone in one hand and an orange Pez dispenser in the other. She's not clicking the side. That makes noise. She's too much of a professional to do that, but that's crashing her anxiety.

Her friends—the ones who know what's going on—cheer her on.

She clears her throat.

"Can you start again?" Skye asks Becca.

After a second, the song comes on again.

The words flash across the screen with stock footage of a mountain range in the background.

She's frozen solid in front of everyone. The second verse rolls by without a song.

"Skye," Becca calls, waking her up, "you don't have to."

"I'm sorry," she replies. "Maybe later."

Fátima applauds. "We love you!"

Scattered clapping from her friends. Some whistling. Skye gets offstage, leaving it ready for someone who'll get up there to butcher a song with a serrated knife of a voice while she's down here thinking she's not good enough to be who she wants to be.

Fuck that.

If anyone's going to butcher a song tonight, it'll be me.

"Becca!" I jump up to the front.

The pink-haired girl looks up from her laptop screen with a look that asks what the fuck I think I'm doing. The pianist plays a few chords to fill in the silence.

"I'll sing it," I say.

"Um, okay?"

Skye comes up behind Becca and deploys every worry line in her forehead. Justifiably. Logan, who only loves his work and his wife, comes to the front with Liam. And Byron, the original stone-cold asshole. Dante, who was never known to have a heart until Mandy. Lyric, who's monetized her entire life—all of them stand there just to guarantee my entire family can mock me for decades' worth of Thanksgivings.

If I'm going to suck, I might as well suck all the way.

"Don't," I say when Becca is about to push her little button. "I got it." I jerk my thumb toward the piano. "Is that mic live?"

"It can be," Becca says.

"Do it."

The pianist gets off the bench.

I speak into the mic to make sure it works. "Nice. It's warm. Thanks, dude." I get some laughs, playing a few chords to loosen my fingers until it dies down. "Spoiler alert. I suck, but so do all of you." The opening chords prove I'm no musician. Knowing the science of music and playing it are two completely different things, obviously, because I sound as if I'm hitting the keys with sausages, but I know the song by ear. "Except Skye. She doesn't suck."

Okay. Here we go.

"*There's a saying old, says that love is blind/Still we're often told, seek and ye shall find.*" There are few words in the English language for how bad I sound, and no math to measure how little I care. "*So I'm going to seek a certain lady I've had in mind.*"

"Stop!" a voice rises from the crowd.

But I don't. I'm committed here, and I'm kind of having fun.

"*Looking everywhere, haven't found her yet.*"

"He's the big affair I cannot forget." Skye's voice comes through the speakers. She's at the stage, pulling the mic from the stand as she takes the next verse. "*Only man I never think of with regret.*" She's looking at me, having changed *ever* to *never* as a message to me and everyone else.

"Go!" I play better without having to sing, and she takes over.

"*I'd like to add his initial to my monogram. Tell me where is the shepherd for this lost lamb?*"

She's perfect, perfect, perfect. It's like being alone in the studio with her all over again, except when she doesn't take the next verse. I look over to see if she froze again. She hasn't. She's looking at me.

"Next one's yours," she says into the mic.

"You're joking."

"You started it."

Laughter and whistles follow along with shouts of *come on* and *do your thing!*

"Shit. All right." I go back a few measures. "*There's a somebody I'm longin' to see

I hope that she turns out to be...*"

She sings with me. "*Someone who'll watch over me.*"

"Help me out here, you guys!" Fuck I can't even stand to hear the sound of my singing with hers. It's like a crime scene. "*I'm a little lamb who's lost in the wood.*"

By *lamb*, a few voices are shouting the lyrics with me. By the next verse, I get more buy-in. "*I know I could always be good/To one who'll watch over me.*"

She's crossed the distance between us and drapes herself over the piano. If anyone in the crowd is singing with her, I can't hear them. There's only her.

"*Although he may not be/The man some girls think of as handsome/To my heart, he carries the key.*"

"Not cool, Skye," I say into the mic for the pause. "Not cool."

The guests laugh and Skye sits next to me on the bench, finishing the torment of this song so I don't have to.

"*Won't you tell him please to put on some speed/Follow my lead, oh, how I need/Someone to watch over me.*"

I play a sweep finale with my sausage fingers that sounds like a cat walking over the keys.

She smiles at me and puts her head on my shoulder. The Garfield rests loosely in her palm. Our friends and family applaud. Maybe some folks we don't know join them. It doesn't really matter.

43

SKYE

It doesn't matter what anyone thinks. Tomorrow morning, I won't even be a twinkle in the eye of Hollywood Blvd.

Poof. Gone.

They may ask what happened to me, as if I blinked out of existence the minute I turned my back. But when I faced a different direction, I could see a path forward instead of an endless void. It's not what I want, but as least I have someone I want to live it with me.

The party is over. We left the staff cleaning and my parents tucked into an Uber back to their hotel. Fátima took Becca home with a laugh and an order that I enjoy my last night in town.

Colton and I burst into my apartment differently than last time. We have a future together. He kicks the door shut. We don't bother with the lights, stripping each other's clothes off as if they're an offense to desire, until we're down to skin cast in the blue of the streetlights.

He slows, brushing his fingertips over my collarbones, appreciating every inch of me. "You were fantastic tonight." He kisses the trail left by his touch.

"A confluence of factors… including you at the piano."

"Am I better than a Pez dispenser?" He bends to kiss my breasts.

"Not as portable." I run my fingers through his hair as he kneels to kiss my belly. "Do you regret promising to leave with me now?"

"Nah. I'm up for an adventure." He picks me off my feet.

I gasp in surprise, but there's a wall behind me to lean against. He gets under my knees so they droop over his shoulders while his face burrows between my legs, licking and sucking with wild abandon.

My orgasm breaks through without warning. He holds me up while I jerk and arch into him, maintaining the same rhythm when it all becomes too much.

"Stop, stop, you're killing me."

He stops. His face is slick and wet, and when he drops my legs to his waist and kisses me, I taste myself on his tongue. I want to lick it all off, taste what he tastes, hear what he hears, crawl inside him and feel us together as one person.

Attached at the mouth, he carries me to the bedroom, and we lie together on sheets that have to be stripped in the morning, exploring how our bodies fit together until avoiding that one, last, ultimate way is too much to bear.

"I need to get inside you."

"I packed the night table drawer," I say.

"I have it."

The willpower it takes to get out of bed, go to the living room, and come back with his wallet is more than I expect any man to exhibit without at least five more minutes of negotiation about pulling out or whatever.

Thus, Colton's dick is inside me in under sixty seconds.

I love him for this.

"I'm going on birth control." I groan, pushing him deeper. "The minute I get there. By the time you come..."

"You feel too good."

"I'll be ready to fuck without."

"I'll last three minutes with you that way."

We're on our sides. I'm on top, then he is. We're a constantly moving organism. He pulls me into his arms, burying his face in my neck, and drives deep, staying there with a push against where I'm sensitive, then does it again.

"Can you come with me?" he asks, deep in the crook of my shoulder.

"I think, I..." I push and writhe side to side, stimulating my clit with him, discovering how close I am. "I can."

We come together, just as we'll go together.

———

My head rests on his shoulder and my hands rests on his heartbeat. I don't want to go, but he'll be there with me. He'll make sandwiches and carry my books. He'll be the relief from my misery which I'm sure is what we've dreamed of being to someone our whole lives and—

But wow.

What the fuck?

I'm leaving today.

I sit upright in bed with a gasp.

The sun is up. I'm alone. I must have fallen asleep with

that thought and woken up asking myself what I'm doing here at all.

There was no dream trying to illustrate the obvious. No words that came to me in a clear voice. Just me asking what the fuck.

I'm leaving today.

What was I thinking?

Why am I doing the hardest, most complicated thing?

Voices come from outside. Men discussing something I can't make out. I throw open the blinds. Out the window, my car is parked at a wonky angle, trunk open, and Colton is handing my father a box. They both look at me.

"Stop!" I shout.

"It's more efficient this way," Dad calls.

I have no idea what he's talking about and could not care less. Throwing on sweatpants and Colton's hoodie over nothing but skin, deciding I have no time for shoes, I run outside. Mom is under the eaves, sitting on a five-gallon bucket and writing the contents of the plastic bags onto little white labels.

"Stop, I said!"

"Skye!" Mom exclaims, pointing down with her pen. "Your feet."

I face Colton and my dad, standing together in front of my open trunk. The back seats are down to fit a neat row of boxes.

"I'm not going."

Blinking eyes. Blank stares.

"I'm not leaving." I figure the rephrase will help.

It's enough to get Colton to lean against the car and get my dad to shake his head as if he's trying to get bees out.

"Tomorrow's too late," Mom says from behind me. "You'll miss orientation."

"You're not understanding me."

"Unless you fly," she adds, proving she didn't hear a word I said. "And Colton here can take the car."

Colton's arms are crossed, and his face betrays nothing, but he understands me. He's already predicted what I'm about to say.

I position myself to face both of my parents. "I know I promised. I know you agreed to support me for a whole year if I'd apply to med school after that. You cosigned the lease for year two if I agreed to go when I got in. I'm so grateful to you guys. You supported my dream. It means everything to me, and I'll pay you back every penny starting now."

"Whoa, sweetheart." Dad holds up his hands like a traffic cop. "It wasn't quid pro quo. It was just about making a backup plan."

"This isn't it, Dad. Mom."

Her mouth is a tight line—the opposite of a smile—and her legs are crossed. The wet end of the felt tip sticks out from her folded hands like a meat thermometer.

"I know you guys don't get why anyone would want to live here. It's loud, it's crowded, it's just so... full. But I like my life here, and I love this man too much to drag him across the country so he can be with a miserable woman who's miserably miserable. I won't do it to him. I won't do it to myself."

Silence. Colton's trying not to smile and failing. My dad's looking at the boxes as if trying to game out the best way to undo the puzzle he's put together in his head.

"How long?" Mom asks. "How much more time do you

need before you realize none of these people care about you?" She shoots Colton a look. "Not talking about you."

"We're good," he replies.

"How long?" she reiterates to me.

"Forever."

"You want to be an old woman still begging for approval?"

When my mother wants to cut, she cuts to the bone.

"I'm tired of dreading my life. I haven't given myself enough room to succeed. I haven't even had time to fail properly. I'm just stopping because I promised you I would." This is true, but there's more to it, so I take a breath and continue to unload. "There's something comforting about failure. Like I don't have to be responsible for my work or my choices because... whoops, I failed, color me shocked. Oh well, no big deal. And it's easy, right? I don't have to improve. I don't have to face the next stage. I don't have to learn. Tamika was right. I'm weak, but sometimes weak is a choice."

Colton straightens quickly, bouncing from leaning on the car to standing on his feet. "She called you weak?"

"I mean, she was right."

"She and I are gonna have a word." He falls back to leaning on the car again.

"I'm sorry," I say to him. "I don't want to jerk you around."

He shakes his head slowly and mouths, "You're not." Then says out loud, "I should go."

"Help me get these back in first." Dad's squinting into the car with his hands on his knees. "How about you push from the front and I'll catch them on this side?"

"Stop it!" my mother shouts, fists balled. When she stands, the sheet of labels fall onto the ground and fan out like cards.

She points at Dad as if this is all his fault. "How can you do this?!"

"It's not personal, Kimberly." My dad stands with a sigh of midlife exasperation.

"I'm aware of that, *doctor*," she barks at him before getting back to me. "How can you do this to yourself? You can have everything. You can be secure for the rest of your life. Instead you choose to do... what? This? You don't even know what it is or how to get there. There's no school. No test. No certificate. You can't see two feet in front of your own face. How is it possible you'd choose this?"

"Honestly, Ma, I don't have a choice."

She looks at Colton, who has one hand tucked inside his elbow and the other over his mouth. "Can you fix her?"

He untangles his arms and holds them out to me, as if the answer's right in front of everyone. "She doesn't need fixing. She's kinda perfect."

"Tell her this is going to end badly."

"Ma!"

"I mean, it might," he says with a shrug of acceptance. I've gained some fluency in his vocabulary of shrugs and this one means he accepts me and whatever I choose.

"Tell *her*!"

Colton comes to me and takes my hands. With a gaze that both warms and chills, is intense and casual, he says, "This may end badly. It could be shit, Skittles. You think Gene is bad? You should meet Barb Fenton. She'll get in your way for kicks. You ready for that?"

"I am."

"You ready for disappointment?"

"Yes."

"You're going to fuck up," he says.

"That's what I worry about."

"Can you keep going even when your heart's racing?"

"Maybe?"

"Fair." He looks over his shoulder at my mother. "I told her." He drops my hands and speaks directly to my parents, who are now standing together by the pile of garbage bags. "I'm nobody here. You don't know me, so this won't mean much to you. That's cool. But I just want to say that I know it's hard—what she's trying to do—and I can't protect her from everything you'd want me to. That's just the world. But I have her back. No matter what gets thrown at her, she's got me, whatever that's worth."

My parents are side by side. Dad's standing, rocking on the balls of his feet, hands in his pockets. Mom's still sitting with her thumb on the back end of the pen. Dad takes one hand from his pocket and puts it on Mom's shoulder. In the way I've learned to interpret the subtleties in Colton's shrugs, they don't even have to look at each other to communicate anymore.

My mother clicks the pen once. "Well, at least I don't need to make more labels."

My dad reaches out with one arm and pulls me into him.

"I'm sorry you wasted the trip," I say.

"Not a waste." He kisses the top of my head as if I'm eight years old again. "I do have to get back though. There's a tumor with my name on it."

"Will you guys come visit?"

"I'm not staying in that hotel again." Mom clicks the labels into a neat stack. "It's too loud."

"You should stay with my parents," Colton says.

"We would never impose." She stands and starts arranging the already-arranged bags.

"It's a really big house. Actually, they're going to be kinda put off if you don't. So, you know, there's that."

The silence in the back alley is thicker than a production of *Wicked* with a broken smoke machine. Then a police siren cuts it open. Mom freezes with her hands on a bag, eyes closed as the siren gets lower in the distance. When it's gone, she snaps around and looks at me.

"I love you so much, Skyebird."

"I love you too, Ma."

"You've grown into a strong, smart woman who can make her own decisions."

Not sure if she's telling me or trying to convince herself, so I don't respond.

"I want you to succeed. And if you don't, I want you to know something." She points at me. "It isn't you. You're perfect. If whoever rejects you can't see that, that's their problem. Not yours. You understand?"

"Yes, Mom."

My arms wrap around her and we hold each other, rocking back and forth while she tells me how much she loves me. I believe her. I always believed her.

My mother doesn't like LAX, and I can't blame her. No one likes it. Now that we've gotten my parents into the terminal despite the chaos, I have to drive us out, if you can call this driving, which you can't, because we're not moving.

Colton taps Lemony. The little yellow man swings back and forth on his spring. "So, what's the plan, Skittles?"

"I think I can get my job at Starbee's back."

"Good."

"And I don't think Fátima's found anyone to rent my room yet." I stop at the last light before traffic breaks at Sepulveda. "Will you stay at Logan's?"

"For now, I guess. There's no rush. I can take care of Halley and see how it goes. If I'm there long enough to help with the baby, that would be all right."

"Oh, can I help too?"

"You like babies?"

"What kind of person actively doesn't like babies? What's wrong with you?"

He leans across the seat with both arms and kisses my cheek for so long I have to nudge him off when the light changes.

"Come to my place," he says. "We haven't fucked in the living room yet."

"I'll come wherever you want."

"Pull into the driveway," Colton says when we turn onto Hudson.

"The actual driveway?"

"No, the theoretical one."

I turn in and stop at the fence. "It's really roomy. Like, my whole apartment is this wide."

"I'll get you a clicky thing so you can park by the studio." He's out of the car before I can demand an explanation.

I shut the ignition and get out, meeting him at the gate. He puts his arm around me that casual way he does—with his elbow crooked at the back of my neck and his forearm draped over my shoulder.

"The code is 1320." He presses it in, then clicks the pound

sign. "That was my first address in Memphis. We'll set you up with your own code."

"Doesn't Logan like the driveway clear?"

"That's why you're going to park in the back when you come over." He pecks my cheek and opens the gate.

From the lime tree, a mockingbird sings the tune of a car alarm. The sky is crisscrossed with contrails, the pool filter *whee-whurrs*, and the sun shines hot on all of it.

Taking another step would be taking it all for granted.

"You okay?" Colton asks, dropping his embrace when he stops with me.

"I can't believe I get to stay."

"You do."

"I really don't have to go. There's nothing hanging over my head. No date. No timeline." I look up at him for some indication that it's all fake, but all I see are blue eyes, the dance of his hair in the breeze, and a kindness so authentic it can't be a dream. "I can really stay."

"You can."

"I can't believe it."

"Me neither." He looks a little dazed in the bright sun— like a man waking up after a nap and finding an entire day has gone by.

"You having second thoughts?"

"Hell, no. It's just that I tried to do something, thought I fucked up, and it worked out anyway. I *won* and it's... you know, a lot."

"You won?"

"Yeah. And you're the prize." He wraps his arms low on my waist, hooks his hands together, and picks me up. "Deal with it."

He carries me past the pool to the guest house. We giggle

like kids as he barely holds me up with one arm and opens the door with the other.

Then we're in, kissing and tugging at each other's clothes.

We land on the living room couch, tangled limbs and groping hands exposing skin to exploring lips. I laugh and squirm as we peel off shirts, shoes, socks, and when we're finally, perfectly, skin on skin, he remembers what I'm too aroused to even think of.

"I'm going on the pill tomorrow."

He spits the foil strip and rolls on the condom so fast I barely have a second to blink. "Up to you."

When he's back on the couch, I pull him close, wrapping my legs around his body to draw him inside me.

My gasp isn't surprise or even pleasure, but the feeling that everything is where it fits best. No tension. No anxiety. No games. No lies.

Just Colton and me and everything. Now.

EPILOGUE

ONE YEAR LATER

COLTON

The sun set an hour ago. The sky is as dark as it gets, but though the backstage lights are pretty dim, it's too much to see the shooting stars. Skye's next to me, taking measured breaths in through the nose, out through the mouth. After our year together, the clickety-click of her fingernail against a Pez dispenser soothes me as much as her.

I want to ask her if she's okay, but I won't interrupt like I did before her set at The Mint in January. That went south so fast the G-force gave me a nosebleed. Lesson learned.

My job is to let her do her thing so she can do her thing.

Drake at UTR Records nominated Skye for the showcase thanks to Liam's ball breaking. Without any pressure to make it in, and with a string of club gigs under her belt, she had room to be both pleasantly surprised and too busy to make it into a big deal.

Glendora Records's nominee for the showcase is singing

her last song. Halley's a natural. No nerves. No hesitation. Jabri, though, is off to our left, rubbing sweaty palms hard enough to set his hands on fire.

He glances at me like a lost puppy. I give him a thumbs-up. He adds a little too much enthusiasm to his return. Poor fucker's faking it too hard.

Lyric bursts past the tent flap, press badge flapping, phone gripped in her right hand like a callous. She punches Jabari's arm, gives him a thumbs-up, points to the stage, then does a chef's kiss.

"Skye!" she whispershouts, heading our way. I hold her back. "Hey, get off."

"Don't talk to her now."

"You her handler or something?"

"Yes. I am."

"Well, I need a pre-set clip or my post won't make any sense." She leans over to address Skye, holding up her phone. "Hey, *psst*. You in the silver dress!"

"Are you fucking with me?" I ask.

Onstage, Halley finishes and the applause roars.

"You asked me to post. And now—"

"You should have done this two hours ago. But you're irresponsible and disorganized."

Her mouth drops, because if in this entire world there was ever a pot calling out the kettle's color, it's right in front of her, wearing Chuck Taylors and a black leather jacket.

"I am so sick of this shit," my sweet little sister growls. "All I do is post this and post that. It's the same crap every day." Out of the corner of my eye, Halley jumps into Jabari's arms. "I'm so 'excited' for this, and I'm 'thrilled' to tell you that. Nothing—and I mean nothing—has been even a little bit exciting or thrilling for a year and a half until tonight.

Yes, I really am excited your fucking girlfriend is doing this show, and I can post and be actually and really authentic and yippee over something instead of typing 'excited' from the toilet. And here you are, King of the Grown-ups, on your throne of shit-that's-not-fun, wearing a crown of fucking boredom, making me want to literally *die*."

"Wow, Lyric that's... I mean, if you don't like your job, you can just—"

"Hey, Lyr," Skye says from behind me. "You okay?"

"Your bodyguard's turning this into an entire slog but... you look *amazing!*"

"Thanks!" Skye's too full of stars to be faking it.

Her anxiety must be put to bed, or at least down for a nap, so I let Lyric make a video of my girlfriend's silver shoes and whatever else.

The next band goes up. Squealing guitars. Screaming. Big we-don't-care-if-you-like-us vibe while strutting around like testosterone divas.

"Median!" Halley squeaks the name she gave me in the studio to describe the utter middleness of my size, and jumps for me, still high on performance dopamine. "I am so happy. Thank you thank you!"

"I didn't do anything."

"Yeah, hello," Jabari says. "That's enough with the leprechaun assault."

Halley lets me go. "Did you hear it? Was I good?"

"You know you were great."

"I do!"

"Damn right," her boyfriend agrees. He wipes his brow with a linen handkerchief.

"Halley!" Skye calls, waving her over to where she and Lyric are making a video.

Halley dashes for them so they can hug and squeal and make Lyric's social media post.

"When are you going to do it?" I murmur to Jabari.

"I thought about it. I don't think the ring is right."

"Look at you, man? You're sweating like a... fuck it, I don't know. A really nervous guy."

"A square-cut emerald is too much statement. She's a classic beauty. She needs a classic stone. I fucked it up."

I've known this dude more than a decade, and I've never, ever seen him doubt or second-guess himself about anything.

"She's going to say yes."

"I don't want her to think I don't know her. She's a traditional lady. Six-point round in platinum. You're the one who should be getting a square-cut emerald, living Downtown together like two heathens."

"Breathe, buddy."

He actually listens to me, taking a few deep ones. When he's done, he puts his hands out as if his equilibrium has been restored, but then he glances at the women all clustered together. Lyric has her phone on a stick, listening while Skye shows Halley her Garfield Pez.

"Shit. Look at her." His nerves of steel bend all over again. "She's everything."

"Ask her and when she says yes, let her pick the ring," I suggest.

"How's that work with me getting down on one knee? Here's a ring, but we can take it back? You gonna do that when you ask Skye?"

No, I'm not gonna do that. I don't know how I'm going to ask her. I only know that I will.

"Forget the knee. If she wanted a man beneath her, she'd—"

"Marry a squirt like you?" He claps me on the back.

"Fuck you, man." I curse him while laughing. He grabs me in a hug so hard I make a show of suffocating. "Save me," I choke out to the stage manager, a skinny dude carrying a clipboard with a pen light clipped to it. He's all in black except for a white earpiece, and he's not impressed with my cry for help. Jab lets me drop.

"You're Skye Phillips?" the stage manager asks.

"No, but yes."

"You're next. Take your place."

He's gone before I agree.

"Good luck out there, big guy." Jabari claps me on the back again.

"Yeah." I walk backward a few steps. "And stop stalling. Give her the emerald."

343

EPILOGUE

SKYE

I am so cool. Ice cold. Calm as Dockweiler Beach on a windless day.

Sometimes I get lucky and feel like this. Sometimes it's harder. But since I let Dr. Solomon put me on an old-school medication that hasn't been used in a while—no commitments, no promises, just a test—I've been able to make it through the worst of it as long as I keep up the calming techniques.

More than any of that though, knowing that there's not a date hanging over my head has lifted a lot of panic. I can fail. I can fuck up. I can embarrass myself. All that stuff will spin me around and around and it's upsetting, but it's not the end of my world.

And there's Colton. Three months after I decided to stay in Los Angeles, we moved into a loft Downtown, not too far from Becca and... four months later... Fátima. I love living with him. He grounds me. He reminds me that no matter what I fail at, I've succeeded at loving him.

I love the way he moves, the way he smells, the way he laughs. I love the way he looks at me as though I'm the only woman in the world. I love that he's a good man, and I love that he's not afraid to be bad.

"Colton gave me this," I tell Halley and Lyric, holding the Garfield Pez up to the camera phone. "Whenever I feel anxious, I rub the letters on the side."

"They're worn out." Halley's observation is performative. We've already discussed this. "How anxious can you be?"

"I have really bad anxiety attacks, especially around performing. It can be crippling, and I thought it was all my fault. I thought everyone hated me."

"Oh my actual God," Lyric cries. "Everyone loves you!"

"Stop it!" We hug and squeal for the camera. "Hey, did you hear Halley!"

"Cut!" Colton says.

"Ass. Hole." Lyric lowers the camera and punches the record button. "You fucked it up."

"Get an editor. Skittles." He holds out his arm for me. "You're almost up."

I duck under his arm and let him pull me into him the way I like to be held—with his hand drooping over my shoulder.

"Good luck," Halley says with a thumbs-up.

"I want some pre-stage jitters," Lyric says, eyes on the phone as she follows us to my place. It's louder here, close to the rock band's last song. "Just let me tag the location."

"Are you ready?" Colton asks.

"Totally."

He cranes his neck so he can see the sliver of sky between the tent's cover and the dark stage, holding up his free hand to block the backstage lights. "It started."

"The meteor shower?"

"Yeah. Block out the light from here and you can see."

I do as he says and catch a light streaking across the Milky Way.

"Two!" I gasp. "Three. Oh, this is fantastic."

"Totally worth waiting an extra year for." He smiles down at me.

I kiss him, because he's right. I was rushing, and now I'm chill.

Everything now sometimes means you have to wait for everything to fall into place.

The stage manager approaches with his little clipboard light as the last song ends with a squeal in C sharp. The crowd cheers, holding up glow-in-the-dark sticks.

"Trey is on piano with you," Colton reminds me. "Breakdown behind the curtain."

"Right." I inhale hard and exhale when my lungs are so full they hurt. "I know how to do this. I'm fine." I scratch my Pez dispenser.

"You're great," Colton says. He looks behind us. "These the pre-stage jitters you wanted?"

"I'm fine," I keep chanting. "I know how to do this."

"Something's wrong," Lyric says.

"She can't do another whole bit about a Pez dispenser right now."

I'm fine. I don't even need to say it. The anxiety is back down to some base-level hum.

"My account," Lyric says with a distracted softness. "It's locked."

"I'll do it again," I say, sensing a fellow woman in the throes of an anxiety attack. "See if Halley can join."

"No, I mean... *locked*. I have the video, but I'm logged out and my password is... this is weird."

"Go figure it out over there," Colton says. "You're stressing *me* out."

"Take it easy on her," I whisper to him.

"I'll take it easy on her after your last song."

"I love when you protect me."

"I love looking out for you."

I kiss him. His lips are soft, but his intentions are firm. I can barely breathe, but for now, I don't need to. He is my breath and my thoughts and the softest beats of my heart.

"You're on in..." The stage manager counts down on his fingers.

From behind me, Lyric panics. "TikTok too? What the—"

"And, go."

"—actual fuck?"

I step toward the stage. Colton squeezes my hand before I turn. He's standing as straight as a man who knows who he loves and what's important.

He's not the same man I met at the karaoke bar or the same man who put dumplings on my plate or who demanded to join me in my personal hell.

Which is fine. I'm not the same woman I was when I met him.

I let go of him, take a deep breath, and walk onstage.

AND EVERYONE LIVED HAPPILY EVER AFTER

(*Halley said yes. And the emerald was perfect. She may be a traditional lady, but she still has taste ffs*)

Hey. So!

Liam was supposed to be next but Lyric spoke to me. Her problem, and her man were so urgent and so hot that I could not deny them for one more moment.

CROWNE JEWEL is available where you expect it to be.

ACKNOWLEDGMENTS

1. In 2001, a few weeks before September 11th, my husband and I drove across country—New York to Los Angeles—in a 1988 Honda Accord. No little box on top. No trailer behind. Everything except our books was in that car, and our bikes hung from a rack. We left a gap in the stuff for the rearview mirror to see behind, but the backseat windows were blocked with the contents of a one-bedroom in Brooklyn. Did we get over the Rockies without a problem? We did. Did the car overheat in the Utah desert? It did not. Did we need new shocks at the end of it all? You betcha. Would Skye have made it home under similar circumstances? Yop.

2. "Golden sunshine all through the day" – hat tip to David Lynch.

3. Speaking of the above speech—it took me an hour and a ton of fiddling. I'm a professional writer. How did Colton just blurt this shit out? Seriously. There's a writer's trope that says you should kill your babies, and I really thought I should cut it for that reason. Then I decided to let it be the sore thumb. In my Los Angeles, love makes men into poets. Also, I love squishy babies. I will not be taking any questions.

4. One of you is asking if the speech inspired me to name her Skye, or the other way around. I'd love to be cagey about it, but I've been waiting to use that name for a long time and I didn't know what I was waiting for. Apparently, I was waiting for Colton. The name inspired the speech.

5. You may have noticed Colton has a very low realism rating. Likelihood a dude in his garage, alone, could produce a viable EP? 61%. Likelihood he could install that studio without ripping apart the garage to the studs? 35% How much I worried about this kind of thing? 0%. I can drive myself crazy with research (read *Girl on the Edge* if you want to see this shit in action), but I'm here to create the best possible world, not the most probable.

I ALSO WROTE THESE

Iron Crowne ~ Enemies to Lovers

Crowne of Lies ~ Marriage of Convenience

Crowne Rules ~ Forced Close Proximity

Fake Crowne ~ Fake Relationship

Crowne Jewel ~ Enemies to Lovers

You might also like:

The *New York Times* bestselling Games Duet

Adam Steinbeck will give his wife a divorce on one condition. She join him in a remote cabin for 30 days, submitting to his sexual dominance.

Marriage Games | Separation Games

Monica insists she's not submissive. Jonathan Drazen is going to prove otherwise, but he might fall in love doing it.

COMPLETE SUBMISSION

CONTEMPORARY ROMANCES

Hollywood and sports romances for the sweet and sexy romantic.

Star-Crossed | Hardball | Bombshell | Bodyguard | Only Ever You

CPSIA information can be obtained
at www.ICGtesting.com
Printed in the USA
BVHW032324080223
658190BV00010B/412